the clouds roll away

A RALEIGH HARMON NOVEL

SIBELLA GIORELLO

THOMAS NELSON
Since 1798

NASHVILLE DALLAS MEXICO CITY RIO DE JANEIRO

Published in Nashville, Tennessee, by Thomas Nelson. Thomas Nelson is a registered trademark of Thomas Nelson, Inc.

Thomas Nelson, Inc., titles may be purchased in bulk for educational, business, fund-raising, or sales promotional use. For information, e-mail SpecialMarkets@ ThomasNelson.com.

This novel is a work of fiction. Any references to real events, businesses, organizations, and locales are intended only to give the fiction a sense of reality and authenticity. Any resemblance to actual persons, living or dead, is entirely coincidental.

Reference in chapter 33 to George Kennan, *Tent Life in Siberia: An Incredible Account of Siberian Adventure, Travel, and Survival* (New York: Skyhorse, 2007).

Library of Congress Cataloging-in-Publication Data
Giorello, Sibella.
  The clouds roll away : a Raleigh Harmon novel / Sibella Giorello.
      p. cm. — (A Raleigh Harmon series; 2)
  ISBN 978-1-59554-534-3 (pbk.)
  1. Women geologists—Fiction. 2. United States. Federal Bureau of
Investigation—Officials and employees—Fiction. 3. Civil rights—Fiction.
4. Richmond (Va.)—Fiction. I. Title.
  PS3607.I465C56 2010
  813'.6—dc22   2009048448

Printed in the United States of America
10 11 12 13 RRD 5 4 3 2 1

One exile holds us both, and we are bound
To selfsame home-joys in the land of light.
Weeping thou walkest with him; weepeth he?
Some sobbing weep, some weep and make no sound.

—CHRISTINA ROSSETTI,
"They Desire a Better Country"

For Richmond

chapter one

Winter rode into Richmond on the chattering breath of the Atlantic. Each year the season blew itself into existence. The ancient elms crystallized and frost crocheted the birches into lace doilies. On this particular December morning, with a bright sun overhead, I drove out New Market Road past fields that glistened like crushed diamonds. For this moment, my hometown looked cryogenically frozen, preserved for future generations to discover Richmond's wide river, verdant soils, and the plantation lifestyle forged through generations— gone tragically, humanly awry.

But the reverie was shattered by two elephants. Carved from white granite, they stood on either side of a black asphalt driveway with a steel sign naming the property: Rapland.

The scene of the crime.

I turned down the asphalt driveway. It was a long drive, rolling over fenced fields where satiny horses were grazing, their breath quick clouds that evaporated in the sun. At the other end, an old plantation house faced the James River. The historic clapboards were painted polo white, the copper cupola green from exposure. But pink stucco additions rose starkly on either side, modern additions with plate-glass windows that stared down on the historic middle and made it look priggish and stuffy, like a dusty repository for outdated books.

A muscular man stepped from the guardhouse as my car

came around the driveway's final curve. His thighs were wide and carried him in a twisting, muscle-bound stride. In his right hand he held an assault rifle.

I stopped my car behind the gray Bentley parked in the driveway and reached under my blazer, placing my right hand on my Glock. With my left, I opened the car door six inches, preparing to use it as a shield if necessary. The man stood beside my car. He wore mirrored aviator sunglasses. In the reflection, I saw myself, my old white car, and the new pink additions to the house.

"Agent Raleigh Harmon with the FBI," I said. "We got a call this morning."

"I need to see the ID."

My right hand remained on the Glock. I lifted my credentials with my left. He stared at the picture with the Bureau's blue-and-gold insignia and then flicked his chin, indicating I could put them away.

"What're you carrying?" he asked.

"Pardon?"

"It's a .45, isn't it?"

I gave him my official smile—the smile of an armed public servant. "The phone call we received this morning sounded urgent," I said.

"We can get to that after we play show-and-tell." He popped gum between his white teeth, a brisk scent of spearmint filling the air. "If you're not carrying a .45, then it's a nine."

"Nine millimeter?"

"Yeah."

"Wrong. It's a forty. The game's officially over. Who's in charge around here?"

He strode back to the guardhouse, slid open the pocket door, and picked up the telephone. "The Feds are here," he said into the receiver. "And the G-man? It's a girl."

The historic part of the house smelled pungent, like clove cigarettes smoked after a spicy meal, and another guard greeted me at the front door. He wore combat fatigues and a three-carat diamond stud in each ear. When he extended his hand, it was three times the size of mine. I saw a .45 in his hip holster.

"I'm Sid," he said. "You want to talk to RPM? He's upstairs. Top of the steps, turn right, walk down the hall."

I counted twenty-two steps, the exotic wood shining like polished onyx. At the top of the stairs, I turned right and crossed a landing decorated with framed records—seven gold, eight platinum. At the end of the landing, the last door was open.

The famous rap musician and producer known as RPM was sitting in a green leather chair, a cello balanced between his long legs. Eyes closed, he bowed the strings, caressing a slow largo that sounded grieving and nocturnal. His fingers pressed the board as if staunching a deep wound. For his sake, and mine, I did not want to break the music. I stood in the doorway, listening until the piece descended to its final note, the lowest G on the scale.

When he opened his eyes, he looked startled.

"Pardon me," I said. "I didn't want to interrupt. Raleigh Harmon, FBI."

"You're the FBI agent?" His voice had a quiet tone, in a deep register.

I nodded. "'Sarabande'?" I gave him my card.

"Yes. Bach's my favorite," he said. He pivoted the cello on its spike, resting it on the chair. Sharp creases in his slacks extended his lean physique, making him appear even taller than the six-foot-three I was guessing.

"Did my guards give you a difficult time downstairs?" he asked.

"Only the one outside." I smiled.

"My apologies. They're on high alert after what happened last night."

"After what happened last night," I said, "no apologies are necessary."

He nodded. "Would you like to see where they burned the cross?"

≈

The cross had burned the back lawn like a branded emblem. The main beam seared twelve feet, four inches. The intersecting beam scorched almost five feet of grass.

Releasing my aluminum tape measure, then letting it rattle closed, I wrote the numbers in my notebook and took several photographs. RPM stood to the side, quietly watching as I snapped on latex gloves, kneeled, and pinched the soil. It smelled of soot and scorched minerals, like a doused campfire. But I pinched another sample and waved it back and forth under my nose, detecting something else. It smelled bitter and acidic.

Hate didn't have a smell, I told myself. But maybe I was wrong.

"I suppose this is one way of telling me to get out of the neighborhood," he said.

I glanced over my shoulder. He wore sunglasses now but I could see his long eyelashes, the almond shape of his dark eyes, the face seen on countless magazine covers. I found it difficult to look at him and not remember he was among the fifty most beautiful people.

"What time did this happen?" I asked.

"The sheriff wrote down that information last night," he said.

"Our investigation will run separate from the sheriff's. I need to get the information from you directly."

He drew a deep breath, nodding. "Yes, I understand."

But he didn't respond further, and I knew fresh wounds

required time. Kneeling again to my work, I reached into a black nylon satchel and removed a sterilized paint can. I wiped down my pocketknife with an alcohol swab and popped the paint can's lid. With a sterilized garden trowel, I dug into the scorched cross and deposited a large section inside the can, pressing the round top in place, hammering it shut with the trowel's handle, making sure all the volatile compounds were sealed inside.

When I turned to look at the famous man again, the rising sun had drawn a bright aureole around his head. It was as if nature was saluting his celebrity. But like most famous people, he let fame perform his introductions. A Southern girl, I wondered how to address him. He was known in the music industry as RPM, but that sounded odd, particularly for the elegant gentleman standing before me. I preferred formal titles—Mr., Miss, and Mrs.

But seriously: Mr. RPM?

Deciding to avoid the issue, I took out my notebook.

"I was playing music in the house." He stared down at the river that rolled like a long shiver to the Chesapeake Bay. "There was a sudden flash of light in the window. I thought perhaps it was lightning. But it grew brighter and brighter. I walked over and saw flames shooting from the ground." He paused. "And I saw that the fire was in the shape of a cross."

"Did you see anything else?"

"Such as people?" He shook his head. "I called 911 and ran outside. My bodyguard and I threw buckets of water from the kitchen—"

"Just the two of you?"

"Yes. I have children in the house. I didn't want to scare them."

"And your bodyguard . . ."

"Sid. You met him on the way in."

Right. The man at the front door. I wrote his name in my notebook. "Sid's last name is?"

"Dog."

"Pardon?"

He smiled apologetically. "The spelling is even worse. D-a-w-g. Seeing Eye Dawg, otherwise known as Sid."

"Okay."

His smile grew. The teeth were so straight and white, they were spellbinding. "Welcome to the world of rap music, Miss Harmon. Linguistically speaking, it won't make much sense. You'll have to bear with us. It is 'Miss,' isn't it?"

"Yes. Was Sid nearby when you saw the flames? Is that how he heard you calling?"

"Excellent question. The sheriff didn't ask about that. I feel better already. My house is equipped with an intercom system. I don't like to raise my voice, ever. Sid was in the theater, watching a movie with his lady friend. With no windows in the theater, he couldn't see the fire. I reached him by intercom."

"How many people were here last night?"

"Sid and Cujo, the other guard you met outside."

I let Cujo's name go. For now.

"There's a cook and a maid," he continued, "who are like family. And the rest are my actual family. My wife, some of her extended relatives, and our children." He smiled again. "I grew up an only child. I'm enjoying the full house I missed back then."

"And none of them saw the fire?"

"Correct. The fire began right after 11 p.m. The women and children were in bed, so was the help. When the fire truck finally arrived, the sirens drew everyone out of bed. But by then Sid and I had put out the fire. We told the children there was some misunderstanding; the women took them back to bed. I would tell you to talk to them, but you'll need a translator."

I looked up from my notes. "What do they speak?"

"African," he said. "More specifically, a tribal dialect from Liberia."

I flipped through my notebook. "When you called the FBI this morning, you said the sheriff's department was . . ."

"Lackadaisical," he said. "This is a cross burning. Somebody trespassed onto my property and set fire to a cross. You see how close it was to my house. It could have burned the place down—which might be the whole point of this hateful exercise. I complained to the sheriff, but he acted as if this was a friendly barbecue. For all I know he's covering up for these history fanatics."

Since "history fanatic" described most of Richmond, I asked, "Could you be more specific?"

"That historic preservation committee, those people living along the river. They've complained about my remodel for years. My home improvements undermine the plantation's authentic history, they say. Perhaps they decided to just burn us down."

I made more notes following his statement and said, "If you don't mind, for the official paperwork, I'll need your legal name."

"Robert Paul Masters. When I started in the music business thirty years ago, I decided to use my initials: RPM. Marvelous stage name. Albums were called RPMs. For revolutions per minute?"

"I grew up with CDs."

"Ancient history." He sighed. "How long?"

"Pardon?"

"How long until we find out who did this?"

"Hate crimes are a priority with the FBI," I said, sounding like the official investigator. "The evidence will get fast-tracked by the lab."

He smiled. "Miss Harmon, please. You do not have to spare my feelings. How long? I can handle the truth."

The truth? Cross burnings were nocturnal acts of bitterness, popping up in rural areas where physical distance separated neighbors and allegiances snaked back generations, particularly in the South. Figuring out who burned this cross would be like unraveling a Gordian knot glued down with hate.

But it seemed cruel to tell him, no matter how politely he insisted. The weight of last night was still on him.

So I gave him another truth, one I could be sure of.

"I will stay on this case until we know who's behind it," I said. "You have my word."

chapter two

I headed west from Rapland and just before Battlefield Park,
turned down an oyster-shell drive. The fractured calcifer-
ous layers glowed like broken pearls and led to a plantation
dating back to a 1662 land grant from King Charles II. The plantation prospered until its slaves were freed, until carpetbaggers
and federal soldiers carried away everything that wasn't nailed
down. When the Depression hit, snakes slithered through the
rotting pine floors and the French wallpaper hung like discarded
bandages from the walls. It took a Yankee to save the place. James
Flynn drove south from New Jersey in 1948, bearing a self-made
fortune in the commodities of necessity—sugar, corn, bootleg—
and the curse of so many Irishmen, falling for underdogs. Flynn
spent years restoring the grand house and eventually Belle Grove
returned to the small coterie of historic plantations along the
James River.

His granddaughter ran the place these days, and when I
walked around to the back of the main house, Flynn Wellington
was in the glass conservatory, scooping soil into gilded pots. The
air was moist and tasted of trapped chlorophyll. To either side,
wooden pallets displayed poinsettias with burgundy leaves lush
as crushed velvet.

"Why, Raleigh, how nice to see you." Flynn lifted both
hands, her cotton gloves smothered with black soil. "I'd give you

a hug but you'd be picking dirt off your clothes the rest of the day."

Flynn and I had been classmates at St. Catherine's School and were acquainted through her mother's penultimate husband. There were five husbands in all. Number four was an attorney my father liked—there weren't many—and on sweltering August afternoons, we would drive out to Belle Grove so the adults could sit on the wraparound porch drinking iced beverages while Flynn and I swam in the river.

"I heard y'all moved to Oregon," she said.

"Washington. It was only temporary."

"I can't imagine leaving Virginia." She picked up the spade, folding the soil again. Her blonde hair bounced with the motion. "How is your mother?"

She pronounced it the Old Dominion way, *muh-thah*.

"Fine, thanks. Yours?"

"She moved to Florida with what's-his-name. What can I do for you, Raleigh?"

"Last night somebody burned a cross at Rapland."

"Please. 'Rapland' sounds like a theme park. You know very well the name of that plantation is Laurel."

Yes, I knew. I knew all kinds of things. By junior high I could recite long passages of internecine gossip about families who traced their heritage to the House of Burgesses, but I only had one foot in that world. David Harmon married my mother when I was five years old. To this day, I couldn't trace my paternal heritage back one generation to my birth father. Not that I needed to: David Harmon was every girl's dream dad.

"The gentleman who owns Rapland thinks you're trying to run him off his property. Is that true?"

"Are you implying something?"

"I'm not implying, Flynn. I'm asking flat out."

"He's ruining that place," she said. "I don't want him there. I've never said otherwise. I've been saying it since he moved in four years ago."

The fine bones in her neck looked as brittle as glass rods. The pretty girl I once knew was lost to hard work. Several years ago, to keep up with expenses, Flynn and her husband had turned Belle Grove into a bed-and-breakfast.

"Flynn, there were people in the house. Children. The flames were burning ten feet from the door."

She dropped the gardening tool, wiping the back of her wrist across her forehead. "It's been awhile since you've been out this way, Raleigh, so let me explain it to you. My guests pay good money to stay here. They want a romantic retreat. They expect a visit with the historic past. We were doing fine until that rapper took over Laurel. Ever since, it's been rap music blaring down-river, party boats up and down the water. How do you think that's affected my business? Is this something I can call the FBI about?"

"That fire could have burned the place down."

"Good."

"Excuse me?"

"Good," she repeated. "Then maybe he'll leave and somebody could rebuild Laurel. Somebody who will treat that beautiful property with the dignity it deserves."

I leveled my gaze. "Flynn, I want you to answer truthfully. Did you have anything to do with burning that cross?"

She picked up the tool, waving it. "Look around. Do you see what I'm doing? I don't have time to terrorize anybody. I'm working. But we're old friends, so let me be very clear: when that guy goes back to Hollywood, or New York, or wherever he came from, I'm throwing the biggest party Richmond has seen since Antietam."

"Thanks for the warning."

"Oh, you're invited."

"I'll pass."

Her blue eyes flashed with indignation. "Here you come to Belle Grove and insinuate—"

"Flynn?"

We both turned.

At the back of the conservatory, where fanned banana palms brushed the peaked glass roof, the stalks parted to reveal a man walking toward us from the door to the house. He looked familiar in some distant way, somebody I'd met but couldn't place again.

"Oh, Stuart." Flynn pulled off her gloves. "Time got away from me. I've got everything ready. It's all in the parlor room."

He wore tan chinos and a blue cashmere V-neck, his face more hard than rugged and capped by blond hair shaved to the scalp. He turned to me.

"This is Stuart Morgan," said Flynn with perfunctory politeness. "Stuart, Raleigh Harmon. Raleigh was just leaving."

I shook his hand. He gave an automatic sort of smile.

"Raleigh was just leaving," Flynn repeated.

Just for that, I took out my card and held it out to her. After staring at it for a long moment, she accepted it with a noble sort of weariness. I walked down the aisle, feeling their silence behind me, and stepped outside. A man wearing an I ♥ NY sweatshirt and jeans sat in a rocking chair on the front porch. He smoked a cigarette and flicked ash on the floor.

I drove down the oyster-shell road. A column of walnut trees reached for the blue sky like ancient black hands. It was mesmerizing land and I sympathized with Flynn's devotion to it. But as I pulled onto Williamsburg Road, heading back to town, I wondered about the past's magnetic hold. Flynn clung to her history like someone afraid of perishing, someone drowning who succeeds only in taking the saving grace down with her.

But most of all I wondered about her statement and the question it left hanging in the conservatory's moist air.

She did not have time to terrorize an unwelcome neighbor, she said.

And if she did . . . ?

chapter three

Having it my way, I ate two Whoppers with large fries and a Coke at the Burger King on Williamsburg Road in Sandston. For entertainment, I watched heads swiveling to look at my K-Car.

A certifiable bucket of bolts, my Bureau ride was apparently designed by engineers hoping to wipe covetousness off the face of the earth. It was a white rectangle with windows like sandwich boards. Inside things got worse. The AM radio barely worked, the heater blew cold, and the bench seats were smothered with grooved vinyl. Over the years, the sun had bleached the plastic to a color resembling dead skin.

And yet, as I licked salt from my fingers and headed back into town, it didn't matter.

I was home.

Home.

In September I got shipped out on a disciplinary transfer initiated by my supervisor, Victoria Phaup. She sent me all the way to Seattle but like a bad boomerang I came right back. The bosses above Phaup lifted my transfer for work above and beyond the call, and I was home for Thanksgiving. More importantly, I was home for the dreaded anniversary of November 29, the night four years ago when somebody shot my dad in an alley and left him for dead. His murder remains unsolved.

Phaup was no dummy. Rather than reassign the hideous

K-Car that she had handpicked for me in the first place, she kept it waiting for my return.

But as I drove into town, my heart skipped at the sight of magnolia trees dark green even in the winter, and downtown Richmond where the buildings glistened in the sun like perfect crystals, and the mighty James River, rolling over its boulders.

For all its troubled history and racial strife, this place was home.

And few things ever feel as good as coming back to where you belong, and realizing the place waited for you.

Since I wanted to stay, I went straight to Phaup's office after parking at the Bureau compound off Parham Road. Among her accusations, she claimed I operated too independently. If daily check-ins kept me in Richmond, I could swallow my pride.

My first instinct when I saw her office door was closed was to walk away, heart skipping with joy. But my second instinct made me ask her secretary, Claudia, how long before Her Highness was available—not in those exact words. Claudia picked up the phone and told Phaup I was here. After eight minutes I picked up a magazine from the coffee table in the reception area. A publication for retired agents. People who started another life after the Bureau. I read it twice.

Thirty-six minutes later, Victoria Phaup granted me an audience.

She was a stocky woman with short brown hair threaded with gray. She must have been pretty at one time, but twelve years of clawing her way through Bureau management had compressed her small features into a persistent expression of defensiveness, her eyes like fractured gray pebbles. Thin mouth locked, loaded for counterattack. And her office smelled like dry ice.

"I appreciate your sending the e-mail this morning, Raleigh."

"Yes, ma'am."

Taking no chances, I notified Phaup after speaking to RPM on the phone. My e-mail gave the time and place and that I was leaving to check it out. Baby-agent stuff.

But hey, I was home.

"Perhaps you've learned something from your transfer," she said.

I nodded. One thing I'd learned was to keep my mouth shut.

According to office gossip, Phaup had been a rising star in the Bureau until she sent an e-mail to the wrong recipient—in fact, to the supervisor she criticized. Since then, she had rotated among field offices, a path she clearly hoped I would experience too. When she landed in Richmond five years ago, it put her within physical striking distance of D.C., and while I was away, she was named head of the Richmond field office.

I never doubted that my career—or its death—was part of her campaign to return to headquarters.

Her desk grew paper in accreting layers, and she reached into one of the stalagmites, extracting a manila folder. She read to herself, then said, "Update on the cross burning."

Speaking to the top of her head, I described my interview with Rapland's celebrity owner and explained my collection of forensic evidence. I said that right now the only leads were his suspicions, which included the preservation society. "They've apparently filed petitions against him. They don't like his remodel. His other suspicion is . . . well, the county sheriff."

She looked up. "You're surprised about the sheriff?"

"I've only met the sheriff once, but—"

I stopped.

I'd met the sheriff once, last summer, when I got myself into a compromising situation. By the mirthful expression on Phaup's face, she remembered it too. The compromising situation that precipitated my disciplinary transfer.

"I don't know the sheriff personally," I said finally. "But it sounds like a long shot. I think the man was venting more than anything else."

"Cross burnings do not happen in a vacuum, Raleigh. That county might be twenty miles from town but it's a century away from the rest of the world. It's much too small for any hate group to operate independently." She closed the file. "You will report directly to me. I want updates, continually. I'll send the information to the hate crimes coordinator in D.C. And since this involves a celebrity, I've alerted media relations." She didn't sound disappointed by the last part. Phaup relished the attention, provided we looked like good guys. "And open a file on the sheriff."

"We're going after the sheriff?"

"'Going after' is not the correct term," she said.

"Ma'am, there are better places to begin—"

"And I don't want any dramatic permutations. Do you understand?"

"Yes, ma'am."

She rolled her right shoulder. I looked away, watching a string of cirrus clouds stretch a veil across the blue sky. Phaup could have been demoted for a misfired e-mail, but she also could've been banished to the hinterlands for adjusting her undergarments in public. The woman tugged, pulled, and shifted things like a third base coach at the bottom of the eighth.

"The hate crime is your priority," she said, extracting the hand from her blouse. "But we're short on manpower. Holidays, vacations. The flu going around. Pollard Durant needs help on his task force. It would require three days a week, at least."

Suddenly caught off guard, I hesitated. She was offering task force work—a plum assignment—after what we'd been through? It didn't seem possible. But then, maybe this was an olive branch.

Maybe, like me, she was trying. And maybe, just maybe, I'd been wrong about her.

"Thank you," I said. "I'd be happy to work the task force."

"No overtime. Headquarters isn't compensating for anything over fifty hours a week. But that shouldn't be a problem for you."

I waited. "Because . . . ?"

"Because you're on phones."

Phones. The dullest part of a task force.

I wasn't wrong about her.

She smiled. "All right, then. Off you go."

Yes, I thought, standing to leave. *Off I go.*

≈

My new desk was tucked into a corner of the third floor, right next to the back stairwell. Four feet, three inches from the stairwell to be exact. Yes, I measured. To reach my chair, I had to duck under the heat vent, and when I sat down just before noon, I could hear an army marching down the stairwell to lunch, the voices echoing off the five-story cavern of concrete and steel.

My old desk had been a pleasant fire hazard of notes, memos, triplicate forms, and weeks of snacks stashed in the desk's bottom drawers. It had also been in the main squad on the second floor. Not only was the K-Car waiting, but Phaup put an entire floor between me and the rest of the squad. Reciting my chant about home, I pulled a bag of Fritos and a can of Coke—never, ever Pepsi—from my desk and consumed both while typing a letter to the forensics lab in D.C. Trained as a geologist, I came to the Bureau as a forensic technician in the mineralogy department. When my father was murdered, I went to Quantico, hoping to turn grief into something productive.

In the letter, I explained to the technician that the soil inside the paint can was evidence from a hate crime, an automatic expedite for the lab. I wanted to know what substance was used to light the fire and what minerals were in the lawn soil itself, in case it could be matched later to somebody's clothing or shoes. Ignoring the one-sided cell phone conversation echoing down the stairwell—"Hello? Are you there? Hello?"—I sent Phaup an e-mail offering a tedious blow-by-blow of my procedure. Ducking under the heat vent, I walked down to the second floor.

The main squad room sat empty. For several moments I gazed at the gathered cubicles, the cartoons taped to partitions, the running gags and inside jokes, and suddenly I felt isolated and lonely, as if everyone had left for a party I wasn't invited to.

Giving my mood a swift kick, I rang the buzzer beside the Dutch door to Evidence Control. *Get over it*, I thought. *Get to work.*

The top half of the Dutch door opened.

"You're back," said Allene Caron.

She wore a yellow satin blouse that lay on her brown skin like filaments of polished brass. Picking up my paperwork, she raised her chin and ran her dark eyes over my request.

"Here to stay?" she asked, looking over the top of the document.

"That's the plan."

She harrumphed and circled a section of my paperwork. Fifteen years ago, Allene started here as a clerk. She now ran Evidence Control and nothing could convince her that agents wrote competent paperwork. She tapped the red pen on my intake form.

"What day is it, Raleigh?"

"I'm guessing it's not the sixth."

"Not in this world."

"But I got December right."

Raising an eyebrow, she corrected the date, December 7, then initialed the correction. She stamped her official seal and assigned a bar code to track the evidence through the FBI system. Just before closing the Dutch door, she threw me an expression that conveyed her suspicions concerning my survival.

"Be good, you hear?"

"I promise, I'll be good."

Harrumphing again, she closed the door.

chapter four

The Title III surveillance operations—known as the T-III room—was stashed with the heating and cooling equipment behind a gray door on the third floor. With half of the ceiling's acoustic tiles missing, the place had a ghoulish jack-o'-lantern appearance. But it made it easier for the tech guys to run cables for routers and modems and phones and monitors.

On Wednesday afternoon I opened the gray door and heard the loud whooshing of air pumps. An almost chubby young man sat at a dinged-up stainless steel table, his back to the door. Bose earphones connected to the laptop, and when I tapped his shoulder he jumped, kicking a yellow Hardee's bucket, scattering gray chicken bones across the floor.

He pulled off the headset and smoothed down pale tufts of hair.

"Stan." He shook my hand. "Stan Norton."

"I'm Raleigh."

"I know."

"We've met?"

"No. But I came up from Savannah right after you . . . after you left for Seattle. Here, let me clean up this mess."

Brushing the biscuit crumbs off the table into the Hardee's bucket, he picked up the greasy bones, placing the bucket near the garbage can where a delta formed of soggy tea bags, oxidized apple cores, wet coffee grounds, and paper napkins smeared with the primary-colored condiments. Although the room was kept cool for the electronic equipment, putrid odors filled the air. I sat down at the laptop.

In the once-upon-a-time I was only too happy to miss, we recorded conversations on magnetic tape. Because tapes can break or get damaged, agents kept a separate log for each phone line, marking date, time, and every single on-off moment. I'd seen illegible notes blotched with coffee and grease but since September 11, 2001, we recorded digitally in real time, down to a tenth of a second. The work was easier now, but more boring.

"Anything I should know before you leave?" I asked Stan.

"Things stay quiet until about 7 or 8 p.m."

I was certain he wanted to say more, but the gray door flew open with a bang and a woman tumbled into the room calling out, "Halloo!"

She carried a large embroidered bag and headed for the table at a run, hoisting the bag up, letting it land with a thud. She laughed, a high shrill sound. "I cannot believe who they give driver's licenses to these days; is anyone testing these people? By God's grace alone I got here in one piece. You must be Raleigh. I'm late!"

I glanced at Stan. He shifted his eyes to his briefcase, which lay open on the table near the enormous bag. He began stuffing papers, clamping it shut without organizing any of it.

"Excuse me," I said to the blustery woman. "You must have the wrong room. This is T-III surveillance."

"Louise Jackson." She stuck out her hand. "Only nobody calls me Louise. Except my brother. And he's got Alzheimer's so even he doesn't call me that anymore. My name's Beezus. My sister, may she rest in some kind of peace after what she did to me, she never could get Louise out of her cruel little mouth, and, well, you know nicknames. They stick like toad spit on a good dress."

She cocked her head, looking at me carefully. "What do they call you—no, wait, let me guess. They call you . . . Leigh."

"Raleigh. Just Raleigh."

"Okay, 'Just Raleigh.'" She swatted at my arm. "I brought us all kinds of goodies."

From the embroidered bag she extracted two thermoses and a series of Tupperware containers, stacking them on the table like a small Eiffel Tower.

"Don't worry about keeping up your strength. I brought plenty of fuel for us both. I pickled these radishes last summer." Suddenly she stopped, cocking her head again, like a dog hearing a silent whistle. "You know, before we get started, I better use the little girl's room."

Beezus raced out of the room. I looked at Stan.

"Who is she?"

"Beezus Jackson. She's cleared for security, but I've only seen her organizing files and stuff for Phaup."

Ah, the flashing red light. "Was she on phone surveillance before today, or is she a little gift just for me?"

"Um, well, it's a lot for one person."

"Stan, you're working alone."

"Yeah." He stretched out the word, layering it with inflections. "But see, they don't make a lot of calls on my shift. The gang sleeps most of the day. I've got two hours of silence. Your shift's probably different."

I took a deep breath. The stench from the trash gagged me. Or maybe the fact that Stan, a junior agent, only had to work two hours, alone.

"I'm on five hours, Stan."

"Oh."

Beezus blew back into the room. "Reporting for duty," she said.

Stan's face held a pained expression, like a gas bubble pressed against his diaphragm. He put one hand on my shoulder. "Good luck," he said.

I didn't even bother. It was just so obvious.

Luck didn't exist.

≈

The next morning I woke from crazy dreams knotted by two alternating threads: the incessant chatter of Beezus Jackson and the peculiar dialect of Ebonics spoken by gangsters. After a long, hot shower in the carriage house, I walked across the courtyard to the mansion on Monument Avenue.

Built by the Harmons in 1901, the three-story brick was creeping toward serious neglect. Maybe it was already there. Ivy invaded the top floor. Moss smothered the gutters. Autumn leaves, still not raked, swirled across the slate, hissing their opinion.

But a song was playing inside the house, a tune about deep and dreamless sleep, a place where silent stars go by. Nobody was in the kitchen, however. Or the den. The dining room was empty, along with the front parlor where the windows faced General Robert E. Lee's statue on Monument Avenue. I stared at the record, the RPM, spinning on my grandparents' hi-fi. I thought of the man with a cross burned into his lawn, and I listened to verses about hope and fears.

Three cardboard boxes rested on the velvet chairs, dusty tops open.

"Anybody home?" I called out, walking up the walnut staircase to the second floor. I knocked on my mother's bedroom door. No answer. Her four-poster bed was crisply made with red and green Christmas pillows lined up against the headboard. Down the hall, I could hear another kind of music. It sounded nothing like a Christmas carol.

We rented a room in the big house to Wally Marsh, a local

photographer who helped take care of my mother. He'd lived with us for about a year and had proved a loyal friend, although since our return from Seattle, I'd noticed some changes. Like the music, loud enough to rattle the iron hinges on his bedroom door. A rapper rhymed *town, down, crown, frown—*

I knocked. No reply.

I pounded. "Wally!"

The door finally opened. "I didn't hear you," he said.

No kidding. "Can you turn that down, please?"

His flat expression drained warmth from his brown eyes. A cold breeze blew through the open window, lifting the heavy scent of his cologne. Another new element, cologne. And jewelry. The rapper rhymed *dawn, con, turned on.*

"Seriously," I said, "it's too loud. Turn it down."

He shuffled over to the desk, his thin frame swallowed by baggy jeans. He lowered the decibels on the boom box from assault to annoying. The CD player glinted with chrome next to a computer whose monitor measured roughly the size of my television.

"Whazzup?" he said.

I let it go. "I can't find her."

"Nadine?" he said, as if another woman lived here besides my mother. "She's been creeping around the attic all morning, putting on holiday tunes, giving me a headache. I was trying to get some work done."

I glanced at the computer monitor. Four black guys wearing baggy black clothing flexed their hands in gestures that reminded me of dive-bombing crows. After years as a struggling freelance photographer, Wally hit the mother lode. Rappers.

"New clients?" I nodded at the picture.

He crossed his arms. "Be glad I'm not scrounging up rent every month. These guys pay."

I couldn't count the months we bartered dog walks, handyman services, and taking my mother for drives. Freelance photography paid enough to feed a houseplant and I knew that when we signed the lease. "Do you know a guy named RPM?"

He gave a dismissive laugh.

"What's wrong?" I asked.

"RPM? He's the bank. Dig?"

"Pardon?"

"His production company cuts my checks."

The urban patois didn't fool me. Wally's true citizenship was Nerdville. That's what I liked about him. He read the gossip section in the newspaper and argued religion with my mom. His parents, now deceased, sent him to Catholic schools and none of this simulated rap-speak changed my mind. Wally was still a nerd.

"If you run into the bank or anyone in that crowd," I said, "I'd appreciate it if you didn't say anything."

"About what?"

"About your landlady being an FBI agent."

His eyes opened so wide I saw the dendritic veins radiating from the dark irises.

"Me?" he said. "How about *you* don't say anything. Cut my ka-ching, ka-ching. Know what I'm saying?"

"Not exactly," I said.

≈

I found my mother downstairs in the front parlor, singing with Bing Crosby how she'd be home for Christmas, if only in her dreams. I watched her pull a crumpled mass of white tissue paper from a dusty box, peeling it back to reveal a red ornament. She held it to the window that faced Monument Avenue, as if waiting for General Lee's inspection. Winter light leaked through red glass, glistening like fresh blood. The last time I saw that ornament was the Christmas before my father died.

Madame, my mother's small black dog, jumped off the couch. Madame Chiang Kai-Shek, don't ask why. My mother plucked the name from thin air. I petted the dog's soft fur and Rosemary Clooney dropped under the hi-fi needle, insisting our troubles were miles away.

My mother turned. "You'll never guess who stopped by."

"Helen."

"Your sister's too busy," she said without a trace of judgment. "DeMott Fielding!"

DeMott. My high school boyfriend.

"He heard you were back in town and rushed right over."

Flynn, I suspected. If thousands of acres could be considered neighboring properties, Belle Grove was right next door to the Fieldings' estate on the James River.

"He said that 'rush right over'?"

"Don't be difficult, Raleigh. He wants us to come to St. John's on Sunday."

I walked over to one of the cardboard boxes, peering inside. "I'm working Sunday."

"No more moping around," she said. "I want Christmas like we've always had. Exactly like before."

After my dad died, we no longer celebrated Christmas. We survived it.

Inside the box she hauled from the attic I saw my old handmade ornaments, things made for my dad. "You go ahead to church. I'm working."

"What possible work could you have on a Sunday morning?" she said. "Rocks don't go anywhere."

"It's an interview." I pawed through the tissue paper. Even when I worked in the mineralogy lab, I never told my mother my job was with the FBI. My dad knew, but my dad didn't suffer from debilitating bouts of paranoia. His only fear was she'd wake up one day and decide I was investigating her. After his murder, I graduated from Quantico with no family in attendance. My sister, Helen—my only other close relative—believed FBI was English for KGB. I sometimes wondered if she was adopted twice.

"You're going to interview rocks, on a Sunday?"

"No, I'm interviewing another geologist. He's only available on Sunday." I kept my hands inside the box, rewrapping a starfish lacquered with Elmer's glue and red glitter that spelled *Dad*.

"Young lady, you're going to church. It's what we do. It's where we belong."

As I stuffed the ornament into my pocket, Wally came down the stairs.

"And we're getting a fir tree, just like we used to," she continued. "Wally's offered to take me."

"And it better not mess my ride," he said.

"Oh, Wally." My mother smiled at him. "Bless your heart."

It was a whole lot nicer than what I wanted to say.

chapter five

Later that morning, I drove to Virginia's southern half where slumbering rural towns started and ended within a quarter mile. Whenever I drove through these places, with their little gas stations and grocery stores and tidy houses, I had the corny idea that the boys here grew up and married pretty local girls and propagated peace through generations, each generation recognizing the special beauty and safety of small-town life. Of home.

But human nature was human nature, and when I parked the K-Car just outside the town of Boydton, I headed for the concrete block where a fair share of country boys jogged in hooded sweatshirts around a fenced yard, looking like defeated monks in search of lost prayers.

I handed my gun to a female guard inside Mecklenburg prison. She sat in a steel-and-Plexiglas booth and locked my firearm in a safe behind her desk. Picking up the phone, she called for an escort. He was a brown-skinned guard with a neck like a fire hydrant. His badge said Thomas. Last name, I was pretty sure.

"We got the man sedated," Thomas said. "You want to wait until it wears off?"

I shook my head and he signaled another guard sitting inside another steel-and-Plexiglas booth. The guard pulled a lever and tumbling steel cogs automatically rolled back the door. Mecklenburg was the wave of the future thirty years ago, a new design that put correctional officers in sealed booths that protected them from inmates. At the opening ceremony, the governor called the keyless facility "a monument to failure." As if to prove the other meaning to his statement, Mecklenburg set records for violent assaults, death row escapes, and guards who feared for their lives. While the keyless design made theoretical sense, in practical terms the place turned into a detached day care center—for grown men begging for attention. Any attention.

"You need me to stay?" the guard asked.

We were passing down the main corridor, a vacant channel of steel that amplified the sound of tumbling locks. We waited outside the infirmary. Mecklenburg was reclassified for low-security inmates, including hospice patients.

"No, thank you. I'll be fine."

The infirmary door slid back and I saw an emaciated white man in a hospital bed. His arms looked no wider than the side rails, his bony wrists handcuffed to the metal.

Hale Lasker lifted his head, moving his eyes over the guard. "This ain't your day, boy," he rasped. "I'm still alive."

The guard turned to me, his dark features barely concealing his thoughts. "If you have any problems, hit the emergency button over the bed."

Thomas walked away and the steel door slid closed, locking with a final snap. Standing beside Hale Lasker's bed, I showed my credentials. His parched skin smelled sulfuric.

"FBI." He pulled back pale lips. "You're the creeps put me in this hellhole."

"You wrote your own ticket, Mr. Lasker."

"And you're here to make sure I die?"

"Somebody burned a cross down by the James River," I said. "The land belongs to a wealthy black man who—"

"Sorry I missed it."

"Who lives there with his wife and children."

"Your point?"

"That area's your old stomping grounds and I need a name. Who runs the KKK out there?"

"What're you offering—parole?" He pulled back his lips. "I got cancer in the pancreas, toots. I got no need to help the FBI."

Blood pooled in ragged blossoms under his almost transparent skin, veins and arteries extending like plant stems. Nine years ago Ruth Lasker stumbled into our field office, her face swollen and distorted by bruises. Her speech slurred as she described the four-by-six cage where she was kept in a barn outside Lanexa. That morning, when her father left for his local KKK meeting, Ruth's five-year-old sister snuck into the barn and lifted the cage's key from its hook. Our agents had asked Ruth to sign her statement, and when I read through the file yesterday, I saw a shaky *X*.

Every one of Hale Lasker's cells was a palace compared to that cage.

"Do you care what's next?" I asked.

"What?"

"Heaven. It exists."

He almost laughed. A dry sound at the back of his throat.

"Eight years I been in here, eight years with nothing but questions. You're not going to hear my answers."

"But your group believes in God."

"My group? The Kiwanis?"

"I thought those crosses were supposed to put the fear of God in a man's soul."

"It's right there in the Bible, God don't want the races mixing."

"And you believe the Bible."

"'Course I believe it. Heard of Job? That's me. Festering wounds and all."

"With one big difference."

"Job was a Jew."

"God said Job was blameless."

He pointed his finger at me, the handcuff clanking against the bedrail. "Don't come in here high and mighty, toots. Everybody's got something they're ashamed of. Everybody. That includes you. I'll bet you—"

"Give me a name."

"Give me a cure."

"Who burned that cross, Mr. Lasker?"

"Who cares? Those people are gonna wipe out their own race. Shooting so-called brothers in the streets, sticking crack needles in their own children." He drew a wheezing breath, exhaling a fetid stench. "That's where we went wrong. We should've been watching the Mexicans. Those people will eat us alive."

"I'm offering you one last chance. Do something right. Tell me who burned that cross."

He closed his eyes and breathed as though the white blanket was a lead apron. He lifted his right hand, the metal cuff slithering down the bedrail. His bony fingers stroked the air.

"Leave."

I stared at his eyelids. The skin looked as tenuous as parchment.

"Every one of us gives a full accounting in the end," I said.

"You don't know."

"I know you might beg for a hellhole like this."

The eyes shifted under the papery skin but my jab didn't open them. After several minutes of heavy breathing, he seemed to have fallen asleep and I walked over to the steel door, pressing the black button to notify the guard. His reply sounded like words bouncing through a tin can.

I turned to look at Hale Lasker, his eyes still closed, the pauses lengthening between his breaths.

An electronic buzz released the steel locks. The door slid open.

Thomas nodded.

"Ready?"

But suddenly he grabbed his nightstick.

Lasker sprang up, pressing himself forward. The gooseflesh tightened in his neck as he cried, "Take this sinner away! Take her to burn in hell!"

His head dropped and the hospital gown sagged over his concave chest. Slumping on the bed, he rolled his head from side to side, moaning.

I looked at the guard. His brown eyes churned with silt. He replaced the nightstick, lifting the radio. "Tell the nurse, infirmary needs more morphine," he said.

I glanced back as we left.

Hale Lasker was still rolling his head, moaning, staining the white pillow with a greasy halo.

chapter six

My drive back to Richmond felt even longer because the K-Car's AM radio played only static-filled country songs and the heater blew like an air-conditioner.

By the time I pulled into town, I was shivering through Friday afternoon rush hour. I pumped coins into the meter on Seventh Street, covering the twenty-two minutes that remained before free parking kicked in, and jogged past the usual odd mixture of folks standing outside the federal courthouse. Lawyers, defendants, prosecutors, and families—black and white, lawkeeper and lawbreaker alike, all doing that curious tense dance of the South. It took eighty years after the bloodiest war on American soil for Richmond to allow black men to join the police force. And that was because a different war, World War II, drained the still-struggling pool of Southern white men, leaving the first black officers to hold accountable the very people who controlled their freedoms, from drinking fountains to schools to jobs.

Today, sixty-plus years later, Richmond's police force was predominantly black. And so was the criminal element, something I left to the sociologists to figure out.

In the police annex's compact lobby, I showed my credentials to the receptionist while two officers—one white, one black—listened to an elderly black woman. She wore a ragged wool coat and her rebukes sliced like knives.

"Right on your car it says 'Serve and Protect,'" she was saying.

"So how come I never see you when bullets are flying past my grandbabies? You want to tell me where you at?"

The receptionist buzzed the door and I walked down a hallway lined with softball trophies. A police cliché, but softball was the game for this job, leaving time for deceptive small talk. You hear about the old woman who wouldn't leave? Claimed her family's blood was on our hands. She's crazy, right? Right?

Just after the vending machines, I found the pebble glass door with one name removed. It said DETECTIVE J. NATHAN GREENE.

I knocked, waited for word to come in, then got the look salesmen get used to.

"You don't look happy to see me," I said.

"I'm surprised," he said. "They let you come back?"

Since the last time I saw Detective Greene, his thick mustache had sprouted gray and new lines etched his brown face. Though not yet forty, he looked old, especially around the eyes. Six months ago his partner, Detective Michael Falcon, plunged six stories to the sidewalk. Another man fell too, both killed on impact. The detective was white, the other man black, and the city divided on race. The mayor called in the FBI to decide if the white cop threw the black man off the roof or the other way around. I was the agent heading up the civil rights case. I was suspended while working it.

"Got a minute?" I asked.

"No."

I stepped inside.

He sighed. "Nothing's changed."

I sat down in a chair so old the wood cried. The cold-case detectives had furnished the small office by diving into Dumpsters behind city schools, and the concrete block room was just big enough for two dilapidated desks.

"Do you have any old files on the Klan?" I asked.

"Why?"

I told him about the cross burning at Rapland and my visit with Hale Lasker. "Lasker's the last thing in our files on the KKK. He went to prison eight years ago. I was hoping you had a cold case with a newer name."

"You need it right now?"

"It's a hate crime."

He nodded, wrote a note, and pushed it over by his phone. It was an old phone, the numbers rubbed off. "How was Oregon?" he asked.

"Washington."

"Whatever. Now you're back. Working another civil rights case. Really moving up in the world."

"I'm working a task force too." I felt pride rising to my defense. And I felt stupid the moment the words left my mouth.

"Which task force?"

"Southside gangs."

"I'm working that." He frowned. "I haven't seen you at any briefings."

"I just started. What's your connection to our task force?"

"Gangbangers create half my cold cases. Nail these guys, I might close twenty cases. Plus I've got the informant you Feds need."

Richmond's cold cases numbered in the hundreds. The files were stored in dented metal file cabinets that stretched behind Detective Greene's desk. One of those files was my dad's unsolved murder and every time I walked in here, I tried to forget it. And failed.

"What part are you working?" he asked.

"Surveillance."

"Whereabouts?"

I stared at the floor. It was the cheapest vinyl, scuffed. "Okay, I'm on the phones."

"Man, she *really* doesn't like you," he said, referring to Phaup.

I didn't trust my voice, or my words, so I didn't say anything.

"Okay, Klan info," he said, changing the subject. "That it?"

"I also need a dictionary."

"For what?"

"For what I hear on the phones."

He pawed his mustache, considering the geometry of things. Finally he said, "You wind up in Poughkeepsie, leave me out of it."

"Totally unofficial translation."

"What don't you understand?"

"I heard something last night that sounded like a prayer. But it was twisted."

"Did it go, 'Now I lay me down to sleep, two shotguns folded at my feet'?"

I nodded.

"We think the local gang's getting recruited by a national group. Something called the Gangster Disciples. Thirty years ago some prison degenerate started lifting pieces of the Bible for his 'book of rules.' Today it's run like a corporation and they pick up local gangs like franchises, do some kind of profit sharing. The locals funnel drugs into small towns and schools. You might hear stuff that sounds like Proverbs but believe me, it's not. And some stuff Gabriel said about respect and freedom."

"Gabriel—the angel?"

"The slave. As in Gabriel's Rebellion?"

I shook my head.

"There was a slave named Gabriel Prosser. Back in the summer of 1800, he planned to attack Richmond, slaughtering every white man, woman, and child. But another slave ratted him out. They hanged him. But this gang worships him. Or they used to. Now it's all about cash. We think the money's coming from the Gangster Disciples, but we can't say for sure. Yet."

"Drugs?"

He nodded. "My snitch buys from them. Who are you reporting to on the task force?"

Shame washed up my throat. Under normal circumstances, I'd report to the agent in charge of phone surveillance, who then reported to the agent in charge of the task force, a guy named Pollard Durant. Pollard reported to Phaup. Normal chain-of-command stuff.

"I report directly to Phaup. On everything."

"That's some tight leash," he said.

I feigned nonchalance. "I'll be fine."

"Sure you will," said the detective. "Eventually."

chapter seven

On a cold Saturday morning in December, the monoliths that lined the streets of Washington, D.C., looked like Advent panels nobody would want to open. The frosty wind off the Atlantic Ocean tunneled down streets choked with dirt-caked yellow cabs that honked as black limos slithered past with darkened windows and diplomatic license plates.

I made my way through the maze of a declining capital and parked under the J. Edgar Hoover Building on Pennsylvania Avenue, between Ninth and Tenth. After passing through security, I rode the employee elevator to the Materials Analysis Lab.

My old stomping grounds.

I felt a twinge of envy passing the lab's toys. X-ray defractor. Ion scanner. Mass spectrometer. At one time I thought it was the world's greatest job. Hunt for answers, plug in data, fight crime.

And minerals didn't have personality disorders.

At the far end of the lab a young woman waited for me. She wore a white lab coat with faded jeans and wool socks with Birkenstock sandals.

"You must be Annette." I extended my hand.

"No. I'm Nettie," she said. "Don't ever call me Annette."

Her firm grip felt callused as a rock climber's. She had replaced my favorite colleague who retired while I was in Seattle. Last night she left a message on my cell phone. She had results for the cross-burning soil; she worked Saturdays.

"You said the soil was peculiar," I said.

"No, I said there were two compounds within the soil that were peculiar."

I smiled. She was exactly what you wanted in a lab tech. Not just accurate, but precise.

"Can you take me through it?"

Nettie Labelle pulled on safety goggles and rubber gloves and picked up a sterile syringe. My paint can containing the soil from Rapland sat on a steel table. She inserted the syringe's tip into a small puncture hole in the can's lid, drawing a sample of air, and turned to the large instrument set on the steel table. Its Plexiglas panel revealed an extended capillary tube. As she injected the syringe's invisible contents into the machine's capillary tube, I heard a starting gun go off in my head.

The great race of Gas Chromatography Mass Spectrometer.

"This is my fourth run on these volatiles," she said. "Just so you know I didn't pull these results out of thin air, so to speak."

"Four runs?"

"I thought something was wrong."

Inside the instrument a small furnace heated the vapor within the capillary tube, exciting the compounds and breaking their bonds. As they separated into individual molecules, the smaller elements sprinted through the capillary tube, while the larger molecules lumbered for the finish line. Nettie pushed the safety goggles up on her forehead and keyed up the computer monitor.

Within moments colored bar graphs started rising and falling on the monitor, showing individual weights and speed of travel for each molecule. Call me a nerd; I loved how GCMS was like a track race with no names on the runners. Like being told there's a 119-pound female who does the hundred-yard dash in thirteen seconds. Your job was to figure out her name.

Back in the early days, we matched molecules by combing through chemistry textbooks. These days computers did all the work.

"That's what I'm talking about," Nettie said as the mass spec painted its final graph, tossing names on the monitor. "The accelerant used to light that cross was mustard gas. And something called lewisite."

"Mustard gas?" I leaned forward, staring at the results. "From what, World War I?"

But she was already walking back to her desk down the hall from the instrument room. The smallest forensics department in the lab, mineralogy was tucked into the building's north side. Nettie dropped into a swivel chair, stubbing her Birkenstock into the floor to pivot and reach under her desk, pulling out a folder.

"Mustard gas isn't even the most peculiar compound," she said. "Wait until you meet lewisite."

"Mineral?"

"Deadly chemical compound," she said cheerfully. "All by itself, lewisite is nasty stuff. But add in some mustard gas and the toxicity goes off the charts. Whoever used these chemicals wanted to make sure that cross burned."

She flipped the folder open so I could see.

The clinical photographs magnified five and ten times showed angry rashes that oozed blood and pus.

But Nettie seemed unfazed.

"In addition to the skin trauma," she said, "lewisite produces convulsions, vomiting, and catatonic states. Sort of like what happens to me when somebody hands me a Barbie doll. Mustard gas does about the same. Burns, blinds people. But it smells like geraniums."

"What?"

"Yeah, that's what I read. Who knew? I take that back. Whoever put this stuff on the grass knew. Or they're dead from contact." She tossed me the folder. "Your copy, all the data."

Opening the file, I glanced over her notes. Her penmanship surprised me. Scrolled and flourishing, as feminine as a wedding invitation, somehow it made the medical photos even more gruesome. "I appreciate the quick turnaround. Thank you."

"But you're going to tell me something's wrong."

"This happened in rural Virginia. See what I'm saying?"

She nodded—a quick, excited gesture—and combined with the spray of freckles across her nose and the faded jeans, she looked all of fifteen. "I wondered about that too. So I went through the lab's back files on cross burnings. To check accelerants."

"And?"

"Nothing's even close."

"Nothing?"

"They mostly use gasoline and lighter fluid. For all we know, these yahoos are drinking it too. Cross burnings aren't rocket science. At least, not until this one came along." She cocked her head, her long braid of brown hair dangling to the side. "What else are you thinking?"

"The Klan's in its fifth and sixth generations. Is there a way to figure out if these compounds are fresh?"

She sat up, excited. "You mean, if they came from somebody's great-grandfather who fought in World War I? Then the questions would be, can mustard gas dating from World War I still work, and if so, what conditions are needed to preserve it and keep it flammable?"

So young, so eager. So much like myself when I started in the lab, thinking science would solve the big puzzle of human cruelty.

"Those are good questions," I said.

"Are you asking me to look into it, officially?"

"I'd appreciate it."

"You got it," she said, as if I'd done her a big favor.

chapter eight

Sunday morning I drove my mother's 1966 Mercedes Benz sedan down the city's silent Sabbath streets. Flicking my eyes between the rearview mirror and the road, I watched Wally, who sat in the backseat staring out the side window. His ebony eyes were bloodshot and jaundiced. His skin bloated from interrupted sleep.

But something else, something I couldn't quite name, bothered me more.

"You all right?" I asked.

The bloodshot eyes glanced at the mirror. "I'm fine," he said.

"You look tired."

"Working late, that's all."

My mother sat in the passenger seat and reached over, patting my leg. "He's nervous about going to church."

"I'm not going in the church, Nadine. I told you, I'm taking pictures of that boneyard. That's all."

She smiled. "That cemetery's close enough to get touched." Her voice filled with defiant cheer. "Wally, there's nothing to be afraid of. God loves you."

"Talk about being afraid," he said. "Look what you're wearing."

She was wearing a red boiled wool jacket, a color that nearly matched the leather inside the antique Benz. The jacket's brass buttons shone like badges but the matching skirt dropped three inches below her knees and the low-heeled shoes were incapable of offense, the footwear a candidate's wife takes on the campaign trail. This was not a good sign.

She turned all the way around to look at him. "What's wrong with what I'm wearing?"

"You didn't check it out?"

"I'm wearing church clothes."

"Church *uniform*," he said. "That looks nothing like you."

It was true. My mother usually wore exuberant prints, heels like stilts, and skirts one inch embarrassingly short.

"You look afraid of not fitting in," Wally said.

"Hey," I said. "Take it easy. Nobody's forcing you into that church."

He glowered out the side window as we passed downtown's old department stores. Thalhimers and Miller & Rhodes, closed years before, abandoned for free parking and food courts at the suburban malls. On either side pawnshops sprouted up and furniture stores rented sofas for 20 percent interest monthly. Steel bars covered the windows.

But this was my city. Richmond. Noble and sad. Heroic and fallen. Forever on the verge of turning around. So much potential it hurt.

I glanced over at my mom. "You're not nervous?"

"Whatever for?" she chirped.

For the memories, I wanted to say. For the anticipatory ache I already felt ten blocks away. My father's church, the church for generations of Harmons, all the way back to 1775, when Patrick Henry stood up and delivered his ultimatum on liberty and death. St. John's was also where we had his funeral.

After that, I couldn't go back. Neither could she.

But now my mother asked to return and my goal was to make her happy, so I parked the Benz on East Broad Street where sloping porches made the wooden row houses look drowsy and walked around the front of the car to open her door. Wally ignored his usual courtesy and headed down the sidewalk carrying a large new Nikon. The church bell bonged with unalloyed tones, reverberating down the long white steeple.

"Nadine?" the greeter called out. "Nadine Harmon—is that you?"

Wally immediately stepped off the brick path and headed for the cemetery.

"LaRue?" my mother said.

"Nadine, bless your heart," the woman said. "It's been ages!"

They gave each other hugs while I turned to watch Wally, his thin legs lost inside the baggy black jeans. He stumbled on the undulating grass where soil had settled around the graveyard's guests. He kneeled beside a gray marble headstone and brushed his long dark fingers over the stone's front where weather and time had erased names and dates. His face remained remote.

"LaRue, you remember my daughter, Raleigh Ann," my mother said in her new singsong voice.

Suturing a smile to my face, I shook her hand. She said something I couldn't hear because DeMott Fielding was coming toward us from inside the church. Far, far away, I felt the woman releasing my hand. My heart thumped in my chest.

He stood beside the woman. "Hi, Raleigh."

My response was ready—I'd practiced it all day yesterday. But when I opened my mouth, my heart beat even faster, turning my words into an incoherent mumble.

"DeMott!" my mother exclaimed. "Raleigh, look, it's DeMott."

As if I didn't see him. As if my face wasn't crimson. As if right here on the front steps of St. John's Church I wasn't having a myocardial infarction.

DeMott smiled and took my mom's elbow, leading her inside.

Feeling numb and confused, I followed and tried to breathe. But the odors of wool and mulberry and perfume choked the narthex. People streamed past us, hurrying as the pipe organ bellowed its prelude to worship.

"Come sit with us," DeMott said. "We have plenty of room in our pew."

"Thanks, but—"

"We would *love* to," my mother gushed.

He guided her down the crowded aisle. She chattered away. "You have no idea how much I've missed men with manners. Seattle certainly is beautiful, but the men? They have no earthly idea of chivalry. I had to open all my own doors. Can you imagine? And poor Raleigh. She could not wait to get home."

DeMott turned, grinning again. "Is that right?"

I looked away, heartbeat racing, telling myself it was some kind of homesick reaction. Nothing to do with DeMott Fielding. *Calm down.* But my mind refused to cooperate. It kept conjuring up his words from last summer, when he told me he knew the perfect guy for me and opened his arms wide and said, "Someday you'll figure it out."

He opened the box pew. The Fielding sisters, Jillian and MacKenna, sat on the dark wood bench and my mother settled in beside them. I stepped in after her and suddenly realized my mistake. DeMott closed the short door and sat next to me.

A tight fit.

I wiggled out of my coat. In 1741 when the church was built, these wooden box pews retained heat when parishioners carried hot bricks and stones to St. John's services. My mother tried recreating the sensations, scooting closer, pushing me into DeMott. I tried to sit back. DeMott shifted, stretching his right arm across the back of the pew, and heat bolted across my shoulders.

No way would I make it through this service.

"So you met Stuart," he said.

"Pardon?"

"Mac's fiancé. Stuart. He says he met you over at Flynn's."

So that's how he heard I was back. Phaup got one thing right: Charles City County was too small. I glanced over at his sister, Mac.

"I thought she got married in September."

"That was the plan," he said. "You left before all the fireworks."

I wanted to ask, but the pipe organ burst with fresh vigor and the congregation stood. Feet scuffed the old wooden floor, hymnals fluttered open, and our voices joined the chorus, each of us proclaiming joy to the world and wonders of his love.

And wonders, and wonders of his love.

chapter nine

Later that Sunday, I walked into the Bureau's wiretap room with two bags of fast food. I was branching out. One bag from McDonald's, one from Burger King.

Stan was cleaning up his mess, moving with a speed uncharacteristic for a man his size. Beside him, Beezus Jackson talked over the dead audio feed.

"If I tried to eat the food you people bring in here, why I'd be doubled up for weeks. And if you don't mind me saying, you look a little bloated. Have you ever been tested for gluten?"

Stan tossed his trash in the tall garbage can, which had been emptied at least once since Thursday and now was only three-quarters full. The stench hovered just below pass-out proportions.

"They kept busy last night," Stan said. "Asleep all day today. Pollard wants updates after every shift."

"Got it."

"They're talking like a hit's about to go down. We're still trying to decipher the code, so keep your ears open. And call Pollard right away if anything sounds imminent."

"Are you saying they're going to kill somebody?" Beezus said.

Stan walked out the door and I set my greasy feedbags on the table. Taking a seat at the laptop, I put on the Bose headphones. The cursor pulsated on the audio feed, ready for a phone call.

"Did I hear him right?" Beezus said. "A hit?"

I unwrapped one Big Mac, careful not to knock any sesame seeds off the bun. My mouth watered. I was one of those junk food addicts who could recite the Big Mac's ingredients by heart, but even I doubted the all-beef part.

When Beezus started to say something, I held a finger to my lips. "We need to be very quiet tonight," I said before taking the inaugural bite. "No talking. Okay?"

"My lips are sealed," she said. "You won't hear another word out of me. You just watch. I can keep quiet with the best of them. That's why Ms. Phaup put me on this assignment." She placed her finger to her lips. Bright fuchsia lipstick made her mouth look like she'd just eaten a Popsicle.

I bit into the two supposedly all-beef patties with their special sauce, lettuce, cheese, and onion—no pickles for me—and Beezus reached into her embroidered bag and lifted out two shawls. She silently offered me one. With a stab of shame I accepted her generosity, and we settled in for a long, cold night of listening.

"What's up?"

That was the usual greeting. Never hello. Not even hi.

"You hear from him?"

I kept paper beside the computer, jotting down words, anonymous pronouns. *Him—who?* Beezus leaned toward me. She wore her own headphones but liked the conspiratorial atmosphere.

"Yeah, he called. Going down tomorrow night. In time for Christmas, baby. Santa's coming to town."

Laughter.

"You watching the game over here?"

"Who's there?"

"Mule's bringing Peanut, Hooligan, and Smoke."

"Can I bring Zennie?"

"Aw, dawg. Peanut's bringing broads. Zennie ain't cool with that."

"I'm just asking."

"Ask all you want. But Zennie Lewis ruins it for everybody. You hear what I'm saying?"

I clicked off the digital receiver, counting silently to fifteen. My teeth clenched.

"Oh, hurry," Beezus said.

But there was no hurrying. Title III wiretaps were written in very specific language. They covered only certain topics of conversation, and we were forbidden to listen beyond the stated boundaries. This wiretap, for instance, specified criminal gang activity. Personal affairs, including watching a basketball game and arguing about "broads," were off-limits, and highly paid defense attorneys liked to examine our wiretaps making sure we obeyed the law. Any topic change from crime required cutting away from the conversation for at least fifteen seconds, then cutting back in to see if the topic had changed again. Since the recordings were digital, anything less than fifteen seconds meant the defense attorneys could buy more Maseratis.

At fifteen, I snapped the tape back on. The caller said, *". . . be there for the tipoff."*

Then the phones went dead.

Beezus snapped a carrot. "Rats."

But the second line suddenly lit up.

"Goody," she said.

"Yo, baby," the caller said. *"I was sitting here thinking about my Z-girl."*

"The *girl*."

"You are, baby, you are."

"Granny says she'll watch Zeke. Come get me."

"Yeah, little change in plans, baby. Here's the thing. I gotta work tonight."

There was a significant pause.

I waited, hoping he would say something about work, something that was even vaguely criminal.

"*You said we'd watch the game together, Moon,*" the woman said.

"*Baby, that's what I want. But XL, he just called. Says I gotta work. Pow-wow on the Christmas party, know what I'm saying?*"

"*XL? You're hanging at XL's?*"

Beezus glanced at me, raising her eyebrows.

"He's lying," I said, trying to stretch my limit. "Lying is criminal."

"*Man's the boss,*" he said. "*I gotta work, girl. You hear what I'm saying?*"

"*I hear you, Moon, I hear you good. I hear you choosing homeboys over me.*"

"*Zennie, be cool.*"

"*XL,*" she said. "*He's extra large, all right. Extra-large liar.*"

I hit the digitizer, starting my count to fifteen.

"He's still lying," Beezus said.

"But now it's a lovers' quarrel." And I'd already stretched jurisdiction. Six . . . seven . . . eight . . . nine . . .

"But what if their argument tells you something about the gang? Doesn't that make it okay to listen?"

"Not according to the lawyers." Thirteen . . . fourteen . . . fifteen . . .

"*I'm blocking your number, Moon. Don't call me.*"

"*Baby, I'm telling the truth. I swear. I'm working tonight.*"

"*Yeah, working your zipper.*"

She hung up.

I watched the monitor, sensing it wasn't over. And sure enough, the man named Moon dialed the guy named XL—or Extra Large, if the woman could be believed.

I wrote the names on my notepad, waiting for the line to pick up.

"How bad I gotta be there?" asked the man named Moon.

"Girl runs you like a pony. All the booty in town, you gotta pick Zennie Lewis?"

"I asked you"—Moon's voice was almost growling—*"do I gotta be there?"*

"I don't know, Moon. You wanna see the fat man come down the chimney or not?"

There was a pause.

"Moon, what's the book say?"

"My brother and I are one, for I know what he's done."

The line went dead.

"Men," Beezus said. "They always stick together."

I was writing notes, trying to capture the words and slang, when the monitor lit up again. The number belonged to the guy named XL but the number he dialed came up "unknown." I wrote the local area code so that Pollard Durant could decide whether to subpoena the phone company for a name and address. While the FBI was sworn to uphold laws, the rest of the world used Google, and judicial approval for our wiretaps sometimes took longer than the phone's free minutes—meaning the cell got tossed in the trash and we had to start all over again. Cell phone surveillance was a long, rotten game of darting mice chased by a lumbering cat.

"Keep your eyes on Moon tonight," XL told the caller.

"Whazzup?"

"You don't need to know. You need to do what I say."

"Just asking."

"Everybody asking," XL said. *"Nobody wanting to obey."*

"So what do I look for?"

"Loyalty," XL said. *"We might got a loyalty issue."*

When XL hung up, he called Domino's and I cut the line. Pizza orders weren't exactly criminal, unless they mugged the driver. I stayed off until XL started dialing the 212 area code. New York City. I made a note for Pollard. The gangbanger asked long odds on tonight's game with the Chicago Bulls and I didn't cut the line because gambling definitely qualified as criminal activity.

"Betting is so foolish," Beezus said.

I put my finger to my lips.

XL said, *"I need some quick turnarounds, Minks."*

"Depends on how dice gets rolled." His voice was foreign, the *r* rolling.

"What if I need to call in a favor, Minks? Can I do that?"

The pause lasted three seconds. Four, five.

"I grant such favors. For you," said the man in New York.

"Cool. That's cool, Minks. I like you. Really, I do."

Then the line went dead.

"He didn't even explain the favor," Beezus said.

Later that night, two more calls connected to the man named Minks. More bets. I added them to the note for Pollard and when my shift ended at 9 p.m., the game headed into overtime. Two agents came to take our places, young guys from the cybercrimes unit, and Beezus toodle-ooed a good-bye. I walked to my desk by the stairwell door and typed up notes, e-mailing them to Pollard Durant, cc'ing Phaup.

My old files sat on the floor by my desk, still packed. Dates scrawled in black marker.

I dug through the years, searching for notes from another task force. Also for drugs. Also gangs. It had put half a dozen men behind bars and kept one man out.

His name was Milky Lewis. And I was hoping he had a smart-mouthed relative named Zennie.

chapter ten

Monday morning's sky pulled up a blanket of washboard clouds, agreeing as I hit the alarm's snooze button—twice. After showering, trying to wash troubled T-III voices from my brain, I walked over to the big house.

My mother stood at the kitchen stove making pancakes.

"Ready for breakfast?" She wore pressed wool slacks, a white sweater with a giant green tree smothering the front, and black velvet flats, a bad sign. Down the hall, Judy Garland hoped I had a merry little Christmas.

As I sat down at the table, her dog, Madame, curling at my feet, I closed my eyes, silently praying for a gracious attitude toward whatever landed on my plate. Pancakes, in my mother's kitchen, consisted of wheat-germ-and-honey monstrosities, dense disks that tasted like chemistry textbooks.

But I opened my eyes to two perfect silver dollars, golden and light, and a platter of wavy bacon strips glistening with melted fat.

"Is that real bacon?"

"Of course it's real bacon!" she said, as if she'd never served soybean strips stained pink to resemble pork.

In moments like this, I usually caught Wally's eye, sharing in the bewilderment that was my mother. Sometimes they were good moments, when she tottered on high heels and uttered piercingly accurate wisdom; more often, though, bad moments, when her mind stumbled across an invisible string that stretched across her soul like a trip wire, sending up paranoid explosions.

"Where's Wally?" I asked.

"I knocked on his door." She went back to the stove.

"And?"

"And he said he wanted to sleep. The third time I knocked, he said he had a stomachache."

Having used these same sleep and stomachache excuses myself, I was tempted to tell him it was real food this time. But she was shuttling among the stove and sink and fridge, working like a woman preparing brunch for twenty.

"Is Helen coming?" I asked.

"Helen?" She took orange juice from the fridge, decanting it into a glass pitcher. No carton for this morning. "Helen has finals this week; she's much too busy."

She poured me a glass of OJ, using the good leaded crystal, and I glanced down at my plate again. Tiny holly leaves danced around the gold rim. Her best Christmas china.

"So who's coming?" I asked.

"For what?"

"Breakfast."

"Nobody."

"Just me?"

"But she promised to see us for Christmas."

"Who?"

"Helen." She tilted her head to the side. Normally it was one of her most endearing gestures, the long, dark curls cascading next to her porcelain face, a gesture of pure femininity as she looked at me with a mother's evaluative love. But today her hair didn't move. It was stuck, sprayed stiff into some dark helmet. And she didn't seem to see me.

"Is something the matter with Helen?" she asked.

"No." I picked up my fork. "Helen's great. Helen's always great."

She watched me take the first bite. The golden crust broke delicately, a fluffy texture inside. I smiled, chewed, smiled, and within seconds a sharp metallic flavor seeped across my tongue. My throat closed, tasting aluminum. Baking soda. Way too much baking soda.

"How are the pancakes?" she asked.

"Wow." I grabbed the orange juice. "It's been a long time since I tasted something like this."

"I've got plenty more where those came from," she said. "Eat up."

───

Just as his secretary said, the sheriff for Charles City County was sitting at the small table beside the window facing Route 60, eating his breakfast at Jean's Country Diner in Providence Forge. Newspaper in one hand, biscuit in the other.

"Mind if I sit down?" I asked.

He looked up. Reading glasses perched on his small Irish nose, his blue eyes flickering with unspoken assessments.

"Best biscuits in town." His voice drawled rural Virginia, the vowels slow and undulating.

I took the seat across the table, my stomach aching from my mother's metallic pancakes. But I'm a girl who never refuses good food, particularly good Southern food, and the diner smelled of butter and salt, milk and flour. Hot biscuits. Food heaven. The sheriff raised his hand, signaling the young woman behind the counter, and slipped his glasses into the chest pocket of his brown uniform. He glanced out the window, his eyes following a truck thundering past the diner, heading east on the Pocahontas Trail.

"What can I do for you, Agent Harmon?" he asked.

"I'm sorry to interrupt your breakfast, sir. I wanted to speak with you in private."

"You tell my secretary you were with the FBI?"

I shook my head, sliding my card across the table. Last summer the sheriff took my statement down by the river. It wasn't a professional encounter; it was victim and law enforcement, and we never spoke again. His sparsely populated county—as close to Williamsburg as Richmond—consisted of working farms and river plantations and boasted one of the lowest crime rates in the state. Our records showed just one FBI arrest, nearly a decade ago. Hale Lasker.

He picked up my card, slipping it behind the reading glasses. His old skin looked weathered and ruddy, the face earned by a committed fisherman. "Y'all looking into the cross burning?" he asked.

"Yes, sir. Your department responded to the 911 call, is that right?"

"I was there."

"Can you tell me what you saw?"

"You investigating me?"

"Sir, I—"

"I'm old, but don't treat me like a fool."

The waitress appeared, a pretty girl in faded blue jeans, and set down a plate of steaming biscuits. She poured me a cup of coffee, topped off the sheriff's mug, and walked away.

"I don't consider you a fool, Sheriff."

"But you want to come here and talk to me, real casual, to find out if I'm covering up something. And I'm not supposed to figure out that's what you're doing. So either I can act like that fool or you can quit playing games."

"How would you handle this, in my position?"

He leaned back, casting his blue eyes out the window again.

"First thing I'd do is take a good look at my deputies. They're white, they're black, their grandparents couldn't sit at that counter together, but we get along. We get along just fine."

"Somebody isn't getting along."

"You think I can stop that? You want me to wave a magic wand? But here you come throwing gasoline on the fire."

"The man who owns that property claims your department isn't taking the threat seriously. The FBI agrees."

"Take what seriously?" He picked up the newspaper, shaking it. "We had somebody spray-painting swastikas over at St. Peter's cemetery. I had reporters calling from Virginia Beach to D.C. I even had a TV reporter stand outside my office for two days, demanding we do something about the county's 'white supremacist' problem."

"When was this?"

"September."

I was in Seattle. "Hale Lasker—"

"They kept bringing up Hale Lasker too," he said, heat rising in his voice. "Hale Lasker, the guy is literally a dead horse. Everybody accused me of not taking it seriously. They wrote stories for weeks and pretty soon we had swastikas in every cemetery. And then what happens? More stories. More reporters. That woman even showed up from New York—the news girl?"

I shook my head.

"My wife used to watch her in the mornings. She looks like a troll. Katie somebody."

"Katie Couric?"

"That's the one. She came down here and did an 'in-depth' look at our 'white supremacist' problem. I kept saying knock it off. But soon as she ran that story on national television, Karl Stein's plumbing truck got covered with swastikas. Karl Stein. The guy's a Lutheran, for crying out loud."

"Sheriff, where—"

"Right before Thanksgiving I caught the sons of guns. Bunch of bored teenagers who read about Nazis and went to the cemetery on a dare. Dumb kids but the media made them famous so they kept going. And you know what? Not one of those graves was Jewish. They were German, like Karl Stein. If you pay too much attention to this nonsense, it just gets worse."

"Sheriff, this particular cross burning goes beyond a teenage prank."

"That's your theory."

"No, sir. It's based on evidence. Forensics."

"Doesn't matter," he said.

"Pardon?"

"Best thing to do is ignore it. Let it die. Somebody got it out of their system. Now it's done."

"Sir, do you expect the people in that house to ignore this? The fire could've burned the place down."

His blue eyes flickered. "You're right. What do I know? I'm just a backwoods sheriff."

"Sir, I didn't mean—"

He stood.

"Enjoy the biscuits, Agent Harmon." He picked up his hat. "They're on the house."

Tipping the hat, he walked out the door.

≈

I drove along the county's winding rural roads, catching glimpses of the James River through the bare trees. The water flashed like channeled mercury and when I reached Rapland, a van with a satellite on its roof was parked in the driveway. Cujo stood in the guardhouse, waving his permission, and Sid met me at the front door.

The foyer looked like an airport baggage claim. Suitcases

were piled against the walls and more were coming down the stairs, carried by two young guys in dark nylon sweat suits. To my right, the pocket doors were slid back and music thudded from the speakers in the old parlor, rhyming *rain* and *pain* and *complain*. White boxes stood in rows, each labeled. Vaccines. Shoes. Toys. Bandages. Syringes.

I was about to ask Sid a question when two little boys bolted across the hallway, screaming with joy, followed by a woman whose dark figure seemed shaped by Modigliani. She wore a batik wrap skirt and a University of Virginia sweatshirt. She called out to the boys in a foreign language, her tone more tired than angry.

I looked at Sid.

"RPM's wife," he said. "Wonkehmi."

"Beautiful."

"I'd introduce you, but she don't speak English," he said. "Her name means 'only she who takes action can know the outcome.' And the woman takes action; they got four more kids around here somewhere."

"It's usually like this?"

"Loud and crazy?" He grinned, his gold tooth glinting. "Man likes a full house. And he's gonna be real happy if you came to tell him who burned that cross."

I gave my official smile. "Where can I find him?"

Sid pointed toward the stairs and I started the climb while a little boy scooted down the stairs on his bottom, followed by an older boy who appeared to watch over him. Neither acknowledged me, just one more person in the house.

At the top of the stairs, I turned right and walked past the fortune-making records to the door at the end of the hall where a bright light was shining within. I stood outside, listening.

"Are you considering moving, now that you've been the target of a hate crime?" A deep voice, perfectly modulated.

"I refuse to let something like that intimidate me," RPM replied. "My ancestors faced worse."

The reporter asked several questions about RPM's work in Africa. The questions floated as slow-moving softballs that RPM knocked over the fence.

Waiting for the interview to finish, I stared at the old photos hanging on the wall, the black-and-white pictures frosted silver like daguerreotypes. The people wore high-collared suits and layered dresses, and behind them palm trees grew in powdery soil. There were no white people in the photos.

As the reporter concluded the interview with a profuse thank you, I stepped into the doorway. The cameraman folded a reflecting panel set beside RPM, who stood by the fireplace, wearing a gray seersucker suit.

"Miss Harmon," he said as I came into the room. "I could use some good news. Have you come to tell me who's responsible?"

The reporter swung, hunger in his eyes. "You with the police?"

"Miss Harmon is an FBI agent," RPM said. "She's looking into the hate crime."

The reporter shifted his coyote eyes to the cameraman already picking up his camcorder again, flicking on the light.

"Don't bother," I told them. "My comment is no comment."

The reporter shoved the microphone at my face. "How long do you think the KKK was planning this attack? Do you have any leads on this cross burning? How serious is the white supremacist problem in this area?"

I wanted to say something, but the only bad film was silent film. I looked over at RPM. He raised his eyebrows, expecting me to answer. In his world, publicity was a good thing.

"What will you do if there are more attacks?" the reporter asked.

When I didn't respond, RPM stepped forward. He touched the reporter's arm gently, almost deferentially.

"I understand your need to pursue the truth," he said. "But it appears Miss Harmon would prefer to speak to me in private. Could you give us that courtesy?"

The coyote turned into a sheep.

"Oh, of course, I didn't mean to get in the way." The reporter continued apologizing, performing a celebrity genuflection, and RPM promised to call as soon as "we" knew anything. I waited for them to pack up and watched them walk down the hall with their equipment. Down the stairs, out the door. I watched until they crossed the driveway.

"You'll have to excuse them," RPM said as I came back into the room. "They're from *Entertainment Tonight*. My publicist tells me the phone has not stopped ringing since news of the burning got out. And here I moved to Virginia for privacy. So much for that endeavor."

I closed the door. "We need to establish some boundaries. If you or your publicist talks to the media, I can't keep you entirely up to date."

"Oh, certainly, I understand," he said. "All right. You have my word. No more interviews. Not about this. And to be quite honest, I was speaking with them only to highlight my upcoming trip to Africa. I was hoping to raise awareness." He paused. "Do you find that crass?"

"Not at all."

"Good. Now, you have my word, I will not repeat anything without your permission. Tell me who did it."

"I wish it worked that quickly. Our lab managed to pinpoint the chemicals used to light the cross."

"Pardon me for asking, Miss Harmon, but how does that help anything?"

"They're obscure chemical compounds."

"Yes?"

"Do not repeat this," I said.

"I gave you my word."

"One is mustard gas."

He frowned. "World War I veterans are after me?"

"We don't know who's behind this. Yet. But these rare compounds are like fingerprints."

"Fingerprints. Provided you discover the hand behind the crime."

"Correct."

"And how much longer will that be?"

"We're moving as quickly as possible."

"Just how much patience do you expect I'll need, Miss Harmon? And is my family safe while I'm waiting?"

I let the jabbing questions go, and he drew a deep breath, holding it a moment before releasing.

"I'm sorry," he said. "I'm very sorry. I don't like leaving my house under these circumstances."

"Where are you going?"

"Liberia. We're taking over aid supplies to my wife's village. The need is appalling."

"Can I reach you if something comes up?"

"You can leave messages with Cujo; he's staying to guard the house. I don't take business calls on these trips. It distracts me from the good work we're doing over there."

Suddenly, I understood the daguerreotypes. When I asked, he smiled.

"Yes, how observant of you. My ancestors recolonized Liberia. Freed slaves. I grew up hearing the stories and decided to continue the mission, if you will. Then I met my beautiful wife—our children are half Liberian—and things have come full circle." He paused. "Which reminds me. May I ask you a question? It's about Wall-Ace."

"I'm sorry—who?"

"The photographer? I believe he lives with you."

"Wall—you mean Wally Marsh?"

"That's his given name, I'm certain, but in the rap world he's known as Wall-Ace." His smile turned apologetic. "As I told you, the linguistics don't make much sense. He asked to come on this trip with us, to take pictures. Sid did a background check on him—that's what Sid does—and his landlord came up as Raleigh Harmon. It seemed inconceivable that Richmond could have two Raleigh Harmons."

"I prefer to keep my personal life private."

"Oh, certainly, certainly. I struggle with that myself. I simply found it a curious coincidence."

"Wally Marsh rents a room from me, yes."

"Is there some reason we shouldn't take him?"

"He's an excellent photographer."

"Good. We're excited for him to document the trip. And he'll be compensated generously," he said. "You're sure this isn't a problem?"

"Yes."

"You seem surprised."

"When will you come back?" I asked.

"It's difficult to pinpoint a day, Africa operates on its own time. But perhaps when we return, you'll know who burned a cross on my property."

"That's my sincere hope," I said.

chapter eleven

There was more ballast for dinner—stuffed mushrooms, soggy as dish towels—but I ate second helpings of everything, hoping to make my mother happy, hoping to get used to the incessant cheerfulness that seemed as authentic as a plastic garland.

Immediately after dinner, despite the dark and cold, I pulled on my running gear and sped down Monument Avenue to my sister Helen's office.

Even as a kid, I could have predicted Helen's future career. My family couldn't drive down Monument Avenue without her commenting on the Civil War statues that made the street so famous, and tonight, as I jogged down J.E.B. Stuart, I could still hear my sister's critique. The war's most famous cavalryman sat on a rearing horse, the animal's right foot raised. The general was turning in his saddle, also to the right, which incensed my sister.

"He should be turning left," she said when she was ten years old. "His body should counterbalance the horse's movement."

My own thoughts were more prosaic, even back then. I was bothered by the traffic pattern around the statue. The one-way street headed east so drivers could only see J.E.B. Stuart's face in the rearview mirror. Helen said that was symbolism for you.

And now she nested in academe, a professor of painting at Virginia Commonwealth University. Her books on Vincent van

Gogh produced effusive reviews in the Sunday *New York Times*. She was lithe and agile and beautiful, and she irked me to the point that I empathized with van Gogh's urge to sever his own ear.

As I walked into her office off Broad Street, she said, "It's Mom, isn't it?"

I was still panting from the cold night run, pulling off my knit cap and gloves, my fingertips stinging.

"Well?" she said.

A nice office. High ceiling. Picture window overlooking Broad Street. Nothing like my hovel next to an echoing stairwell.

"What's going on?" she demanded.

"She decorated the house like it was five years ago. She's trying to cook with white sugar and white flour, which she normally considers poison, and the Christmas carols are playing twenty-four-seven."

"Raleigh, I'm in the middle of finals. Can't you come by the house next week?"

No way.

Helen lived in bohemian splendor on Oregon Hill with an abstract painter named Sebastian Woodlief. Spawned by prestigious British boarding schools, Sebastian considered himself a passionate supporter of the workingman, despite never having a job himself. My dad prayed Helen wouldn't marry somebody like this. Unfortunately his prayer was answered. They weren't married; they lived together.

"Why don't *you* come by Mom's house?" I said. "She hasn't seen you since Thanksgiving and she keeps asking about you."

"So what's the problem?" Helen plunked down behind her drafting board. "She's decorating, celebrating Christmas, and this is a problem because . . . ?"

"She wanted to go to St. John's on Sunday and wore some

outfit from Montaldo's. She sat frozen stiff through the entire service, then said it was *perfect*. Does that sound like her?"

"Be glad she's not with those nutty Pentecostals."

After my father died, my mother gravitated toward charismatic services.

"It's not about the church, Helen. It's about why she's going. She's forcing herself to perform duties she doesn't even enjoy or believe in. Maybe it's guilt or fear or some paranoid obligation, but it's like living with a robot."

"Leave her alone. Vincent said all religions are equal. Buddhist, Christian, Muslim. They're all the same, so it doesn't matter where she goes."

Queen of the button-pushers, my sister maintained an annoying habit of referring to Vincent van Gogh by his first name, as if they were intimate friends. But nothing sent me over the edge faster than when she moralized about my faith using the words of a guy who sliced off his own ear after an argument with his mistress.

"Helen, what if I said all paintings were the same?"

"What?"

"It's all paint," I said. "So we shouldn't judge *Sunflowers* as any better than somebody's amateur watercolor."

She crossed her arms. Her enormous gray sweater hung on her tiny frame like a dress. "You are," she said, lifting her fine chin, "the most annoying person on the planet."

"I love you too."

She rolled her eyes. Beautiful eyes. Almost turquoise. "What do you want me to do?"

"Come see for yourself. She's acting like a wind-up doll. Something's about to snap."

"As soon as finals are over."

I sighed. That meant next week.

"Are we done?" she asked.

"Almost," I said. "Is Milky around?"

She shook her head. "Not this again."

≈

A 265-pound former crack addict, Milky Lewis had a face that looked like it sped through puberty so fast it missed the exit. Soft and rounded, with bones that didn't seem quite set, his brown face grew a wispy black beard sparse as tumbleweed. His child-like appearance disguised a bitter childhood, a childhood spent guarding the front door while his mother prostituted herself for drugs. Later Milky sold crack to support six younger siblings.

Leaving Helen's office, I ran down to the Lucky Strike building, a former tobacco warehouse on Canal Street. Shuttered by Philip Morris decades ago, the gouged pine floors still reeked of the sweet and bitter scent of curing tobacco leaf. I found Milky in one of the studios, swirling an acetylene blowtorch over frayed steel cables. An artists group had converted the warehouse into studios and a gallery.

"R-r-raleigh?" He pushed up the protective visor.

Milky's stutter was terrible, but it had saved his life. Without it, he'd be in jail.

"How are you doing, Milky?"

"I-I-I thought you moved to Oregon."

"Washington."

He shrugged, signaling the truth. Most of the East Coast, particularly the South, saw Pacific Northwest states as one big indistinguishable region.

Twisting off the blowtorch, Milky asked what I thought of his sculpture. It was a mess of soldered steel and I offered him the same response that I gave my mom for her food.

"Wow."

"Ye-yeah," he said.

"Helen says you're working down here in the art gallery."

He nodded, telling me about the art show, and I listened carefully. But he would always be streetwise and finally he stared down at his beefy hands.

"Wh-why are you here?"

We would never be friends. I never pretended otherwise. The FBI had picked up Milky as part of a joint drug task force operation. I was a relatively new agent, assigned to the interrogation room. Milky's stutter improved when I talked to him. To keep himself calm, and get around difficult words, he drew pictures. When the task force ended, successfully, Milky served four months on a plea. His buddies did years. I showed his drawings to Helen, who pulled him a full scholarship to VCU. Probationary.

"Are you related to a girl named Zennie Lewis?"

I watched another layer of betrayal settle into his dark eyes.

"Wh-why?"

"I can't tell you, Milky. Is she family?"

"C-cousin."

"Close cousin or four marriages and two half-brothers removed?"

"T-tell me wh-what she's done."

Close cousin, I decided. "I need to talk to her. That should tell you enough."

He wanted to know what we were offering her.

"We talk first; any deals are later. If there are deals."

The soft brown flesh buckled across his forehead. "You hear about any other L-Lewises?"

"Just Zennie."

But the pained expression on his face said he didn't quite believe me.

≈

The cold bristled in my lungs as I jogged from the tobacco ware-house, heading up East Main. Although I didn't like running at night, at times like this, happiness really was a warm gun, and when my cell phone rang, I didn't stop but unclipped the phone from my waistband, glancing at the LCD display.

The sheriff from Charles City County.

"Miss Harmon?" he said in his slow drawl.

"Yes?"

"I thought you'd want to know."

"About what?" I was passing the Jefferson Hotel, so lit up the white stone glowed.

"In case it's true, y'all might want to get out to Rapland right quick," he said. "Somebody just called in a bomb threat."

chapter twelve

Fifty-four minutes past nine o'clock, I sped the K-Car down Rapland's driveway. Blue-and-white police lights criss-crossed the dark. I counted six cruisers lined up bumper-to-bumper behind a white EMT van, its back doors open.

When I stepped out of the K-Car, the air smelled of inciner-ated rubber and scorched metal and a strange peppery scent. The officers stood together beside the EMT van, using it as a shield against the burning mess on the other side.

Outside the eight-bay garage, the gravel had blown away, the garage doors splintered with shrapnel from the torn vehi-cle steaming and smoldering on the rocks. The windshield and part of the roof were gone and a stick shape leaned out of the vehicle, as if trying to see around a blind curve. One append-age dangled, terminated in red jelly and I glanced at the head, once. Soot-streaked bone. Melted hair. Restraining the gag reflex, I swallowed, tasting the green and peppery air.

Geraniums.

Yanking my turtleneck over my nose and mouth, I ran toward the officers. Safety glass crunched under my feet. The sheriff was speaking to the EMTs. I swallowed again, throat burning. The peppery scent blew in waves, riding a breeze off the river.

"Sheriff."

He turned, startled by my hidden face.

"Sheriff, get everyone away from this scene now."

"What?" he said.

"Call Hazmat. Get these men in their vehicles—"

"I already called the bomb squad." He sounded defensive. "We don't know if the gas tank already blew but we're not stupid; that's why we're standing over here."

My eyes burned. "Can you smell that?"

"What?"

"The smell, like geraniums? It's a deadly poison. Get your men out of here or you—"

"I don't see—"

I turned to the medics, speaking to the older one. "Do you have gas masks?"

He glanced at the sheriff, almost laughing. "No."

"This isn't a joke, Sheriff. Please. It's a poison, used as a fire starter."

He ran his flickering eyes over my face. His expression shifted from suspicion to realization. "Everybody in their cars—now!" he yelled. "Now!"

I looked at the medics. "Start treating everyone for exposure to vesicants."

"For what?"

"Blister agents." Still speaking through the fabric of my turtleneck, I squinted to limit the fumes' contact with my eyes. "Get everyone to the nearest hospital. Wash the skin. Check the lungs."

I glanced back at the main house, thirty yards away. The lights were on. Cujo stood on the front porch, his muscular form looking squat and thick.

"He refuses to talk to me," the sheriff said.

"Get to the hospital, Sheriff. I'll wait for Hazmat."

"But you're—"

"I haven't been exposed as long, and the wind is carrying it away. Were you here when the bomb went off?"

"No."

"Good. Get to the hospital anyway."

I ran for the house. The security lights blinked on as I moved across the lawn, throwing a long shadow on the ground surrounded by glass fragments that glittered like diamonds. On the porch, Cujo held an assault rifle, the muzzle pointed toward the porch floor.

"Quick, get inside." I reached around him, opening the door. "Are any windows open?"

"What's going on?" he said.

"Are they open!" I slammed the door shut.

"No," he said. "It's cold out, why would—"

"Keep the house sealed tight. Don't open any windows. Where are the chil—"

Hearing a whimper, I turned. The woman in the batik skirt and UVA sweatshirt sat on the stairs, looking down at us. Four little boys in pajamas clung to her skirt, their brown eyes widened with fear. Another two, older, stood behind her with assorted women, all black, all scared.

"Were they outside?" I asked.

Cujo shook his head.

"Don't let them out; the air is poisonous right now. Do you know who was driving that car?"

"Some local kid. Cleveland."

"That's his real name?"

"I don't know. We just called him Cleveland."

"What was he doing?"

"Starting all the cars. You know, to keep the batteries running in the winter. RPM's got eight cars out there, and they don't get driven—"

"How often did he do that?"

"Cleveland? Once a week."

"Was it the same night each week?"

Cujo thought about it. Then nodded.

"When the bomb went off, where were you?"

He pinched his black T-shirt, ringed with sweat. "In the gym. I heard something sounded like the end of the world. I grabbed my gun, ran outside—"

"How long were you outside?"

"Long enough to see the flames."

"How long?"

"Couple of seconds. Everybody was screaming so I came back in here."

"RPM's left for Africa?"

"They took off about eight o'clock."

"When did this thing go off?"

"About nine thirty," he said. "I had the TV on in the gym, my show was almost over."

I heard a siren blaring and glanced out the window beside the front door. Two fire trucks barreled down the driveway, red lights spinning. When I looked back at Cujo, his eyes had turned to anthracite.

"Yeah," he said, as if answering a question.

"Yeah what?"

"Notice how they didn't call the fire truck till now? This is why RPM called the Feds. Whole house blows up, and what, I'm gonna get us all out in time?"

I glanced up the stairs. One boy had buried his face in the woman's skirt. She patted his back. He whimpered. The others just stared.

I turned my back, dropping my voice. "Cujo, put the children somewhere they can't see or hear anything. Please. I'll send a medic in to see if there's been any exposure. But above all, stay inside where it's safe."

"No kidding," Cujo said.

I pulled my turtleneck back over my nose and mouth, opened the door, and ran for the K-Car.

Windows up, vents closed, I watched from inside the car as gas-masked firemen sprayed down the blown-up vehicle. It still smoldered in the cold, gray clouds rising from its scorched form. When the state Hazmat team arrived, I flashed my headlights and somebody wearing a yellow protective suit and visor lumbered toward my car. I cracked my window two inches, introducing myself. My throat stung. I hoped it was just the cold air and my run earlier tonight. I introduced myself.

"Tom Brennan," he said, speaking through the plastic helmet. A black tube connected an air pump to his suit.

"Tom, it's an obscure but deadly vesicant," I said carefully. "There might even be two blister agents, but I smelled one in the air when I got here. It's something called lewisite, it smells like geraniums. You might also be dealing with mustard gas."

"So why are you still here?" he asked.

I slid my card through the window. He fumbled it with his thick gloves, managing to pinch it between his thumb and forefinger.

"When you're finished here, call my cell," I said. "I'll tell you where to send the evidence."

There was a sudden flash of light and we both jumped. But it was a large security light on the side of the garage, triggered by a Hazmat technician who was waving both arms. The bright white beams made him look like an actor onstage.

Tom Brennan began walking over and I turned the key in the K-Car, driving slowly around the keyhole curve, cutting around the fire engines. The spotlighted technician was kneeling now, trying to pick up something. The object was large and unwieldy, and as Brennan approached, the technician stood, holding a rectangular slab of metal in both hands. One edge was torn. The gray surface dented.

But even from here I could see it was the car's door. And I could read the paint. The letters were red, dripping like blood.

KKK.

chapter thirteen

Winter sparrows greeted Tuesday's dawn with their song about poor Sam Peabody, Peabody, Peabody, Peabody, but as I walked across the Bureau parking lot, all I heard was: dead body, dead body, dead body.

And upstairs, Phaup was waiting.

"Did you get an ID on the deceased?" she asked as I took a seat in her office.

"Nothing confirmed." I cleared my throat. It felt a little raw still. "The man who works security out there says he was a local kid."

"He wasn't in the car?" she asked.

"Who?"

"Who do you think, Raleigh?"

"RPM is in Africa."

"So they missed him."

"Probably."

She raised both eyebrows, feigning dismay. "Probably?"

"Somebody's watching that property. They lit a cross and planted a bomb without being seen under huge security lights with armed guards. They made sure the bomb went off after he left."

"You opened a file on the sheriff?"

"Yes, ma'am."

She reached into her taupe silk blouse, tugging. I glanced out the window.

"I spent one year in Mississippi," she said, "another two in Louisiana, now five in Virginia. The South is racist and that infects local law enforcement. Take a good look at that sheriff. And I want this case resolved before the new year."

"But my work on the phones—"

"I'll find a replacement—you're not exactly essential to the task force. Word got out on the Internet about this bomb. I've already taken calls from four reporters this morning. You want to hear their angle? The FBI is dragging its feet on this because he's black. So if this isn't closed by—"

"I got it."

She stopped.

I ran the tip of my tongue against the back of my teeth, pressing out the rest of the words. "No disrespect meant, ma'am. I've been up most of the night tracking the evidence and getting a medical checkup for exposure to—"

"Sounds like you need a less active field office."

For several moments I held eye contact. But she was better at this, and I was wrung out. Shifting my eyes, I stared at the lapel of her crisp navy suit. The clothing that was climbing gear for the FBI ladder.

"If you want to stay here, Raleigh, this case gets closed by the end of this month," she said. "Do we understand each other?"

"Perfectly," I said.

≈

Next to the echoing stairwell, I typed up a version of last night's events, removing every ounce of emotion from the crime scene, pushing aside the image of the dead kid and the scent of burned flesh among deadly geraniums. I typed facts into a wall that could repel armies of invading defense attorneys, and with my standard precaution I printed everything in triplicate: one copy for the Bureau, one for the U.S. Attorney's office, one for the fiery catapult launched by the defense. With my hoarse voice, I left a message for Nettie Labelle in the mineralogy lab.

"You'll be getting a package from the state today," I said, explaining what was inside and what happened. "Obviously the case is an even more serious expedite, so I'm thanking you in advance for your time."

Most of the material would go to explosives, but Nettie was the first person in the chain of command since she received the first pieces of evidence in the case. By rights, the sheriff had jurisdiction over the crime scene, but it didn't take much last night to convince him to use the FBI's lab. When I left Rapland, I found him and his deputies and a state trooper at the Medical College of Virginia's emergency room. One man was vomiting. Another complained his eyes were on fire. A state trooper was taking a shower. And the sheriff's normally ruddy complexion looked almost green.

After directing the paperwork to its respective homes, I drove to McDonald's and ordered hot tea with extra honey and an Egg McMuffin. I tried to choke down the food, then I drove out New Market Road under a midmorning sky that couldn't decide whether to cloud or clear. The gray cumulus shapes fulminated like sea foam before breaking, exposing the blue that lay beyond. And then covering it up again.

Twenty minutes after leaving town, I reached the point where the James River divided into an oxbow and followed a colonial-era road down to the water, passing sheep fields and slave quarters and barns that once hid soldiers wearing blue and gray. The three-story house at the plantation's center was set on a bluff overlooking the hairpin twist in the river. It was a place the Chickahominy Indians called Weyanoke—meaning "where the water turns around." Robert MacKenna named his plantation after it, and the Fieldings who followed never changed it.

As I pulled up, DeMott Fielding was lifting a wooden mallet, cracking a croquet ball across the estate's perfectly level front lawn. A dozen people stood with him. Guys in down parkas and chinos. Girls clad in bright scarves and wool coats. His sister MacKenna turned, watching DeMott jog to my car.

A green croquet ball sizzled across the cold grass. The girls jumped around, hugging each other. The guys groaned.

DeMott didn't turn to see what happened. His skin was russet from the cold, his smile wide and white. My throat was feeling better after the hot tea and honey, but when I looked at DeMott, it started closing again.

"What's going on?" I asked.

"Mac's making up for lost time," he said. "Throwing party after party before the big day. Not that I blame her after a grand jury bumped her wedding."

Harrison Fielding, their father, held vast reserves of money and did things with it that the FBI frowned upon. His grand jury indictment was tangentially related to one of my cases.

I cleared my throat. "I didn't create that situation, DeMott."

"No, you didn't." His blue eyes were luminous. "You want to go for a drive or something?"

"DeMott!" MacKenna called across the lawn.

A girl blessed with gazelle legs, and knew it, Mac wore her standard outfit, jodhpurs and black riding boots. Her leather-gloved hands held a silver tumbler, making her look plucked from imperial India.

"DeMott, your turn!" Her honeyed Virginia accent carried an edge.

DeMott waved the mallet. "Stuart can take it." He dropped his voice, muttering, "He can cheat up a win for the guys."

"Can I talk to you?" I said.

He pointed the mallet toward a stand of old tulip poplars,

their dark limbs unraveling against the marbled sky. We stopped beside the icehouse, a short round building that tunneled into the earth. At one time, the plantation's only refrigeration.

"Did you hear anything last night?" I asked.

"You mean the bomb?"

"You know."

"I thought it was thunder. I went outside and saw the sky turn bright pink downriver. So I called Flynn. She told me a bomb went off at Rapland."

"You called Flynn?"

"Who else would I call? The girl pins her ear to that beloved ground every morning."

"You could call the sheriff," I pointed out.

"Flynn's got the dirt on everybody and everything. Much as I respect Tink."

"Tink?"

"Sheriff Tinkham. Ron Tinkham. Around the county, he's known as Tink. What's all this about anyway?"

"Did Flynn happen to mention that a kid was incinerated? That women and children were inside the house? Did she tell you that?"

"Hey, Raleigh, take it easy." He held up the mallet like a crossbar. "All I know is what I just told you."

I glanced back at the croquet party. A tall man with a buzz cut wrapped his arms around Mac, pulling her close. Stuart, the groom, the man I met in Flynn's greenhouse. Despite his affection, Mac stared petulantly toward us. I was ruining her party.

"How well do you know the sheriff?" I asked.

"Don't go there, Raleigh."

"It's a simple question."

"All right, here's what I know. His daughter's a meth addict. She's in prison. Tink and his wife are raising her two kids. The kids happen to be black and they love them to pieces. That's what I know."

"That's all great. But this entire county has the population of one small town. He's been sheriff out here nineteen years, and he thinks Hale Lasker was the end of the road for racists."

He tapped the mallet against the side of his boot. "If I could give you the name of somebody to talk to, would you return the favor?"

"Who is it?"

"You won't be disappointed."

"What's the favor?"

He laughed. "You're one careful girl, Raleigh. Mac's throwing a fancy shindig Friday night."

I tried to read his expression, whether this was casual or serious. "You're asking me for a date?"

He nodded.

"But we're making a deal for it?"

"Because I know you. If some purpose isn't attached, you won't come." He continued to bounce the mallet against his boot, then looked down. "And I didn't know what you'd say if I just asked you. Because of what happened last time."

Last time. Prom night. Ten years ago. When I woke up with DeMott passed out next to me and half my clothes off. He assured me nothing had happened, but when he asked me out again and again, I said no and no, then left for college, thinking I'd never look back.

"Mac won't mind? I'm not exactly her favorite person."

"Do you really care?"

"Actually, I do."

"Way I look at it, once you land on somebody's list, you might as well ride it all the way down."

He smiled.

Snap went my heart.

"Seven o'clock Friday night," he said. "Deal?"

"Deal," I said. "What's the name?"

≈

The sky gave up the ghost on my way back into Richmond, turning to lead. It suited the mood in Detective Greene's office.

Sitting at his desk, he gripped his head between his hands. Even after I stepped inside, closing the door, saying, "Hello?" he continued staring down.

Finally he swung his dark eyes up. The whites were jaundiced, as if the brown irises were leaking. His brown skin seemed covered by a layer of gray ash.

"You okay?" I asked.

"Sick." He winced. "Don't come in."

I was already in. "So go home."

He shook his head, winced again. "Can't. Task force. Tonight."

The small room had a fevered scent, thick, almost rancid. But I couldn't leave. It was the first time I'd ever seen a hint of vulnerability in him.

"Can I do anything?"

"Leave."

I opened the door.

"Sorry," he muttered.

I closed the door.

"I checked," he said. "No KKK files."

"Okay, thanks."

But when I didn't open the door, his bloodshot eyes darkened. "Ask," he growled.

"Maybe it can wait."

"Don't even—"

"The sheriff in Charles City County, you know him?"

He nodded, winced, squeezed his eyes shut. "Tinkham." Perspiration beaded like pearls on his dark forehead.

"Your honest opinion, would he ever cover for the KKK?"

His eyes filled with a baleful expression. "Right now, you gotta know this? You can't let me die first?"

"You can't work tonight. The task force should find somebody to cover for you."

"Can't. Can't trust them."

"You can't trust th—" I stopped. "Oh. Your source."

His nod was feeble, barely perceptible. But it told the whole story.

He worried the FBI would steal his informant. Cutting into his territory, smothering the meager thunder that came from the parsimonious sky. It was a legitimate threat, exacerbated by informants who weren't exactly altruistic types. In bidding wars the Feds usually won.

But I would never admit it out loud. The Bureau was like family: I can insult my sister, but you try it? I'll take you out.

"I'm hurt," I said. "Truly, deeply hurt. You don't trust us with your source?"

He dropped his face into his hands again, groaning.

"Even me?" I persisted. "You don't even trust me?"

chapter fourteen

I slept four hours in the carriage house. Woke at 9:09 p.m. Took my second shower of the day. Dressed in my warmest clothing. Dashed across the courtyard to my mother's house, starving.

She was baking cookies. An entire regiment of gingerbread men cooled on the wire racks, dressed in frosting vests with cinnamon dot eyes, a delirious scent of nutmeg filling the kitchen.

"Help yourself," she said in the singsong voice.

I decapitated one of the cookies. It tasted like sand marinated in molasses and allspice.

"How are they?" she asked.

"Wow."

"I'm so glad you like them." She smiled. "Are you going out?"

"I'm meeting a friend at the movies."

This was almost true. The real truth was coming from down the hall. The song told of a world long in sin and pining in error. To make up for my fib, I kidnapped eight gingerbread men, thanked my mother, kissed her cheek good-bye, and walked outside, wishing my soul felt its worth.

At five minutes to ten, I pulled into the parking lot behind the Grove Theater, waiting for the detective's informant, Steve Sullivan, known as Sully.

But fifteen minutes later, Sully still wasn't there. The K-Car's

heater was cranking out sixty-five degrees, the warmest this winter, and after another fifteen minutes, the windshield had fogged,
forcing me to roll down my window. A luscious aroma draped
the cold air, a scent of sautéed garlic and chicken stir-fried in
hot oil. I glanced at the back door of The Peking, a restaurant
next to the movie theater. My stomach growled. I rolled up the
window.

Fourteen minutes later, after I'd flicked the heater on and
off, hoping to jump-start hot air, my stomach sounded like a
bear waking up from hibernation. I flipped open my cell phone
and called The Peking, ordering the Hawaii 5-0. I waited eight
minutes, watching headlights stream past on Libbie Avenue, then
called again, making sure the order was ready. I bolted past the
plaster lions outside, tossed a twenty on the counter, not waiting
for change, and raced back to the car, half-scolding myself for
hoping the detective's informant didn't show up until I finished
my food.

But selfish thoughts bring just rewards. As I took my first
bite of the 5-0—tender prawns that tasted like the sea itself, garlic kissing my taste buds—the passenger door opened.

He leaned down, talking to me across the K-Car's bench
seat.

"You must be the replacement," he said.

"You're late," I said.

Steve Sullivan, aka Sully, dropped his scrawny body into the
car. He bounced the bench seat, testing the busted springs. "Nice
ride," he sneered. "Hey, that looks good. Chinese?"

Closing the Styrofoam clamshell, I slipped my meal back in
the white plastic bag. *Good-bye, 5-0. So long, fortune cookie.* Sully
looked around the K-Car.

"You drive around in this thing?" he said. "You're not, like,
embarrassed?"

I set the food on the floor in the back, bookending it with my briefcase and gym duffel.

"Why don't you drive a Crown Vic like every other cop in town?"

I clenched my teeth into a placating smile and pulled onto Libbie Avenue. At the red light on Cary Street, I glanced over. Twice. Sully had the pasty skin of an Internet junkie. Lank hair not quite brown, not quite black, and long, narrow jaw that reminded me of some nocturnal creature that burrows to hide food. But what disturbed me most were his hazel eyes. Too brown, they obscured more light than they reflected. And there was no mistaking his default setting. Wicked calculation.

"Nate parks down the street on Decatur," he said.

"Nate?"

"He probably makes you call him Detective Greene."

"You two have a routine worked out, is that it?"

Sully glanced over, the muddy eyes calculating. "Didn't he tell you?"

"He said I'd be driving tonight."

Sully scooted back, trying to get comfortable, then ran his hand over the bench seat. "What is this, plastic?"

I glanced out the window, heading into downtown on East Cary. "You know these buyers pretty well?"

"Without me, Nate's got nothing. I'm the key to the vault."

"Is that right."

He looked over, the eyes doing their calculus. "You don't know the situation here?"

"I'm new. You can enlighten me."

"All you need to know is I'm the lead. Nobody else. I go in and tell these guys the way it is."

"Really. What way is that?"

"The way I say it is."

A necessary evil of law enforcement, informants displayed an abundance of qualities that God explicitly hated. Sully went over the top with his extra-haughty eyes, but he seemed like the kind of guy who enjoyed playing both ends against the middle, then snickering as he wiggled out of collateral damage. When he looked over again, I felt another shiver of suspicion.

"You don't believe me?" he asked.

"I'm sure you're a big help to Detective Greene."

"Babe, I'm all he's got."

Stifling a full-body cringe, I glanced out the side window as we crossed the Manchester Bridge. The streetlights illuminated the river below where hulking black boulders snagged the inky water, tearing white strips down the middle. We crossed over to Southside. I turned on Decatur and drove behind one of the many abandoned mills, checking my mirrors for cars and pedestrians and lookouts. All I saw were lonely brick factories, looking as patient and resigned as stones awaiting the erosion that would sift them back into the earth.

I backed the K-Car into a dead loading dock, cut the head-lights, and let my eyes adjust to the dark. I did not want to turn on the dome light. I counted fifties to five hundred dollars, the bills crisp and fresh. It was some sign of respect, the detective had said with a grunt of disgust. "Big egos want big, new bills."

I held out the money to Sully. His attenuated spine pressed against the passenger door. When he reached for the bills, I pulled them back.

"Hey!" he cried.

"Here's the deal, Sully. On your way back, walk across the bridge."

"What?"

"In case somebody's following you." I wasn't taking chances, not with this guy. Instinct told me he wanted to pull something,

something he could blame me for. Not only would I never regain the detective's trust, but by January I'd be working in Topeka.

His muddy eyes confirmed my suspicions. Darting sideways, twice, they finally riveted on me, sizing up the fresh blood.

"Man, that bridge is, like, a mile long!"

"Quarter mile, maybe." I held out the bills. "Meet me at Riverfront Towers. In the parking deck."

He dropped the F-bomb attached to the second-person singular and pointed out the obvious. "It's cold out there!"

"Yes, I know. I waited fifty-seven minutes in the same cold."

"This isn't how—"

"Yeah, but I'm not your buddy. I'm the replacement, remember? So do it my way or we call it a night."

He snatched the money from my hand. "You're a real—"

"Save it," I said. "I got the picture."

≈

When Sully stomped off to the crack house, I was tempted to follow, just to see where it was. That wasn't information listed on our phone surveillance, since nobody in this gang had a landline, only a cell phone. The detective had only told me where to hide the car, waiting for Sully. And I didn't want to blow our cover.

Driving back across the bridge, I parked on Ninth Street preparing for Sully's approach and reached into the backseat. A thin skin had coagulated over the Hawaii 5-0, its witty pineapple slice soggy, the white rice dry and stiff. For one brief moment I considered the redneck microwave—sticking the Styrofoam container under the hood on top of the running engine. But that would flag my location.

Bowing my head, I gave thanks again for the food and prayed for a safe night. As if insulted by the wait, the shrimp had curled up on itself. The beef and chicken held their own, but when I leaned forward to read the fortune cookie, catching enough light from the street, I read it twice, making sure. *"You will win the admiration of your pears."*

I folded the paper, slipping it into my coat pocket, remembering that my dad used to say he always expected his fortune to read *"That wasn't chicken."* I laughed at the memory, my breath clouding the cold car as I pushed back the stinging sensation in my eyes.

Twenty-nine minutes later, shivering with the cold, I saw Sully walking across the bridge. He had a slacker's gait, skinny malnourished legs extending from his wilted torso, fists crammed into the front pockets of low-rider jeans. Even from this distance I could detect the passive-aggressive hostility slithering up his spine. When a crisp wind blew across the river, pushing the shaggy hair into his eyes, he flicked it away, neck snapping like a viper.

But no pedestrians followed him. No cars trailed behind. Just Sully, having his twentysomething tantrum.

I drove across the street, turned down the concrete pad under Riverfront Towers, and pointed the K-Car up the ramp so that Sully marched flat-footedly into my headlights. Opening the passenger door, he tossed himself on the bench seat, bumping me upward with the landing.

I held out my hand.

He pulled out a small baggie, pinching it between his thumb and forefinger. He wagged it back and forth like a doggie treat.

I refused to beg, leaving my hand open.

He shifted his arm, trying to drop it out of my grasp.

I caught it midair, then flipped open my notebook. "Who was there?"

In a bored voice he gave several names. Two sounded familiar.

"Moon," I repeated. "What's he look like?"

"He's black."

"No kidding, Sully. How about a real description?"

"Nate knows who they are. Can we go?"

"What about XL, is he the leader?"

"He's black, too, and because you made me walk across that bridge, you're going to drive me exactly where I want to go."

It was like negotiating with a spoiled toddler.

I closed my notebook and followed his directions back to the Fan District. A brick row house on Floyd Avenue was just close enough to VCU's campus to befall the tragedy of converted apartments. And parties.

"Drive around the block," Sully said.

"Don't worry, I won't blow your cover."

"It's the car, stupid. Anybody sees me in this thing, I'd die."

He got out without so much as a good riddance and slammed the door. In my side mirror, I watched him disappear down the sidewalk.

I called the detective.

"Feeling better?" I asked.

"I just unloaded my gun in case I try to put myself out of my misery."

"I don't want to add to your pain, but you know Sully's loose, right?"

"Sully's crooked as a three-legged dog." The detective sneezed, then groaned.

"Bless you," I said.

"Thanks. What'd he do?"

"For one, he was an hour late." I described his attitude, which went beyond the usual informant dysfunction, and how I exercised some due caution.

"You made Sully walk across the bridge?" he said.

"I wanted to make sure he didn't double-cross me."

The detective coughed. "He might. Was anybody following?"

"No. But I still don't trust him."

"He's—he's—" Another sneeze.

"Bless you."

"He's a snitch. You can't trust him. Anything else?"

"I don't know . . ."

"What?"

"He's your source. I don't want to interfere."

He grunted. "I can tell."

"The baggie seems way too light."

"Snitches never work for free."

"I mean *really* light. A fraction of what we paid for." I held the baggie in the palm of my hand. It contained maybe six white rocks, instead of the quarry load that our five hundred bucks should have bought. "I'll put it in an envelope, you can check it later," I said. "But just so you know, he either kept some cash or some product."

The detective coughed. Then groaned.

"When's your next surveillance?" I asked.

"Friday. I'll be fine."

"Yeah," I said, returning his own words back to him. "You'll be fine. Eventually."

chapter fifteen

The flat landscape east of Richmond was once a shallow sea, an ancient outwash accepting sediment that eroded from the Appalachian Mountains hundreds of miles to the west. In fact, the sea received so much sediment that a wide plain of thinly layered soils now separated Virginia's extremes of mountain and ocean. On Wednesday, December 13, I drove down Lott Carey Road and searched for a driveway that DeMott assured me was there.

I finally found the dirt road. It was covered with dry walnut shells that exploded under my tires and made the lowland plain seem even more timeless, as if the fallow fields might suddenly bloom with torn and ragged soldiers staggering home from a lost cause, the air still acrid from an incinerated city. As if I could pass wooden grave markers watered by the blood of the dead and dilapidated plantation houses waiting for once-beautiful women to step inside, their faces etched with bitterness.

Out here, it could still be April 1865.

The road came to an end at a cedar-sided rambler with an attached Airstream trailer. Unfettered leaves filled the yard. Cats lounged on the trailer's front steps, tails twitching lazily.

I parked the car, walked through the sibilant leaves, and reached over the cats to knock on the trailer door.

Angela Crell swung it open. "You're early," she said.

"I can come back."

"My daughter's not here and I gotta feed Daddy." She had a raspy voice. "You mind?"

The trailer smelled of cigarettes and that odd molecular odor that clings to new fabric, apparently coming from the sheets of satin hanging from the ceiling. Red, yellow, blue, white. Angela Crell pushed the fabric aside, like a woman swashbuckling through a satin forest.

In the next room, where the trailer connected to the house, an old man sat in a wheelchair. Calico quilts covered his lap. His emaciated face was set like parched clay.

He stared at Angela Crell. Then shifted his eyes toward me.

"Tina's not back yet," she said in her froggy voice. Loud, as if he were deaf. "It's time to eat."

His eyes filled with emotion.

"Yeah, somebody's here," she said. "But don't worry, she just wants some sewing."

She rummaged through a box on the couch under windows facing the backyard. When she stood, she held a small can, shaking it hard, looking at me over her shoulder. Her eyes were a tremulous green-gray, like tropical fish caught in the netted skin of a devoted smoker. "You're gonna have to hold this a sec."

Standing next to the man, I could smell his rheumy breath and felt cold air leaking through the thin windows above the couch. Angela Crell snapped open the can, releasing a cloying odor of fake vanilla. She handed the can to me and reached under the man's quilt, pulling out a narrow plastic tube. She pried off the capped end and set a small funnel in the opening. With one hand holding the tube, she balanced the funnel with the other.

"Okay, go ahead, pour."

The viscous beige fluid filled up the funnel, slowly draining into the narrow tube. I waited, pouring at her direction.

She gave the old man a soft smile.

"Daddy, 'member this song?"

On a table next to the couch, a small radio played. She sang along in her throaty voice, about what the night wind said to a lamb, and I watched her father's eyes reach out with greedy love and gratitude and an attachment that forced me to look away. I did not want to feel anything. Not for this man.

On the windowsill family photographs showed a pretty woman with rolled hair. A small child grinning from a tricycle. A school portrait of a dark-haired girl with eyes like Angela Crell's. The oldest photograph's sepia hues matched the faded leaves outside. Wearing his Confederate cap, the famous general held an unwavering gaze. There was no telling whether the portrait of Nathan Bedford Forrest was taken before or after the Civil War, before the South came tumbling down, or after, when Forrest launched plans for his family circle, a poisoned-arrow enterprise named with a confusion of Greek and Scottish words.

The Kuklos Klan.

When the can was empty, Angela Crell lifted the funnel from the tube, her voice rasping with words about goodness and light. She pushed the cap into the tube's end and tucked the quilts around her father.

"Ring the bell if you need anything." She reached over, turning up the radio.

We wound back through the satin forest to the trailer. Angela lit up a Salem, taking a long drag, sucking hard like somebody coming up from deep water. Beside her on a wide table sat a sewing machine.

I waited, figuring she needed another hit.

She took it and stared at the floor littered with torn thread.

"You wired?" she asked.

"Pardon?"

"Are you recording me?"

"No."

She waved the cigarette. "Whatever. They didn't do it."

"Who?"

She leaned forward, speaking into my coat. "The Klan did not light up that cross."

I opened my coat, moving the blazer too. Her eyes lingered on my hip holster. "I'm not wearing a wire. What about the car bomb?"

"Wasn't them neither," she said.

"Then who was it?"

She gave a tense smile, revealing front teeth that crossed over each other. "I'm only talking to you because some things need setting straight."

"Things like what?"

"These old guys couldn't light a candle, forget about a cross. You saw my daddy. Does he look like he could do that?"

I glanced around the room, running my eyes over the bright satin. "And you're sewing, what, choir robes?"

She tapped the cigarette against the ashtray. "I'm just saying is, if the FBI's watching my daddy, it's a waste of time. He's done. He can't even talk. The cancer took his tongue. So don't pin this on them."

"Miss Crell, the Klan left its signature at the crime scene."

"And you want me to believe you don't got a wire on. You sure do sound like a lawyer."

"I'm not a lawyer. I don't have a wire."

She waved the cigarette again.

I gave her a moment, studying her face. Her eyes were electric, cheekbones high, her frame as delicate as a ballerina's. And I'd seen the tender smile she bestowed on her father. But her beauty had a corrosive edge to it, as if the attitudes swirling around her had dripped like battery acid. According to DeMott, she once worked as a nurse, doing hospice in the county. She took care of his grandmother and some of the older black women living on land the Fieldings rented out. DeMott claimed Angela Crell treated her patients equally, black and white, but her seamstress talents were one of those open secrets small places whisper about.

"DeMott says you took care of his grandmother."

"Good woman," she said. "I like that family. Well, some of them."

"And you took care of some black people near Weyanoke."

She looked at me, disdain in her eyes. "You think I'm okay with them, long as they're dying?"

"I didn't say that."

She lit another cigarette. "You know what bothers me more? The TV reporters. Making it sound like this guy's totally innocent."

"Who?"

"That rapper, whatever his name is. I saw the story they did on *Entertainment Tonight*. Made me mad as hell. He talked like he's a victim."

"He is."

"You ever listen to his music? My daughter plays it. I hear stuff about how evil the white man is, how great it is to kill cops. If the Klan ever said something like that, I swear, you Feds would come after every last one of them. But this guy does it and makes millions of dollars. Nobody bats an eye. When somebody gives that trash back to him, suddenly he's the victim. Give me a break."

"Miss Crell, a teenager died in that car. He was incinerated. Judging by the satin you've got in here, somebody's holding Klan meetings."

She smashed the cigarette in the ashtray. "I'm trying to raise a kid and take care of my daddy. So I take measurements; I sew robes. I don't ask questions. It's how we get by."

"Do they pick up the robes?"

I saw fear in her eyes.

"You going to haul me into court?"

"I can keep you out of court. With conditions."

"I knew this was a bad idea." She lit another cigarette, fingers shaking.

Dropping my voice, I explained how confidential sources worked. If I could rely on her for crucial information, if revealing her name would compromise the FBI's ability to fight crime, I could keep her identity anonymous. "You've leveled with me up to this point," I said, "and I appreciate it. If you want to stay out of court or jail, keep your business, then . . ."

I let the rest hang in the smoky air.

"I mail the robes," she said, sighing. "Post office boxes only. Kentucky, Louisiana, Arkansas."

"What about Virginia?"

She stared at the floor again. She was a woman who probably never got many choices, who played the hand she was dealt. I saw no ring on her finger, but there was a daughter. No mother, but a father whose neediness pulled like a physical hunger. And a background of bigotry for a nurse who earned a reputation of tenderness and mercy for both white and black patients. Angela Crell knew what most people realize too late: nobody, but nobody, gets out alive.

"You give me your word?" she said.

"Yes."

She spoke staring at the floor, her voice a low rumble. "My mama sewed the robes before me. She taught me how to work the satin. But when I was grown, the orders stopped coming in. You couldn't support a rabbit. I'd stitch a robe for somebody's funeral, something for the man to be buried in." She looked up, giving a soft laugh. "Like Jesus would want to see that, right? I went to nursing school and took up the hospice work because it meant I could stay in the county and be here when Tina came home from school. But about three years ago, the orders started coming in. Robes, emblems. Flags. Lots of them. When the doctors found the cancer in Daddy, he needed help and there was enough sewing I could quit nursing and take care of him."

"So these are new robes, for new recruits?"

Her green eyes filled with turmoil. "You gotta let me keep my business. It's the only support we got."

"I won't interfere. Where in Virginia are they coming from?"

"I never get their real names. They go by Grand Wizard, stuff like that."

The trailer door whipped open and a large girl stomped inside. She stared at me, narrowing her gray-green eyes.

"You was supposed to be here an hour ago," Angela Crell said.

The girl's mouth was red and swollen. "I'm here now."

"Get in the house and start on dinner."

The girl stomped through the satin forest and her mother turned to me, speaking loudly enough to be overheard.

"I'll call you when the order's ready," she said. "About a week. Thanks for stopping by."

I took my cue, silently handing her my card and walking outside. The cats still roosted on the steps, and the wind was picking up the dead leaves, swirling them in the air, stirring them inside an invisible cauldron.

chapter sixteen

Driving back to town, I listened to a voice mail from Milky Lewis, then swung by the Lucky Strike building.

Milky was standing on a six-foot wooden ladder in the art gallery, hanging pictures on the brick walls painted white. In the varnished yellow pine floor, his dark reflected image looked like a shadow.

"You g-gotta help my c-cousin."

"We're talking about Zennie?" I asked.

"I ever t-talked to you about some other c-cousin?"

"Milky, I'm not sure what you mean by helping her, but that's not really my job. I want to talk with her, but I can't make promises."

He jumped off the ladder, landing with a shuddering thud. "Sh-she got herself a k-kid. You know that?"

"Let's take this up after the new year," I said. "I got shifted off that case. And what I'm working right now is urgent."

"Urgent? That g-girl could die." He squinted his amber eyes. "I ever asked you for one f-favor?"

"No."

"No." He handed me a slip of paper with an address scrawled in blue pen. "T-talk to her. Make her listen."

Make her listen. Good one. "Milky, if I led you to belicve—"

"Her boy's not but f-five years old."

I sighed.

"One more thing," he said. "D-don't make her mad."

≈

The hair salon where Zennie Lewis worked was one link in a national chain that stretched across America and boasted cheap haircuts for anyone who walked through the door. This particular franchise was located in the dullest section of Broad Street, an inchoate strip west of town where fast-food joints squeezed in with brick houses rezoned into offices for dentists and chiropractors and the occasional psychic palm reader.

When I opened the salon door Thursday morning, the air smelled of berry shampoo and hot hair. The young woman behind the cash register looked up expectantly. Purple streaks wove through her short black hair.

"Hi there!" she said. "What can we do you for? Trim, haircut?"

"Trim."

"Great! Take a seat. I'll be right with you."

"I was hoping Zennie was available."

"Zennie?" She ran her eyes over me. Dark eyes lined with lavender shadow that struggled to match the hair streaks. "*You* want Zennie?"

"My friend got a great haircut, and when I asked who did it, she told me it was Zennie."

She ran a painted nail—another shade of purple—down the calendar page on the counter. Sawing her jaw back and forth, letting me know that she was insulted or that I was some kind of idiot, she said, "Name?"

"Mary Mitchell."

"Have a seat, Mary."

I sat down in one of the fake leather sling chairs near the door and read gossip magazines dated a week back. Several had stories about celebrities and Thanksgiving. Actors, actresses, pop music stars. There was even a photo of RPM, described as a "rap mogul," volunteering at a soup kitchen in New York with other famous people. Everybody talked about "giving back," though it occurred to me that sentiment never included refunds for bad movies, and a photographer always happened to be present to capture these moments of altruism. That was apparently Wally's role in RPM's latest mission to Liberia. Publicity made the world go round.

"Mary?"

I looked up and saw a face like a golden brown cabochon. Her black hair was straightened, pulled back into a short pony-tail, revealing her rounded cheeks that dimpled with her smile. Like Milky, she had amber-colored eyes, but hers were the size of buttons. And not even the plastic apron could disguise her cur-vaceous figure. Zennie Lewis was what Southern women meant when they said a girl was "cute as a bug."

But when I stood, laying aside the gossip magazine, her smile faded, kidnapping the dimples.

Something had given me away, maybe something Milky had told her.

I followed her back to the shampoo sinks where she reached up and yanked a nylon smock off the shelf, snapping it open like a bullfighter. She closed it tight around my neck, then picked up the sink hose, testing the water with one hand. I eased back on the reclining chair and she leaned over me, her voice a whispered growl.

"Nice try, *Mary*."

"You're going to scald me. Turn it down."

Making a face, she twisted one of the knobs. The water turned cold. Very cold.

"Milky's worried about you," I said.

Her rounded face held a mixture of pride and anger. She began shampooing my scalp, using a force that shook my entire body. I let her, hoping the exertion would wear her down.

It did, a little. The water came back on at room temperature.

"So you two share a grandmother," I said.

"What?"

"If Milky's your cousin, you share a grandmother."

No response.

"Is she still alive?"

"Who?"

"Your grandmother."

"Yeah," she said.

"What's she like?"

"She kills chickens with her bare hands."

Throwing a towel over my head, Zennie rubbed like my hair was on fire and then tied the towel into a turban so tight my eyes had epicanthic folds. I followed her to a chair near the bubble-headed hair dryers. A woman was reading one of the celebrity magazines.

I sat down, Zennie yanked off the turban, and my long hair flopped on the nylon smock. I stared at the mirror, watching her face. What made cabochons so valuable was the radiating star of light emerging from the curved shape. On Zennie, that light emerged from her eyes, the amber color luxurious, mesmerizing. I stared into the mirror, watching her pick up a lank strand of wet hair, gently tugging it to full length. She contemplated my appearance with a certain detachment.

"You always wear it like that?" she asked.

"My hair? Yes."

"Just hanging down around your face?"

"Well, I wear a ponytail sometimes," I said, feeling oddly defensive.

"It does nothing for your face."

I heard nothing harsh in her tone. She spoke with authority, a calm that comes from knowing, and not for the first time, I wondered about people's attitudes, whether half the world's agony would evaporate if each person discovered the talent God gave them instead of squandering days painting by numbers laid out according to someone else's preference. Parents. Peers. Pastors. We read books bursting with self-help, about roads less traveled and finding bliss and all these so-called secrets to life. But they all left out the most crucial factor. We fought an enemy, invisible yet definite, who diligently worked to block us from our intended purpose, keeping us from the one thing that brought joy, that connected us to each other and to our Creator. Condemned and resentful, miserable and uncertain, we filled our minds with chatter from talk show hosts, always hoping for the answer, when all the while one simple supernatural prescription waited: "Come to me."

In the mirror, I saw Zennie move from side to side of the chair, suddenly lost in the graceful dance of her talent, her purpose. The reason behind my visit was suddenly gone. And I let it go.

"What do you suggest?" I asked.

"You need some pizzazz."

"Pizzazz?"

"Yeah, holiday pizzazz. Milky said you were pretty, but you need to play it up."

"What kind of pizzazz are we talking about?"

"Put your chin down," she said.

"Not too much."

"Keep your head down." She began snipping the scissors, still moving from side to side, and when she walked over to the mirror, pulling a comb from the jar of blue disinfectant, I saw a picture tucked into the mirror's corner. A little boy.

"He's got your dimples," I said. "What's his name?"

"Zeke." She placed her small hand on my head, gently tilting. "You got kids?"

I shook my head.

"Hold still. No kids?"

"I'm not married."

"Girl, I ain't married either, but at least I got a kid outta the deal."

"And if something happens to you, what happens to him?"

The scissors stopped.

I looked up, our eyes locking in the mirror.

"Milky's got a job," I said. "Going to school, putting his life together. But the other guys in that gang are behind bars. It'll be decades before they hug their kids again."

She held my gaze in the mirror. She whispered, "Nothing's gonna happen."

"I hope that's true. But if you love your son, you'll get away from those guys."

"Put your head down," she ordered.

I hesitated. I was tempted to say more, but I was dealing with a wounded creature, one who saw every offer of help as another opportunity for pain.

In those cases, it was always best to leave the plate of offered food and slowly back away.

chapter seventeen

It was a haircut that demanded itself. A haircut that would make headlines for an actress who worked a soup kitchen once a year after appearing in terrible movies.

No doubt about it: Zennie was talented.

But for me, the cut was a shock. I was not a pizzazz kind of gal, and when I snuck into the office on Thursday, I was only too happy to stay in my echoing hovel for a day of KKK research.

Our Bureau files showed nothing on World War I weapons caches in Virginia. Or North Carolina or West Virginia, where the KKK claimed strongholds. Mustard gas did show up in other places—Austria, Sierra Leone, Iraq—but lewisite was almost non-existent, an arcane chemical killer. Frustrated by the dead ends, I called Nettie Labelle at the lab and asked about the explosives evidence from the car bombing.

"Pipe bomb plastique was just regular old C-4, duct-taped together," she said. "They're running traces to see if we can track down the tape manufacturer, where it was sold. I'll let you know ASAP about what comes back. But the accelerants—"

"Let me guess."

"Alex Trebek, Raleigh Harmon would like to answer the daily double for one thousand."

"What is mustard gas and lewisite?"

"That's correct. You win. And you lose. All at the same time. But I did get a number for you." She rattled off ten digits so quickly I had to ask her to repeat them, twice. The last time she repeated the numbers so slowly it was annoying. I felt like calling her Annette.

"What's the number go to?" I asked.

"Aberdeen," she said. "As in, bang, bang."

≈

After the United States declared war on the Central Powers of Europe in 1917, our government decided the world wasn't getting any nicer. It was time to expand weapons testing. After a long search, the army chose several thousand acres near the Chesapeake Bay, the same land that saw Jamestown settlers warring with Indians three hundred years earlier. But the stubborn Maryland farmers refused to move. It took an act of Congress, two presidential proclamations, and finally two hundred dollars an acre for the government to relocate several thousand people and their twelve thousand animals. Even the human remains were moved from family graveyards.

Today it was doubtful that anybody would want to move back. Aberdeen employed nearly fifteen thousand scientists over as many acres that formed a literal killing field. The elite force of scientists, researchers, engineers, and technicians figured out ways to eliminate life. I'd always wanted to visit. But when I explained what I was working on, the woman who worked as the liaison to law enforcement told me to forget it. Her name was Hannah Hamer.

"Nobody's here," she said. "And clearance to visit would take weeks."

"I'm an FBI agent."

"Weeks."

"All right. What about the chemicals?"

"We had mustard gas," she said. "But it's old news. The

military never liked it. It incapacitated our troops as much as the enemy. Too difficult to control."

"What about lewisite?" I asked.

"Nettie told me you were interested in that. We had some here, the records show."

"The government made some?"

"Yes," she said.

"Stored at Aberdeen?"

"Yes."

"How much?"

"Why do you need to know this again?" she asked.

I went through the cross burning and car bombing a second time. Once again, it was my description of the teenager's violent death that softened her.

"I do know we kept hundreds of tons of mustard agent here," she said.

"Kept it how?"

"In one-ton containers."

"Any go missing?"

"Agent Harmon, it was guarded around the clock by armed forces."

"And?"

"And we blew it all up."

"When?"

"Last year. We didn't need mustard gas anymore. It was neutralized in the disposal plant."

"Every last bit of it?"

Hannah Hamer sighed. "We keep vigilant supervision over our weapons. I can guarantee the mustard gas is gone."

"Understood, but somebody down here got hold of some."

"They didn't get it from us."

"What about lewisite?"

Another sigh. "I'm very busy with—"

"Please. It's a hate crime."

"I'll see what information we have. But I need to get the information's release cleared first."

"When can I expect to hear back?" I asked.

"Monday at the earliest. But don't get your hopes up," she said, as if this had been one big uplifting phone call. "In case you haven't noticed, it's Christmas."

"I've noticed. But the guys using this stuff haven't. Can you call me as soon as possible?"

"I'll do what I can," she said.

≈

My plans were foiled at 2 p.m., when I got a call from Pollard Durant—the agent in charge of the task force.

"Your phone replacement has the flu," he said. "Any chance you can work tonight's shift, with no overtime?"

"Can I work alone?"

"I'll talk to Phaup."

At five minutes to four, I walked into the T-III room carrying three bags of food.

Beezus Jackson stared with shock. "Raleigh! What happened to your hair?"

I placed three bags on the table, the results of my successful forage for food on Broad Street. Big Macs. Crispy fries from Burger King. An Oreo milkshake from Hardee's. I wasn't going to wallow in self-pity about my hair, but I also wasn't about to deprive myself of salt and grease at a time like this.

Stan stared at my head. "It's different," he said. "But kinda cool."

The right side of my hair touched my collarbone while the precisely cut ends tapered at an angle across the back, layered seamlessly to the other side. When I tilted my head, the hair fanned in sexy ellipse. But I didn't feel like I could pull it off—I felt inferior to my hair. I bit into a Big Mac.

Stan left the room and I tapped the volume button, raising the static in order to block the penetration of any comments from Beezus. After several more bites of the Big Mac, I began to feel better and by the time I polished off the fries, the phone line was popping up. I felt the old thrill coming back. My road less traveled? My bliss? Hunting down the bad guys.

Moon, the guy who blessed Zennie Lewis with an illegitimate child, dialed the number that belonged to XL's cell phone.

"Yo, dawg," he said.

"What's up?" XL sounded sleepy. It was 6:23 p.m.

"You got numbers for the game?"

"Bulls by three."

"Dig." Moon paused. *"I'm supposed to take orders tonight?"*

"Odds are."

"Can't."

There was silence on XL's end.

"I can't," Moon repeated, as if a question was asked.

"You mean won't."

"Zennie asked—"

"Naw, dawg, naw—"

"Listen, she says it's serious. Something with Zeke. The boy's my blood."

My index finger hovered over the Stop button. Technically, this conversation wasn't about criminal activity, unless XL explicitly said something more about taking orders. I waited for the next sentence, hoping, hoping.

"Tomorrow night I'm there. Saturday too. The busy nights, yo."

"Moon."

"You hear from the man?"

I waited, hope waning.

"Moon."

"He's gonna be surprised."

"Moon." XL's voice sounded cold. *"You want the fat man to come down the chimney or not?"*

"Honor the father," Moon said. *"No other gods before him."*

"Now you're talking."

"So I see you tomorrow night. I be there. I promise. And—"

XL hung up.

The rest of the night sounded like the drive-through window at my beloved McDonald's. Dozens of numbers outside our wiretap called XL's cell phone. The voices sounded young and tense, mostly white. They pretended to call for taxis and take-out and tonight's special—all the lousy code language for drug orders. Between sales calls, XL dialed the number that belonged to the man with the foreign accent, the man they called Minks. XL asked if his car was gonna need repairs and whether the man thought he'd be working this weekend. To everything, the man gave one reply: *"Yah."*

"So you got everything for Christmas?" XL asked.

"Yah." But he couldn't pronounce his *w*'s. I heard it when he said, *"Ve haf everything for Christmas."*

I wrote notes and between the calls I gave my own monosyllabic responses to Beezus's questions about my hair. When my shift was over, I drove home and, avoiding my mother and my mirror, fell into bed with much weariness, more questions, and even more gratitude.

Then I woke up on Friday and realized I had a date to keep with DeMott.

chapter eighteen

After work in the morning, I spent the rest of Friday jogging from one end of town to the other, attempting the impossible, trying to run away from myself.

When chimney smoke joined the darkening sky, I settled into the carriage house's claw-footed bathtub for bubbles and *Scientific American*. Soaking in the suds, I read a good story about DNA, marred only by the author's assumption that our double helixes of nucleic acid were the product of chance.

Quite an assumption. It was like saying blueprints could write themselves.

And not just any blueprints. Our DNA contained three billion complex sequences—for each living creature. The statistical probability of this happening by random selection was laughable. It was like saying tornadoes can rip through junkyards and build jumbo jets. Never mind that the second law of thermodynamics proved that over millions of years we grew closer to entropy than order, the opposite of what evolution claimed.

Scientifically speaking, evolution was whacked.

But try telling that to the smart people—the people who believed fish scales turned into feathers and sludge somehow squeezed out higher life forms. Try explaining the degree of planning and order and creative genius necessary for just one hundred working sequences, let alone three billion.

Try it. They'll call you delusional. Go figure.

I tossed the moisture-rippled magazine on the floor and climbed out of the tub, skin blushing rose, and searched my closet for my Mata Hari dress. It came into my life from a consignment shop near DuPont Circle. The perfect velvet sheath, sleeveless. The store's owner claimed the dress once belonged to a CIA agent stationed in Czechoslovakia during the Cold War. The former spy, now in her nineties, was living in a convalescent home around the corner. I not only bought the dress, I purchased the saga.

Three weeks later, my father was murdered. The dress never came out of my closet.

But now, as I slipped sheer silk hose over my legs and shimmied into the charcoal velvet, I looked in the mirror and decided it was great being a girl.

After some minimal evening makeup and a fluff of the new haircut, I stepped into three-inch black heels, grabbed my coat, and hurried to the big house. The night wind blowing against the house felt alternately warm and cold.

In my mother's kitchen, cookies were baking again. More cookies. I opened the oven and counted two dozen chocolate chip. Another dozen cooled on a wire rack on the counter. I picked one up, taking a bite. Ghastly. Like masticated chocolate clay. I spit it out in the sink, guzzling a glass of water, trying to figure out who was eating these things.

"Oh, Raleigh Ann." My mother walked into the room. "You look beautiful."

"Thanks."

"But you can't wear that coat."

"What's wrong with my coat?"

≈

In her bedroom upstairs, tea lights flickered on the bureau, releasing a mulled spice scent. Opening her top drawer, she removed a strand of pearls that looked like cabled moonlight. She dusted my bare shoulders with powder and painted my lips the color of glistening rubies.

I looked in the mirror. Even better being a girl.

"Now this." She held up red velvet.

"What is it?"

"I wore this on my first formal date with your father. It was December fifteenth. Can you believe it? Here's your date with DeMott, the same night. It's a sign."

I stared at the red velvet. I blinked twice to make sure I wasn't imagining it.

"The weatherman called for sleet or hail or something," she continued, "but I refused to wear an overcoat. And risking my health was the smartest thing I ever did. Your father took one look at me and said, 'Nadine, you look like a dream revealed.' Isn't that just—" She drew a quick breath, eyes misting. "A dream revealed."

It was a cape.

A red cape.

Outlandish, outrageous. Perfect for my mother—or was, before she turned into a Stepford widow last month. On me, the thing looked ridiculous.

But I wore it because I saw her smile.

On the freezing cold drive to Weyanoke, I clutched it around me, clutching it even more tightly as I parked the K-Car at the plantation and walked a herringbone brick path to the mansion. A gibbous moon turned the stones pearlescent. At the top of the stairs, I stood for a moment outside the large double doors. The wind blew a final shiver up my spine. Ignoring my frantic heartbeat, I rang the sonorous bell and gave the cape to the maid. I kept my black clutch. It held my cell phone and Glock, as agents were required to be armed at all times. When I started down the wide gallery, walking toward the ballroom, I passed ancestral portraits of the Fieldings and DeMotts and MacKennas who had inhabited this land for hundreds of years.

My heart raced even faster. Standing at the edge of the ballroom, smelling warm pine and sharp gin, I began to worry about my hair. From the coved ceiling, three crystal chandeliers bathed the oak parquet floor with golden light, and a band onstage played a jazzy sort of Muzak. Around the room, tuxedoed men stood with women so well manicured they appeared manufactured. Not so long ago, this was my parents' world. My father, the esteemed judge, descended from a long line of Virginia barristers. My mother, accepted by marriage. But when he died, most of the invitations died with him. The rest died when my mother and I quit going.

DeMott was standing on the other side of the room, speaking to a petite blonde woman. His eyes searched the crowd, but the woman kept her pretty face on him, giving him a perfect smile. Instead of a tux, DeMott wore a black suit with a white shirt and red tie. Somehow, dressed up, he looked even more rugged. He turned, his eyes locking on me. Something brushed the back of my knees.

Turning his body sideways, he walked across the room, carving through the crowd.

Run for the door, I told myself. *You can still make it. You can still pretend you don't care.*

"You're here," he said.

"A deal's a deal."

He nodded. "May I get you a drink?"

"Club soda, two limes."

"Be right back."

The waiter passed by with canapés. I took two.

"Raleigh?"

I turned to see Jillian, DeMott's older sister. The sister who liked me.

"Did he find you?" she asked.

"Yes, he went to get my drink."

Jillian lacked Mac's dramatic beauty, but she exuded a sensible peace, an unflappable quality. And as I'd discovered last summer, Jillian was the person you wanted in a crisis.

Tonight she wore a taffeta gown, the deep eggplant shade matching the sapphire briolettes hanging from her ears like champagne grapes. The earrings swung as she turned to the couple beside her.

"Raleigh, this is DeDe and Leland Morrison. They live near you on Monument Avenue."

DeDe said, "Which block on Monument Avenue?"

I told her.

"Well, my goodness," she said. "We're practically neighbors. Which house?"

I told her.

She almost caught the gasp before it fully left her mouth.

DeMott appeared, offering me a highball glass wrapped in an emerald napkin. He took my elbow.

"We'd love to stick around, but we were hoping to have a good time," he said.

"DeMott!" Jillian said.

He was already turning away, whispering in my ear, "And if Leland Morrison knew how to have a good time, he wouldn't be married to DeDe."

I looked up at him. "Thank you."

"Thanks for wearing that dress," he said. "I like the new hair too."

"Honest?" Suddenly I was sixteen years old. "It's not too short?"

"Raleigh, you could shave your head bald and you'd still be gorgeous."

His eyes, I decided, were his best feature. They were like bi-refringent blue prisms, splitting the light into playful rays.

"I want you to meet somebody," he said.

We were heading back across the room, but suddenly it filled with the tintinnabulation of cocktail forks clinking against crystal. The band fell silent. DeMott stopped and looked toward the stage, frowning. His father, Harrison Fielding, and his mother, Peery, stood on the platform with the band. Peery surveyed the crowd, her unlined face glowing above a peach-colored gown, already very mother-of-the-bride. The tuxedoed Mr. Fielding stepped toward the microphone.

"Thank you all for coming to celebrate my beautiful daughter MacKenna and her groom-to-be, Stuart Morgan." He paused, significantly. "This wedding has been a long time coming."

There was a murmur through the crowd. DeMott leaned down, speaking into my ear. His breath felt warm on my skin. But I shivered. "Care to say something about the delays, Raleigh?"

I tried to glare at him. He laughed.

"My lovely wife, Peery, and I would like to offer a toast," Harrison Fielding continued. "Please, raise your glasses and join us in wishing this young couple a long and happy life together."

MacKenna Fielding stepped onstage with her parents, followed by her fiancé. She wore a fir-green dress, the lustrous folds of satin falling from the narrow bodice. Standing behind her, Stuart Morgan wrapped an arm around her waist.

"Among life's greatest blessings is a loving spouse." Mr. Fielding raised his glass. "May you honor each other. May you remember the great legacy each of you brings into this marriage. May you know that your mother and I, along with Mr. and Mrs. Morgan and everyone in this room, wish you nothing but happiness."

The crowd applauded and cheered and Stuart spun Mac around, dipping her into a luxurious kiss. The crowd erupted.

But DeMott growled under his breath.

I looked over. "What's wrong?"

He shook his head.

Mac wrapped her long arms around Stuart's neck, her hands fluttering a moment, the light from the chandeliers catching in the enormous diamond of her engagement ring. The gleaming spot-light provoked another appreciative response from the crowd.

"That's some diamond," I said.

"She needs it." He took my hand. "C'mon."

The musicians were striking up a song I didn't recognize as we worked our way to the double doors that faced the river. Back when this house was built, air-conditioning was a breeze off the water. And it still worked. Braced open, the doors ushered in a fresh snap of air, diluting the room's heat. Sitting in a silk moiré chair, an elderly man took in the breeze.

"Granddad," DeMott said, "I'd like you to meet Raleigh Harmon."

His tuxedo shined at the seams, his red bow tie sitting cock-eyed. And his hair was a sparse white Caesar ring, almost as white as his new Nike tennis shoes.

"Dennison Fielding." He shook my hand, a surprisingly strong grip. "DeMott, bring Miss Raleigh a chair."

He spoke with the syncopated rhythms of a true Virginian. A word like *chair* had two undulating syllables. *Chair-ruh*. DeMott obeyed the order and carried over a Windsor chair. It looked like it had crossed the Atlantic on the *Susan Constant*.

"Thanky," said Dennison Fielding. "Now go see if your sis-tahs need help."

DeMott excused himself and I sat down. His grandfather leaned over. His breath was brisk with whiskey.

"You're the gal who almost put my son Harrison in the clink?" he asked.

"Yes, sir."

He sat back. "He shouldn't have tried cutting deals with that colored mayor." He paused. "You're not one of those rightists?"

"Pardon me?"

"Women's rights, animal rights, human rights. You take offense when I say 'colored'?"

"I've heard worse."

"True. And personally, I don't care for this new word. *Black.* It doesn't fit. Of course, neither does white. We're pink. But I grew up hearing 'white' and 'colored,' and I got used to those words. I'm ninety-one years old and it's too late to change."

He didn't look a day over ninety. "May I ask you a question, Mr. Fielding?"

"Hang on." He lifted his hand, the fingers rough. Working hands. Signaling the waiter, he asked for a Bushmills straight up. Then he turned to me. "What did you want to ask?"

"Do you know if the KKK is still active around here?"

"Not the small-talk type." He grinned, nodding happily. "I don't particularly care for small talk myself. But I've noticed most people are invertebrates, no backbone to them. They don't appreciate us straight shooters. We come into heaps of discord because piffles rule the world." He reached over, patting my bare arm. "Your daddy was a judge, wasn't he?"

I nodded.

"Then we'll do this like court. I'll ask a question right back. When the federal government took its first census out here, what year do you reckon that was?"

"The federal government? I'd guess about 1800."

"Right close, 1790," he said. "They counted some five thousand folks. White and colored, neck and neck."

"The colored being slaves."

"Not all, not all." He wagged a long finger. "People forget. We had right many free blacks in these parts. Ol' Lott Carey, he was free. They all should've been. Slavery was an evil kind of stupid. And most Southerners knew it had to end. The Yankees just hurried us along. Half a million men were killed in the process."

The waiter arrived with his drink and Dennison Fielding thanked him, taking a long draw. The band was playing a song about an enchanted evening.

"The most recent census," he said, "was two years ago. How many people you figure they counted?"

"I'd rather hear from you."

"You're the girl for DeMott, all right. They counted nearly the same number as was here in 1790. You see where I'm going?"

"No change is the best change."

"You hear me. Folks along the James River want things to stay how they always were. Of course, that gets expensive, holding back time. Take that little gal over there." He lifted his glass, aiming into the crowd. "Every month, she's got to figure out how to cover her bills."

It took me a moment to realize who he was talking about.

Flynn Wellington stood with her husband, Leighton, and another couple. Flynn wore black silk trousers and a white sequined top, her platinum hair combed back with a sparkling headband.

"She's a hard worker, I'll give her that," he said. "Grew all the flowers in here tonight. We paid her right well."

A soft wave of exclamations rippled through the room. The crowd parted as waiters wheeled a three-tiered chocolate cake covered with sparklers. I watched bits of stray sulfur leap and pop in the air.

"All so foolish, celebrating like this before a wedding." He shook his head. "I give MacKenna six months before she runs home crying her eyes out over that boy."

DeMott walked over. "Granddad, they want a toast from you."

Sighing with the weight of ninety-one years, he lifted an arm. DeMott helped him out of the chair. I stood up.

He tugged his worn tuxedo into place. "Don't let her get away," he said.

"I don't plan to," DeMott said.

The old man looked over at me. "And don't you be leaving Virginia again. Stay where you belong."

He headed toward the cake with the sidling amble of a crustacean. DeMott guided me toward the crowd, placing his hand on the small of my back. Heat radiated through my dress, my knees weak again. When I felt something tingle near my heart, I wondered if I was going to be dumb enough to faint.

But when the tingling came again, I took my purse out from under my left arm. I was almost relieved. My cell phone buzzed a third time.

"Excuse me," I said. "I'll be right back."

Dennison Fielding began his toast as I walked down the long hall toward the front door. Stepping outside, the cold air felt like a slap on my bare arms.

Detective Nathan Greene sounded like he was dying.

"He set up a buy," he said.

"Who, Sully?"

"Yeah." He sneezed.

"Bless you."

"We don't show, they get suh-suh—"

"Suspicious? Bless you."

He groaned. "I can't go."

I found a pen in my purse but no paper and wrote his address on my left palm. Closing the phone, I went back inside, searching for the maid who took my cape. DeMott came down the hall.

"Raleigh, what's wrong?"

"I have to go. Can you help me find my . . . coat?"

"Is everything okay?"

"Yes, but I have to go."

He hesitated, then nodded and walked across the room, speaking to one of the maids. He walked me back to the front door.

"Last to come, first to leave," he said.

"But I was here."

"Yes, you were."

We stood by the front door, waiting for the cape. DeMott was smiling, but I kept looking away, the bright light in his eyes making me feel uncomfortable.

"What?" I finally said.

"You get one point for keeping your promise."

"How many points are there?"

"One." He was still smiling. "There's only ever been one."

chapter nineteen

The detective lived in Highland Park, an old neighborhood
north of downtown that showcased noble Victorians and
Queen Annes and ancient oaks that leafed out in summer like stage curtains, concealing the huge homes. Like so many
streetcar suburbs across America, Highland Park's decline began
soon after World War II, when returning veterans wanted newer
homes and the automobiles that carried them farther out. Later,
when white flight swept through, crime marched in. And today
the latest stabbings, break-ins, and murders had an almost conver-
sational air. The detective had the worst kind of job security.

I pulled up to his house on Second Avenue just after 10 p.m.
and glanced at my palm, where I'd written the address. I wasn't
sure I had the right house.

It was pink.

Bright pink.

The house next door was cerulean blue. And across the street,
a cadmium yellow Victorian. I got out, stepping over the cracked
concrete invaded by tree roots. I'd heard young families were moving back to Highland Park, picking up the historic homes for a
pittance, pouring in their sweat equity. The brightly colored houses
with the filigree details reminded me of stern-wheel riverboats.

At the front door, Lisa Greene waited. Pretty and petite and
put-together, she looked like the kind of woman who yanked up
old linoleum without breaking a nail.

She handed me the envelope of cash and said, "I sprayed it with Lysol."

"He's that bad?"

"Quarantined in the guest room," she said. "The kids haven't seen him all day. I've got an open house on Christmas Day. I'm not serving my guests the flu."

I thanked her and was walking back to the K-Car, stepping over the rupturing tree roots, when she called out my name. She was still standing in the doorway, the light silhouetting her tiny figure, making her look like a boxed doll.

"Pardon?" My breath clouded the night air.

"Thank you for what you did," she said.

"I don't know—"

"For Mike."

It took me a moment to realize who she meant. And then I was grateful for the distance and the dark between us. She meant Mike Falcon. Detective Michael Falcon. Her husband's dead partner.

"If that one had turned into a cold case, it would've ruined my family."

I nodded, got into the car, and was shivering before I reached the end of the driveway. Against my legs, the vinyl bench seat felt like a cold compress. The dreaded cape lay on the seat next to me—I had refused to put it on with DeMott watching—but now I swung the thing over my shoulders, snapped the collar, and drove down to Chamberlayne Avenue with my right hand slapping the dashboard. Even if the heater didn't kick on, beating the thing would warm me up. And maybe it would even knock some of the annoyance off me. I didn't want to make this buy, didn't want to see Sully again. And I really didn't want to think about the expression I'd seen in DeMott's eyes. For some reason, it scared me.

Cutting over to Montrose Avenue, teeth chattering, I trolled up and down the road until Sully finally stepped from the shadows of Battery Park.

"So we meet again." He deposited himself on the bench seat. My teeth chattered.

"Nate sounds really sick," he said cheerfully.

I pulled a U-turn, heading south.

Sully slouched down. "How come you're not, like, totally humiliated driving this car? Man, I'd die if somebody saw me in this thing."

The wicked temptation swept over me. I wanted to lean on the horn. Wave out the window. Let the whole world see him in this car. Instead, I drove silently down Broad Street, listening to Sully sniff as though he had a cold. We passed a kooky Caribbean restaurant painted bright green and yellow, some pawnshops, the city's convention center, and at Ninth Street I hung a right and followed the hill down to the river.

With office buildings purged for the weekend, Richmond felt eerily quiet until I crossed the bridge to Southside. It was busy in a worn-out sort of way, like broken-down shoes kicked off at the city's back door.

Sully sat up. "Your hair—"

I looked over.

"Your hair." He sounded panicked. "Why is your hair like that?"

"What?"

"And why—why are you dressed like that?"

"Like what?"

"Hold on." He sat up even higher. "Stop the car."

"What's wrong?"

"Stop the car!" he screamed.

I kept driving across the bridge.

Sully leaned forward, splaying his pale hands on the dashboard. "Don't even think about it."

"About what?"

"Nice disguise, but you can forget it. You're not coming in with me."

Another temptation swept over me. It was harder to resist.

"Why can't I come in with you?" I asked.

"Why?"

"Tell them I'm your girlfriend."

"What're you, crazy?"

"That's it, the crazy girlfriend. Good thinking, Sully."

"You can't." His voice cracked. "You can't do this."

"Come on. I even wore my red cape."

His pale face wadded with worry. I could see all the sneaky ideas, all the schemes and double-crosses, snaking through his narrow mind. Behind him, the bridge's streetlights clicked past, the water sparkling like a jewel.

"Turn around," he said.

"You set up the buy. We have to go."

"I'll make up something. Turn around."

"They'll get suspicious. You know that."

"Okay, how about I tell them some crazy woman kidnapped me?" he said. "How about I tell them she works for the FBI? Huh? How about that?"

When I looked over, I'd successfully wiped the perma-sneer off Sully's face. Stewing in his own rancid juices, his cramped face almost looked human. But it wasn't normal fear. It was the anxiety of the compulsive manipulator, a guy who was afraid he wouldn't get the final twist, the last dig, the ultimate lie. I would have liked to instill authentic fear in Sully, but he belonged to the detective.

And the task force needed him.

"Relax, Sully," I said. "I'm not going in with you."

He didn't move.

"Seriously, I'm not."

"Then why are you dressed like that?"

"I was at a Christmas party."

"And your hair?"

"I got a haircut, that's all."

"You don't look like a cop anymore," he said.

"I promise, you're going in by yourself."

He closed his eyes, sighing with relief. When I pulled into the parking lot of the abandoned mill off Decatur, he was already unzipping his fanny pouch. I counted out the bills. Sully licked his lips, yanking the bills from my hand.

"You're still walking across the bridge," I said.

He stuffed the bills into his marsupial nylon pouch, got out, and slammed the car door.

I drove back across the bridge and up to Main Street. White Christmas lights framed the buildings, delineating their shapes and making them look like enormous presents. Circling down to Seventh Street, I parked where I could watch the bridge that clasped the city's opposing sides like a bejeweled broach.

After ten minutes of rubbing my bare arms, tapping my feet against the floorboard, and slapping the dashboard, I pulled out my cell phone and called my mother.

"Will you be late?" she asked.

"Yes. I didn't want you to worry."

"I'd only worry if you came home early."

I stared out the windshield at Riverfront Towers. Inside, a janitor guided a polishing machine across the marble foyer. On the phone, in the background, I could hear canned laughter from some television show my mother was watching.

"Is it beautiful?" she asked.

"What's that?"

"The party—is it beautiful?"

Something landed on my chest, the full weight of it. The white Christmas lights on the buildings blurred.

"It's a very nice party." I swallowed.

"Who have you seen?"

I tossed out names, tightening my throat as I told her about MacKenna's dress and Mr. Fielding's toast and seeing Flynn Wellington and her husband, and when I finished the lights were rivers of white light.

"Tell DeMott you'll see him Sunday for church," she said.

"We're going back?"

"And I made a Bundt cake for breakfast. And eggnog from scratch, just the way Daddy liked it."

I closed the phone and watched the janitor finish polishing the floor. The K-Car felt like a meat locker. Uselessly, I put my hand over the heat vent. It felt like the air conditioner was on. Pulling the cape around my body, shivering, I stamped my feet to stay warm. By the time Sully came sauntering across the bridge, my teeth were clacking.

Nobody was following him.

Rather than drive under Riverfront Towers, I raced across the bridge, pulling an illegal U-turn to drive up beside him. He didn't seem particularly surprised and dropped on the seat. I hit the gas, holding out my hand for the product.

He sat up, as if suddenly remembering the point of this exercise, and unzipped the little fanny pack. He tossed me a plastic baggie.

My fingers felt like popsicles. There were six stones, just like last time. "Thizizit?"

"What?"

I clenched my jaw, forcing out the words without chatter. "This . . . is . . . it?"

"You look cold," he said. "It's freezing in here. Can you turn the heat on?"

"Money," I said. "Where's the money?"

He reached over, twisting the knob already cranked to hot. "This thing doesn't even have heat?"

"Sully." I gritted my teeth. "What did you do?"

"I bought drugs."

"You had twice as much money. Where's the rest?"

"You think it's some kind of store?" he said. "I walk in and ask for change? Maybe in your little white bread world, that's how it works. But this is the real world, babe. Quit nagging and start driving."

I hit the brakes. Cranking the wheel, I pulled another U-turn and raced across the bridge, heading south. The bridge lights zipped past.

"What the—" Sully said. "What are you doing?"

I headed up Semmes. The light turned red; I slammed on the brakes. Two women on the corner walked toward the car. They were not dressed for the cold and stared at the K-Car, a little uncertain. When the light turned green, I stepped on the gas and looked over at Sully. His pale face was starting to show fear. Real fear.

"Hand it over, Sully."

"I gave it to you," he said.

"Then give me the rest of the money."

"I used it all."

"Don't play games with me, Sully. We've got one rule, and you know it. Stick to the routine."

"I did."

"There's barely enough in that baggie for possession."

"I don't know what you're talking about," he said.

"Okay, I'll just go in and ask them what happened." I turned left on Cowardin. "Are they down this street?"

"You wouldn't."

"Try me. Because whatever you pulled tonight, I guarantee you sent up red flags."

"I didn't. I swear."

My radar went screaming red. It did that whenever a self-serving creep uttered the words "I swear." What could they possibly swear to except themselves?

I stopped at Perry Street. It was nothing but shadows. The streetlights were shot out, the copper wires cannibalized for cash. I felt an urge to lock the doors. But showing fear would give Sully the upper hand. I looked over. Sully was licking his lips, eyes darting.

"When these guys get nervous, Sully, people die. Tell me what you did."

"Prices went up," he said.

I stepped on the gas, barreling down Bainbridge Street.

"Okay," he said. "Okay. Look. It's no big deal. I just took some of the—"

Four men stepped from the shadows. My headlights hit them, twenty yards ahead in the middle of the road. They formed a line, arms crossed, and Sully cursed. When I hit the brakes, the back wheels locked, fishtailing the K-Car to a stop.

The men walked toward us.

Sully cursed again. His voice high and scared.

They wore black jackets marked with the eye patch and crossbones of the Oakland Raiders. The man in the middle placed both hands on the K-Car's hood, staring through the windshield, as the other three moved to both sides, disappearing from view.

A fifth man stepped off the curb.

Sully cursed again.

I kept my voice at a whisper. "Are these the guys?"

He answered with another curse. I glanced in the rearview

mirror. One of them was running his hands over my square trunk. The other guys were somewhere in the shadows. Reaching under my cape, I found my purse and wrapped my palm around the Glock, placing my index finger alongside the trigger.

The fifth man walked over to Sully's side.

Sully was hyperventilating.

"Don't talk," I whispered. "Let me handle it."

He knocked on Sully's window.

"Roll it down," I said.

Sully was wild-eyed, paralyzed with fear. Pure fear.

I leaned across the bench seat, cranking the handle with my left hand, my right still tucked under the cape and inside the purse.

The man leaned down. He was big. His brown scalp was shaved bald, a Raiders headband covering his ears. He placed one hand on the window frame. The other hand went to the K-Car's roof, presumably to signal the Raiders. He stared at Sully, a flat expression in his dark shiny eyes. The dead expression perfected in penitentiaries.

I started shivering again. Not from the cold.

"Yo," he said to Sully. "We got a problem?"

Sully shook his head.

"Yeah, we got a p-problem." I shivered and stared into the big man's eyes, not even trying to hold back my shakes. "How m-much m-money did he give you?"

With one glance, he took inventory of the car. The backseat held my beat-up duffel bag. No briefcase. I wasn't supposed to be working tonight.

"Who am I talking to?" he said.

"His buyer."

Sully let out a squeak.

I lifted the baggie. "I paid a g-grand," I said. "Does th-that look right to you?"

He opened his palm, holding it just inches from Sully's sweating face. I gave him the baggie and he rubbed the grains between his thumb and finger. The expression in his eyes never changed, never exposed one thought or feeling or suspicion, and his next move cracked like lightning.

He grabbed Sully's jacket and yanked him out the window. By the time I realized what was happening, Sully's dirty tennis shoes were caught on the frame, toes twisted backward.

"You stealin', Sully?"

Sully gurgled.

"I asked you a question." He yanked Sully all the way out of the car, holding him in the air like a rag doll. "Check the little purse."

One Raider stepped forward, unzipping Sully's fanny pack. He pulled out a fat roll of bills bound by a rubber band.

The big man let go. Sully dropped like a stone.

Licking his fingers, the man counted the money. My pulse jumped in my neck. I ran through the scenarios, narrowed it down to two. Both ended badly. The third idea started worse, but could end better.

The man scratched the side of his face, flicking fingers across his skin.

He nodded.

The Raiders rushed forward, kicking. Dull, ugly thuds.

Sully screamed. The big man leaned down into the open window, staring at me.

I held his gaze. "Thanks, I—"

"Get out of the car," he said.

chapter twenty

It was a shotgun-style house, one long rectangle stinking of mildew and scorched microwave popcorn. I waited inside as they dragged Sully over the threshold, throwing him on the dirty floor. Dirtier than any floor I'd ever seen.

The bald man had a lumbering walk, scuffing the heels of his Timberland boots. He unzipped his black down jacket, motioning for me to follow down the long hallway where clumps of dog hair stuck to chewed-up baseboards. Somewhere far away music played, a sound muffled by the blood whooshing through my ears. My heart banged against my chest.

The hallway ended at the kitchen. I combed my eyes over the back door, checking the dead bolts. All three were locked. Dogs were scratching on the other side. Their barks were deep and slobbery and hungry. Pit bulls. Rottweilers.

Killer dogs.

Keeping the door to my left, I turned slowly to the right, taking in a torn-up countertop and electric stove whose coils burned crimson under dented aluminum pans. A man stood at the stove and poked a sharp knife at bubbles that rose in a thick white substance inside the pans. He wore horn-rimmed glasses. His eyes were large and sloe and mean.

"You nailed it, XL," the big man said. "Sully was up to something."

I took a swallow of the rancid air and pulled the cape tighter, wedging the small clutch under my left elbow. For several long moments I stared at the cooking white paste, trying to detach. I decided to think about the drugs, not the people. I thought about the chemical structure of cocaine hydrochloride. I thought about how it changed from salt to freebase if heated with an alkali. Staring at the tip of his knife, I listened to the metal-on-metal scrapes until I trusted my eyes to conceal their knowledge.

XL was size S.

Five-foot-five in oxblood penny loafers, he wore a white polo shirt and wide-wale cuffed blue corduroys. With the horn-rims, he looked ready for the Ivy League. His mean eyes traveled from my face down to the cape, to the dress, my legs, finally resting on my high heels.

"He rip you off, baby?" His voice was as sweet as rancid honey, nothing like the cold voice I'd heard on the phones.

I nodded, letting my teeth chatter. I pulled the cape closer.

The big man took off his coat. The kitchen was hot.

"Moon," said XL.

"Yeah?"

"Where's Sully?"

"In the living room, filling his pants."

"You're telling me he came back?" XL glanced into the pan, stabbing the paste.

Moon took him through the details, describing the sight of the K-Car flying down the street, screeching to a stop. As he spoke, I trained my eyes to the side of his face and tried to remember how tiny Zennie Lewis controlled this large ruthless man. Her voice, I recalled her voice. The way she spoke on the phone. She always sounded . . . offended. Inconvenienced.

I let out a short impatient sigh. I shook my head, flicking my hair. Something caught my eye. In the corner. By the back door. Guns. Submachine guns, leaning against the dirty wall like toys.

"Only Sully ain't the narc," Moon was saying. "He's just a thief. Look what he held out on us."

Moon held up the fifties.

"Frisk her," XL said.

"But it's Sully who—"

"Do it, Moon."

Moon scuffed over in the Timberland boots, standing behind my back. He laid heavy hands on my shoulders, patting down my back. I shifted the clutch purse forward, and when his hands came around the front, I pulled away.

"No free feels," I said, trying to sound annoyed. "I already got ripped off once tonight."

Moon held his hands in midair. He glanced at XL.

XL concerned himself with his cooking again. The cell phone on the countertop rang. He ignored it. "Where you at, baby?"

"Baby?"

"Who you working for?"

"What?"

"Answer my question."

I frowned. Then laughed. "Oh, you think I'm a cop."

Moon reached over, tugging on my hair.

"Hey!"

"That's no wig," Moon said. "And dawg, she's driving a grandpa mobile."

From under the long eyelids and horn-rims, XL stared like a malevolent English professor. He'd almost mastered the dead expression, except I was certain XL never had to perfect it behind bars. He was the brains. Other people did his time. People like Moon.

"You got a job?" he asked.

"I'm in school."

"Where?"

"VCU."

"Old for a student. What's your first class on Monday?"

"Painting."

"Teacher?"

"Helen Harmon."

"Call the school," he told Moon, not taking his eyes off me. "See if that's who teaches painting Monday mornings."

I watched Zennie's boyfriend dig into the pocket of his baggy jeans and pull out a small phone. He held it close to his body, his thick finger aiming for the buttons. He dialed 411, then glanced at XL.

"What am I asking for?"

A bead of sweat rolled down my back.

"Virginia Commonwealth University," XL said. "You want the art department."

When he asked the name of the teacher again, I took the opportunity to act peeved, rolling my eyes. It gave me another glimpse of the guns. The wooden stocks were scratched. Heavily used.

"I got a voice machine," Moon said. "I gotta spell the name."

I sighed, irritated, and spelled the name Harmon. Pushing the lettered buttons, Moon placed the phone back to his ear. A sudden burst of relief went through me. Moon's cell phone was on our T-III wiretap, this call was being recorded. No criminal activity yet, but they would keep listening—wouldn't they?

"Look, you got my money," I said, loudly enough to be picked up on Moon's phone. "Quit playing games or I'll find somebody who can fill the order."

"I got the voice mail," Moon said.

XL stared at me. But he spoke to Moon. "Leave your number. Ask her to call about her student. What's your name, baby?"

"It ain't baby."

His smile was arctic. "What is it?"

"Nadine."

"Last name?"

"How many Nadines do you think there are in her class? Just leave the message so we can get on with it."

Moon asked my sister to call about my mother.

Sweat beaded at my neck, rolling down my back.

"So, Nadine," XL said, "where you going tonight all dolled up?"

"Christmas party. Now I'm late."

"Selling?"

"If I ever get the goods."

He asked about the party. I invented rich guys who worked downtown and liked to party hard on weekends, guys whose habit paid my tuition at VCU.

"These rich guys," XL said, "they need more product?"

I held out my hand. "Just give me the goods."

Moon turned, coughing.

XL smiled, but the expression never reached his eyes.

"Go chill in the living room, Nadine," he said. "I'll be right with you."

Moon stayed in the kitchen. I walked down the hall, my heart playing handball against my sternum, my heels clicking hollowly on the wooden floor. It sounded like I was walking across a trapdoor. I looked down. My fingers had crushed the cape's red velvet. Looking up again, I searched for Sully, for an escape. By the front door, a Raider stood holding a submachine gun. Scratched-up stock, just like the ones by the back door.

"How you doin'?" His voice echoed off the bare walls and floor.

"I gotta get something out of my car."

He shook his head and pointed the gun's muzzle toward the living room.

The shag carpet looked like an amethyst ocean of nylon with black leather flotsam. The modular couch, separated into three pieces, formed a horseshoe under a ceiling projector. The only light in the room came from the hazy blue images beamed to the eight-foot screen on the opposite wall. I saw Sully, sprawled on the sectional by the door. His right arm was draped over his face. I reached down, picking it up.

One eye was shiny and swollen shut. Blood leaked from his nose, coagulating on his neck. His left eye was open. It stared at me.

"We'll take care of him," the Raider said.

I dropped Sully's arm over his face. He whimpered.

"I better take him home," I said. "Otherwise his mommy will worry."

The Raider laughed. My heart launched another round of handball.

The rest of the couch was occupied by a woman built like kindling, one stick arm fenced around a little girl beside her. An older boy, about ten, sat next to the girl. I watched the woman's head drifting. When her chin touched her chest, her head snapped up, eyes rolling like blind marbles. Then she drifted off again.

I sat down next to the boy.

He stared at the screen and took darting glances without moving his head. Checking out Sully. The Raider, the gun. Me. At ten, he was already an expert at concealing.

The Raider moved back to the front door. I looked at the screen.

Charlie Brown was dragging a spindly Christmas tree into the school auditorium. I took a slow breath, trying to still my heartbeat. On the second breath, I ran through an escape scenario, working my hand back inside the clutch purse while

Charlie Brown threw his arms in the air, wondering if anybody knew what Christmas was all about.

I glanced over at the children. The boy's eyes shifted back to the screen. The girl sucked her thumb, her braided hair secured by plastic barrettes. The woman's fingers twitched at the end of her long bony arm, and Linus walked onstage. The girl turned to the boy, mewing.

Linus asked for a spotlight, then began quoting the book of Luke. Shepherds abiding in the field, watching flocks by night. An angel appearing, telling them not to fear.

The girl mewed again. The boy patted his leg, and Linus described a babe wrapped in swaddling clothes, lying in a manger. The girl laid her head on the boy's lap, the woman's hand flopped on the couch, and Linus picked up his blanket, walking offstage.

XL stepped into the doorway. He ran his eyes over the woman, disgust on his face. He ignored the children. He glanced down at Sully.

"Next time," he said, looking at me, "leave the trash at home."

≈

The Raiders dumped Sully in the K-Car, making sure his head struck the door frame. As I shoved the key in the ignition, my hands shook. I peeled off the curb, speeding down Perry Street, blind with fear and relief.

I hit a pothole and Sully whimpered, pulling his arm off his face. He looked like a battered Cyclops. "You could've got us killed!"

I found Semmes Avenue. The bridge was up ahead. I decided I would run any red lights just to get out of here.

"Did you hear me?" he demanded.

"I heard you, Sully. You've got it backward."

"What!"

"Those guys can smell fear, Sully. They knew you were playing games. They pegged you for a narc."

"Did not." He sneered, but only half his face responded.

The bridge was coming closer. I glanced in the rearview mirror, wondering what would happen if they suddenly realized the truth. I pushed the gas pedal into the floor. The K-Car whined a solid fifteen over the speed limit.

"That money's mine," Sully said, as though we were discussing it. "My life's on the line here."

"Everybody's life is on the line," I said. "Every cop, every agent out here. So what do you do? Get greedy. Risk everything for a couple hundred bucks. You're alive right now because those guys got the money you were supposed to deliver. But don't bother thanking me."

"Thanking you?"

"If they thought you were a narc, they'd kill you."

"Would not."

"You're right," I said. "First they'd torture you, then they'd kill you."

He was quiet.

I turned right at Riverfront Towers. The city was as silent as a mausoleum.

He said, "And what if I told them about you? What if I told them you were an FBI agent instead of taking your punches? Huh, what about that?"

"You didn't take any punches for me, Sully."

He sat up, pointing to his black eye. "Oh yeah? What's this?"

"A reprieve."

"What?"

"Sully, if you told the truth, we'd both be dead. You took punches tonight. But it would have been a bullet tomorrow."

I suddenly realized I was driving past the governor's mansion, my mind distracted with adrenaline. Snapping on the blinker, I whipped around, swinging up Main Street by the Mutual Assurance building. The light turned red. No need to run it. Nobody was following. I looked over at the digital clock. 11:42 p.m. Temperature, 38 degrees. And downtown Richmond frozen as a still life.

"You know what you are?" Sully said.

The light turned green. He released a string of curses, punctuated with the name for a female dog.

I waited for him to finish, then said, "Sully, you just might be right."

chapter twenty-one

When I first read the biblical account of Eve and the serpent, it seemed way too short. Just a couple dozen words in Genesis. It didn't seem sufficient for explaining the fall of mankind. Nothing in there about Eve's struggle to choose between right and wrong. Nothing about the time she spent contemplating the decision that sealed our fate.

It went like this: The serpent speaks, Eve replies. The serpent lies and bang—we're toast.

But when I was old enough to live through my own falls from grace, those seven short verses began to gleam with wisdom.

Whenever I thought I was right, I forgot to listen for the sibilant whisper. Hearing only my own counsel, my righteous insistence, I failed to hear the asp slithering through the grass. It was only later, in the messy aftermath, that I began to peel away the justifications and rationalizations, the false logic and shifting blame, until I was left with one small dark object, resting in the palm of my hand like an apple seed.

My hasty choice.

Sunday morning in St. John's Church, I sat between my mother and DeMott. The organ piped a Christmas melody. My mother hummed along about shepherds guarding and haste, haste, and I stared at the altar. My mind circled with the images of XL's deadly eyes and Sully. Drugs, guns. Children.

"Mac's having an open house on Christmas Day," DeMott said. "Would you two like to come?"

Mac was not here, nor Jillian. My mother exclaimed her acceptance. "Isn't that lovely? Of course we'll come."

She wore the red wool suit again, the harsh fit trapping her delicate femininity. When she lifted her wrist, checking a new digital watch, the thing made me want to weep. I missed her bangles, the music they used to make.

"Three minutes," she said.

DeMott turned to me. "Thanks again for coming to Mac's party."

I nodded, thinking of those children. Later that night, where did they go? Who fed them? Tucked them into bed?

The priest strode to the front of the sanctuary wearing long white vestments. He asked us to stand and open the Book of Common Prayer. My mother's sensible flats hit the wood floor. She gave the jacket a tug, its all-business style never intended for a woman with her curves. The outfit made her look stout. Opening the book with the rest of the congregation, she recited the lyrical language, centuries old. But the words tasted stale in my mouth, and I remembered when I first learned the other meaning of the word *common*. In second grade, I overheard two adults discussing my family. I was backstage, hiding behind a curtain, waiting to go onstage in a play about the Pilgrims.

"Which girl?" asked one woman.

"The one David Harmon adopted."

"Oh, her. There's also a sister several grades up. Bright girls. But I've met the mother."

"And?"

"She's common."

"Forget I said anything."

Then they laughed.

Among the most violent things I saw Friday night was how XL looked at that woman, and how the children saw it, taking in another dose of shame while the good news played on a cartoon.

The congregation sat. DeMott draped his arm across the back of the pew and I sent up another prayer for those two children. And for my selfish and willful heart.

"Praise Jesus," my mother whispered. Her head was bowed, eyes closed.

The priest continued his sermon.

"Praise his holy name," she whispered.

I glanced at DeMott. He pretended not to notice. But my mother continued to whisper petitions and a man in the pew in front of us turned, glaring at her.

"Speak, Lord," she whispered.

After what felt like an eternity, the priest faced the altar. Holding the silver chalice of wine and the loaf of bread, he recited the new covenant.

"Yes, Lord," my mother said.

The man turned, running his eyes over my mother. He glanced at DeMott.

"How's it going?" DeMott said.

My face flushed. The man turned around.

"Therefore," the priest said, "we proclaim the mystery of faith. Christ has died. Christ is risen. Christ will come again."

"Yes, Lord, yes, Lord, yes, Lord."

The man spun around. I kept my eyes on the priest. But I heard DeMott.

"Don't worry about her," he said. "She's the one who's got it right."

chapter twenty-two

Pollard Durant, head of the joint task force on gangs, had the deceptive gait of a grassland leopard, a relaxed quality that disguised explosive power. I once saw him leap from a standing position and take down a running perp in one fluid motion. As Pollard slapped on cuffs, addressing the criminal as "sir," the perp spat in his face.

On Sunday afternoon Pollard wore dark jogging clothes with no brand-name insignias. His face was flushed from exertion and cold weather, his blue eyes luminous as opals. When I walked into his office, handing him a manila folder, he gestured for me to take a chair across from his desk. The folder contained all my documentation of Friday night's adventure in law enforcement.

"I spoke to Nate Greene this morning," he said. "He wanted to be here, but I can't take that chance. That flu's done enough damage; we're barely covering as it is." He pinched the front of his jogging suit. "I'm wearing this so that when I run into Phaup, I can claim I'm just swinging by for my mail, no overtime."

"You want the two-minute version?" I asked.

"Please."

"The first night I took the informant for the buy, he pinched. I called Detective Greene to let him know."

"When was that?"

"Tuesday."

"This Tuesday?"

"Yes. We both assumed it would be my first and last time out with this informant. So we let it go."

"But you went out again," Pollard said.

"You heard the guy; he sounds like he's dying. I was available, he trusted me, the task force needed help—you want more reasons?"

"So what happened this time?"

"The snitch set up the buy. Looking back, I think he did it because the detective was so sick. I sensed something was wrong the minute he got in my car."

"In what way?"

"He was worried I might go in with him."

Pollard frowned. "Yes?"

"I was dressed up, for a Christmas party."

"Raleigh, the informant claims you *told* him you were going in."

I drew a deep breath. This was where it got complicated.

"The informant's threatening to hire a lawyer," Pollard said.

"I told him I was kidding," I said lamely.

"Why was that even a joke?"

Because Sully was a rat and I wanted to see him squirm. Because I made a hasty, willful choice. "Because he brought up the idea and I ran with it, teasing him. It was wrong."

"And yet it wasn't teasing. You still went in." His voice sounded flat.

"No, he went in alone. When he came back to the car, it was obvious he'd thrown in a change-up. He had one-tenth the product he was supposed to. He told me prices went up."

"So you decided to go in," he said in the same tone as before.

"That wasn't the plan, Pollard. I just wanted to scare him into confessing. I wanted to know if he'd messed up our operation."

"Raleigh—"

"It was never my intention to go inside that house. I didn't even know where it was. I'm on phones, remember? Cell phones. They don't have addresses."

He picked up the folder. All that official paperwork. And no box to check for repentance.

"Consider this next question carefully," he said.

I stared at his desk. Beneath the glass were pictures of his children, his wife. The dog.

"Answer this *very* carefully, Raleigh. I might be asked to testify later."

"All right, go ahead."

"Why didn't you keep driving? Why stop and talk to them? Why get out of the car?"

"They jumped in front of my car. I could have mowed them down—would that be better? And they saw the informant, Pollard. I had two choices at that point. Shoot it out, or go with the scenario that I got ripped off."

No nod, no shake of the head, nothing. When he opened the file, only his arm moved. His preternatural stillness made me feel even more anxious.

"I hate saying this, Raleigh, but it all sounds like CYA."

"No kidding. But somebody needs to start thinking about the good part."

He looked up. "What good part?"

"They had already pegged our informant as a narc. Now they think he's just a thief. Since they pounded him pretty good, maybe it's done."

"Except they think you're a dealer."

I hesitated. "I said the good part. Singular, not plural."

"It was reckless, Raleigh."

"With all due respect, it was a calculated decision."

"Calculated how long?"

"Long as I had."

"A split second?"

"Pollard, if they knew he was a narc, they'd come after him. He's the kind of guy who would give them everything before they shot him. Identities, the task force, all of it. Then they win. We lose."

He skimmed the pages inside the folder, reading, suddenly stopping. "Does your sister know why they called?"

"I told her I'm applying for credit and they messed up the names. I told her to ignore it. She's good at ignoring things."

Placing the file on his desk, he leaned on his elbows. Each movement precise. "Not one thing was by the book," he said. "On the other hand . . ." He paused.

"What?"

He stared at me, blue eyes almost glacial. "Phaup's never been in your corner."

"That's not the other hand. Believe me, I've gone over every conceivable reaction from her. Not one has helped me sleep. So I'm asking you, Pollard, please, what's on the other hand?"

He glanced out the window. As a supervisory agent, he had an office on the same floor as Phaup's, but his window faced soggy wetlands and anemic cattails. "It could be argued that you gained some valuable information."

"Anything else?"

"The investigation wasn't compromised, as far as we can tell."

"You'll tell Phaup?"

"She probably won't listen, and I can't blame her. When I got the call from Nate Greene, I thought you went cowboy on us."

Cowboys were rodeo agents, bull riding solo for acclaim.

"I even wondered if you were trying to win Phaup's respect," he said.

"That's not winnable. Not for me."

"Nate's extremely angry," he said, not bothering to disagree about Phaup.

"I'm working on getting him another source."

"Given these recent developments, Raleigh, run the idea past me."

I told him about Zennie, that she was a girlfriend to one of the gangbangers and had a son with him. I explained that she was unhappy with the relationship, and her knowledge would make her an excellent source, for us and for the detective.

"She's friendly?" Pollard said.

"She gave me this haircut."

He ran his eyes over it.

"It's not Bureau-regulated hair, I get it. But she didn't butcher me. She gave me a nice cut."

Pollard closed the file.

"I'm meeting with Phaup tomorrow," he said. "Between then and now, load up on good ammo."

chapter twenty-three

I left Pollard's office and walked down to the main squad room on the second floor. At four o'clock Sunday afternoon, the week before Christmas, the place was a sea of empty cubicles. Only two agents were working. One typed furiously on his computer, meaning any number of things—urgent search warrant, depositions, even a meeting with Phaup, who was a stickler for details. Just not her own.

And Stan.

Waiting beside his cubicle as he finished a telephone call, I read the cartoons tacked to his partition walls. Garfield, every panel joking about the cat's insatiable appetite. Apparently Garfield was some kindred spirit to Stan.

When he hung up, he said, "Annie Oakley, how's it going?"

"It wasn't like that, Stan."

"No?"

"No." I kept an ironclad unwritten vow about work: never, ever let male colleagues see weakness. Ever. No matter what. When I came back to the lab two weeks after my dad died, I managed to hold it together every day—until I got in my car and my eyes turned into Niagara Falls. There was one rule about women and crying. It was always seen as weak.

So was groveling. But I didn't want to get transferred again.

"I need to ask you a favor, Stan."

He narrowed his eyes. "What kind of favor?"

"Can you get me a copy of the cell phone transcripts from Friday night and Saturday?"

"What for?"

"I'd like to know what they said after the informant left." I paused. "After I left."

"Why?"

"Stan, I can't go into it right now."

"Can't, or you don't want to?"

I could fight. I might even win. But what was the point?

"I need as many facts as I can gather," I said. "I'm meeting with Phaup tomorrow."

"Are you in trouble?"

"What do you think?"

"I think you're lucky to be alive."

"It wasn't luck," I said.

"Okay. So it wasn't cowboy, and it wasn't luck. What was it?"

I looked at him, wondering whether he would laugh when I said it. "Grace."

"What?"

"Undeserved. Without merit. No reason for it. Grace."

He gave me a lingering expression. A smile crept across his wide face. "Sounds like luck to me," he said.

≈

The K-Car was an icebox as I drove west out of town Sunday night. To distract myself, I tried to list all the cities and towns in Virginia named for geologic attributes. Rockbridge, Great Bridge, Blue Ridge. Big Stone Gap, Copper Creek Bluff, Luray Caverns, Watts Island Rocks, White Rock Cliff . . . The game went on for half an hour, and I was still not at my destination. So I turned it around, listing places that named the geology found there. But I had to open it up to the world. Magnesia, Greece, was where magnesium was discovered. Epsom, England, was where local salts proved medicinal. And when I finally reached my destination of Mineral, Virginia, the vagueness of its name annoyed me. "Mineral" could mean anything from arsenic to zinc. It was about as creative as naming a place Animal or Vegetable.

But I found the better-named Chopping Road, just as Milky described, and the mailbox with its large painted rooster. The grass road scraped the K-Car's undercarriage and my headlights raked across weathered chicken coops surrounded by flocks of damaged automobiles. I saw the small white building he told me about, its square windows throwing gold streams into the cold black night.

I parked behind a Dodge truck whose tailgate was secured by nylon rope, and listened to a confused rooster announce the dawn. The air smelled of wood smoke and grilled meat. I heard clapping, rhythmic clapping, and a voice that sounded like wind howling through a cavern.

I opened the door to the small white building.

Dozens of men, all wearing suits, swayed and dipped to the beat. The singer stood under a bare bulb at the front of the room, his black skin glowing with violescent hues. He strummed a six-string guitar with a fist-sized hole in its base and his shoes pounded out the blues beat, the toes curled from weather and wear. But his voice. His ragged voice crawled up his spine and bled into the air. He sang about clouds opening up and seeing Jesus standing there.

The men called it back, pushing their hands against the viscous air.

Milky stood off to the side, his blue button-down shirt soaked with sweat. Seeing me, still clapping to the beat, he nodded and stepped into the crowd. His sharkskin slacks were three inches too short, the material shimmering as he moved, flashing from azure to copper. He tapped a woman's shoulder, the only woman in the crowd, and her circular shape came toward me with an oscillating movement. The walk of somebody whose hips never stopped hurting, her orthopedic shoes worn down on the outer edge. She scooped up a flashlight by the door.

"You come with Granny Lew." She leaned in close to be heard over the singing and clapping.

She took my hand, her skin soft and warm as risen bread dough, and her flashlight beamed across the dark grass. We walked past the cars to a horizontal oil drum set on metal legs. Chickens roasted on a metal grate, coals beneath glowing orange.

"Lookit this," said Granny Lew. "That girl can't even keep her mind on my birds."

She headed across the grass, leaving the grill, rolling forward and picking up speed as she headed for a house behind the chicken coops. I trotted behind, trying to keep up.

"Zennie!" she called. "Zennie!"

A wooden ramp angled over the house's front stairs and Granny Lew came across it like dice rolled out of a cup, her feet churning and clunking. But before she reached the top, the front door flew open.

Zennie looked mutinous.

"My chickens are about burned." Granny Lew breathed hard, her wrenlike chest rising and falling. "What do you expect me to feed those men after the service—feathers?"

Zennie grabbed a coat hanging beside the door. "Zeke had a nightmare," she said. "That crazy music scared him again."

"Five years old and the boy still can't sleep," Granny Lew said to me. "It's not that music," she told Zennie. "That music's from God. It's on account of that no-good man says he's his father." She wagged the flashlight, zipping the beam around. "You listen to me, child, and you listen good—"

Zennie slammed the door, stomping down the ramp, leaping onto the dark grass.

"See that?" Granny Lew said. "She just scared that boy all over again."

Trundling down the ramp after her granddaughter, who was already passing the beat-up cars, Granny Lew murmured in front of me. I lagged behind, wondering if I should come back another time. Gray veils were rising from her mouth, disappearing in the night.

Zennie snatched a pair of tongs from the grill and began flipping the chickens. The skins sizzled on the grate. Granny Lew was rolling up behind her, breathing heavily. When she grabbed Zennie's shoulder, I froze, thinking the fight was turning violent. But Zennie only continued to stare down at the embers and her grandmother squeezed, a wordless gesture, summing up love and anger and laughter and argument. It was a touch that said nothing could ever diminish this woman's bond to her family.

"You listen, child," Granny Lew said again. But her voice was tender now. "And you listen good."

She let go, rolling past. The flashlight beam swung with her gait as she walked to the building where the men were still singing.

Zennie had not looked up from the chickens. I glanced back at the house behind us.

A light shone in the room above the porch. The window was open, a yellow curtain billowing in the breeze.

"What kind of life do you want for him, Zennie?" I asked her.

Twisting her wrist, she snatched the chickens, slapping them down on the hot metal. But the hiss was drowned out by the music coming from the small building. The clapping cracked like electricity through the cold.

"What I want," she said, "is for those ex-cons to shut up."

"They're ex-cons?"

"Milky's fault," she said. "Granny went out to visit him in jail. She never stopped. She promises to feed them if they come worship." Waving the tongs, she took in the coops. "This place is just death row for birds."

I knew what she was doing. I refused to play along.

"Zennie, what do you want for your son?"

Several long moments passed. She stared at the glowing red embers under the grate, the fire exploding as the juices dripped. In the ambient light, her cabochon face looked wounded and stubborn.

"You want him to grow up and join a gang?" I asked.

"Get off it."

"Sure, your grandmother can go visit him in prison. Then he can come out here wearing a suit from the Salvation Army. Are you going to cook chickens for that?"

"You don't know anything about me," she said. "Moon takes care of me."

"He'll take care of you all right."

But I didn't get any further. The doors burst open and the men came tumbling out of the building, gasping at the cold air. I saw Milky and another man carrying Granny Lew, lifting her by the elbows. The singer was the last person out. He held the damaged guitar by its neck and moved as though he'd donated every ounce of his blood.

"You gotta eat," Zennie grumbled.

"Thanks, but—"

"I ain't inviting you," she said in a tone that said as much. "Granny Lew's got a rule. Nobody leaves here without a meal."

The men swarmed around the grill, exclaiming over the scent. Several others slid coolers from the truck beds and held cold soda cans to their sweating faces. Granny Lew rolled among them, admonishing, pushing them back until the ex-cons formed a loose circle. In the night, their dark faces were almost invisible, but I could see their bodies, still swaying, still moving to the raw music.

Granny Lew took my hand and squeezed it. Then she told us to bow our heads and give thanks.

chapter twenty-four

Monday morning I sat in Phaup's office and stared out the window, watching clouds heather into soft washboards. When I glanced back at her, she was sitting behind her stalagmites of memos. I went back to counting the ripples in the cloud's washboard. When I reached nine, Pollard Durant cleared his throat. He sat to my right.

Phaup looked up.

Dread crept across my heart.

"Raleigh." She closed the file a little too slowly. "I'm curious about something."

"Yes, ma'am."

"You maintain that your actions Friday night were not out of order. Do you plan to stick by that . . . theory?"

I didn't move.

Pollard cleared his throat again. He wore a dark blue, nearly black suit with a white shirt and blue tie. "In all fairness," he said, "Raleigh changed their minds regarding our informant. We have that on tape. They suspected our informant. But Friday night's events changed their minds."

"It's valiant of you to defend her, Pollard. But she's once again in my office, expecting me to agree when she steps outside the protocol."

"I'm not expecting anything like that, ma'am."

"We've been down this path before, Raleigh, and from what I

can see, you've learned absolutely nothing from your disciplinary transfer. In fact, you seem determined to go one better."

"I learned from my transfer," I said.

She raised her brows.

"Ma'am," I added.

"What did you learn, exactly?"

"When I went into that house Friday night, I had my gun with me."

"You're missing the point. And you know it. The issue here is that you placed yourself in harm's way, again. No backup. I'm beginning to believe you actively seek out opportunities to work this way." She looked at Pollard. "You disagree?"

I didn't let him speak.

"The informant pulled the change-up," I said. "I reacted to it."

It was like being a gnat.

She continued looking at Pollard. "I can understand why you're supporting her. You want to see the task force continue. I can appreciate the strain of keeping that operation going when you're shorthanded." She smiled, and it scared me. "So I'm willing to let Raleigh remain on the task force, with one alteration."

I didn't even attempt to breathe.

"She's now the drug buyer."

"You want—" Pollard stopped.

"Is there a problem with that?"

The man without fidgets was a statue. "My understanding was the Bureau didn't want agents doing street buys anymore."

Her cold smile warmed with victory. "Then you agree it was dangerous for her to go in there?"

Pollard glanced at me. His eyes held a mixture of disgust and admiration. Phaup was so terribly good at painting people into corners.

"Thank you, ma'am," I said. "I'm honored by your trust in me."

She opened her mouth. Then closed it. Her lips tightened.

"Pollard," she said, "give us a moment, will you?"

He walked across the room, all too eager to leave. When the door closed, Phaup reached into her red blouse and tugged.

"Any undercover work will be strictly part-time," she said. "Your top priority remains this hate crime, which I guess I need to remind you is still open. Have you seen the news stories, Raleigh? Either you close this by month's end, or—"

"I'm heading out there as soon as we finish here."

She smiled, frigidly.

"Then go," she said. "We're finished here."

≈

In the whistling cold of the K-Car, I drove past the roadside elephants and down the long driveway. The guard shack was empty and covered with gold tinsel.

Climbing out of the car, I saw fresh gravel smothering the blown-out blackness where the teenager had died inside the vehicle. Crime scene tape had been removed from the garage, and new doors hinged each of the garage's eight bays. Walking across the grass, I counted the days. It was just seven days ago that the bomb detonated. Yet now there was no sign of it.

Beside the stucco additions, a long white box truck was parked on fresh mulch. The truck's metal tongue touched the wood chips, guiding men who marched like ants down the ramp. They carried white chairs across the mulch and set them inside an enormous white tent. One of the flaps was rolled up, exposing round tables that dotted the Astroturf floor. I stopped counting the tables at twenty-six.

Cujo stood next to the truck, chewing his spearmint gum. The rifle was slung across his back. "RPM's in the house," he said.

"What's going on?" I asked.

"Christmas party," he said.

I walked across the mulch to the formal brick walkway laid centuries ago. As I stepped on the porch, Sid opened the door. He was smiling.

"RPM's got an interview," he said, still smiling.

In fact, Sid was smiling so hard it looked painful. A diamond glittered in the middle of his gold front tooth. It matched the two white stones in his ears. His broad smile seemed to be waiting for me to acknowledge his new accessory. I didn't particularly care for jewelry in mouths. Or noses or eyebrows or any unmentionable locations. And at strained moments like this, my background in science reared its head, filling my mind with clinical descriptions. Everybody had their coping mechanisms; this was mine, thinking that the half-carat white diamond was affixed to the anterior number nine tooth, on the maxillary upper horseshoe.

"You like it?" Sid said.

"Is it new?"

He nodded. And although it didn't seem possible, his smile broadened. "You like it?" he asked again.

"Wow," I said. "Is RPM around?"

"He's talking to a reporter. You can wait in the photo booth."

Motioning me to follow, Sid walked across the foyer. At the bottom of the wide stairs, a pair of ebony figureheads sat encased in bubble wrap, apparently brought back from Africa.

"How was the trip?" I asked.

"Good." Sid continued down the hallway. "Sounds like we missed some fireworks around here."

I nodded, glancing at the rooms we passed. It was decorated chaos. Plastic children's toys and suede loungers and big-screen televisions. But no people.

"Quiet today," I said.

"Everybody's sleeping," he said. "Getting ready for the party."

He turned into a square room, the walls painted the color of cloudy emeralds.

"I'll tell him you're here," Sid said.

Photographs covered the green walls, frame touching frame like a jigsaw puzzle. I walked the room's perimeter, the famous faces staring back. Actors, musicians, starlets. Faces I'd seen only in magazines. Here they partied with RPM on yachts and walked red carpets and held up champagne flutes. In one picture, the governor of Virginia stood with RPM. It appeared to be some kind of ribbon-cutting ceremony. Their arms were around each other's shoulders like old friends.

But at the corner, the photos suddenly shifted. No champagne flutes. No movie stars. I stared at the dry grass huts. Swollen dark bellies. Naked children. Women staring at the camera with dull eyes, holding listless babies. I leaned in closer. The skin on the women's arms was marbled pink and brown.

"Hey."

I whipped around. Wally stood at the edge of the room. His face looked wan and tired. Except his eyes. They were strange, almost scary.

"What are you doing here?" I asked.

"What are *you* doing here?"

"Working."

"Me too," he said. "What happened to your hair?"

I felt as ridiculous as Sid. "You like it?"

He shrugged. "Not too bad. You here about his car getting blown up?"

I nodded.

"He's negotiating with *Newsweek*." Wally feigned casualness, badly. "He wants them to use my photos. *Newsweek*, you believe it?"

RPM's deep voice was coming from down the hall. As he walked into the room, he was speaking to Sid. He laid his hand gently on Wally's shoulder.

"You'll be hearing from the photo editor shortly," he said.

Wally reached up, grabbing his head as if it might explode. "Are you serious?"

RPM's eyes twinkled. "I'm always serious."

Wally looked at me.

"That's great," I said, smiling.

But something passed over his face, an expression that said he doubted I shared his joy. Turning back to RPM, he thanked him again. And again. RPM chuckled.

"May I have a moment alone with Miss Harmon?" he asked.

Wally raced down the hall.

Sid stayed.

"*Newsweek*," I said.

RPM nodded. "They're writing a story about the hate crimes. I told them I had no comment but I sent them some of Wall-Ace's photos of Africa. He's quite good."

"Yes, he is." I glanced at Sid. "Would you excuse us?"

Sid looked at RPM. He was not smiling.

"Five minutes," RPM told him.

When Sid left, I said, "I'm not sure how much you've been told."

"Enough." He shook his head, then walked over to the wall. He pointed to a photo of a man from late-night television, known for his lantern jaw. "I bought that Bentley from him. When he heard the news, he called my New York office nearly in tears."

"I'm sure that kid's parents are even more upset."

"Oh, of course," he said, turning to me. "I didn't mean to make light of that tragedy. Do you have any leads?"

"Not that I'd want shared with the media."

"You have my word."

Still, I kept it vague, telling him the plastic pipe was fairly ordinary, along with the duct tape holding it together. "Our focus is the explosive compounds."

"Why?"

"They're connected to the cross burning as well."

"Ah, mustard gas. Was that it?"

I nodded. I decided not to say anything about lewisite, in case it slipped during his interviews.

"But you don't know where it's coming from?" he asked.

"Not yet. We'll be stepping up the search this week."

He lifted his wrist, checking his watch. It was encrusted with diamonds. "I'll trust you to keep me informed," he said. "But right now I've got to get ready for my party."

"Given what's happened, I don't think a party's a good idea."

"I'm pleased to hear your thinking," he said. "But that's what they want me to do. Live in fear. Hide. Leave for good. I refuse."

"The fear's legitimate."

"Yes." He nodded. "You're correct. That's why I've hired private security."

"Local?"

"Oh, absolutely not. I've brought them down from New York. They came highly recommended."

"By whom?"

He smiled. "I appreciate the good grammar, particularly after what I listen to most of the day. Some friends in the entertainment world recommended this security detail."

I imagined Phaup's reaction if something happened. "I'll be here too."

Sid came to the doorway. "FBI—at a party?" He wasn't smiling. "I don't think so."

"I'll be unobtrusive," I said. "Please."

RPM nodded. "I would appreciate it. Some of these people are dear friends."

"When's the party?" I asked.

"Tonight," he said.

"Tonight?"

"Is that a problem, Miss Harmon?"

chapter twenty-five

The sheriff was leading a woman to the parking lot outside his New Kent office. She was black, late fifties, and kept a handkerchief pressed against her mouth. He opened the door to a red Pontiac, helping the woman into the passenger side. Another woman drove, also black, and the sheriff spoke to her for several moments and then the car backed out.

Both women waved to him.

"Her son's the boy who died in that car," the sheriff said when I walked over. "He offered her fifty grand. Compensation."

"Who?"

"That rapper. He's being so generous she won't talk to anybody unless he tells her it's okay. She talked to *Newsweek* about her tragedy. But she won't tell me diddly about what her boy did over there." His blue eyes flickered. "Maybe she'll warm up to the FBI."

My official smile appeared. "There's a party tonight at Rapland. Are you aware of that?"

"Aware and unprepared. Half my men are on vacation. The other half are sick as dogs." He turned to me, the wind whipping between us. "You want to level with me, or do we keep playing games? I got guys who still can't breathe right."

Judgment calls. It was all judgment calls. One side was Phaup's leap in logic, all her stereotypes about the South. The other side was the man DeMott described, the man I saw walking that lady to her car.

"Some of it's mustard gas," I said, watching his face for reaction.

He looked startled. "Where's the Klan getting that?"

"If it's even the Klan."

He wiggled a finger in his ear, as if he couldn't hear. "You know, I do have a confession to make. I'm half-hoping somebody makes a move on that place tonight, just so y'all can stop suspecting me and my men."

"I didn't—"

"You don't have to say it."

"We're dealing with chemical warfare, Sheriff. That's a big step up for the Klan."

"You going out there tonight?"

"Yes, sir. Are you?"

He sighed, looking out the window. It faced the parking lot and Courthouse Road. "He doesn't want me or my men on his property. We can come beforehand and check for bombs. So that's what we'll do."

≈

A sheen of ice crystal covered the elephants that night, as if the granite had sprouted more quartz. When I rolled down my window, trying to ignore the embarrassing sound of cold rubber stuttering against the glass, a county deputy, a state trooper, and a sleek German shepherd were standing on the side of the road, just off the driveway. I showed my credentials to the deputy. Leading the dog on the leash, the trooper walked through the condensation clouds of my exhaust.

"She's FBI," the deputy called out. He handed back my

credentials. "Bomb dog. We checked the house and the tent. We're checking cars as they come in."

I glanced over at the trooper. He touched the brim of his blue hat, a gentlemanly gesture.

"We have our own K-9," said the deputy, sounding agitated. "But he's a drug dog and he said we couldn't bring him. I know why. They're smoking weed in that house."

I glanced at his thick jacket. Brown nylon, his name stitched on the left side. Erlanger.

"Deputy Erlanger, who said you can't bring the drug dog?"

He hesitated, suddenly uncertain of his indignation.

"I just need to know the boundaries for tonight." I smiled.

"It wasn't the sheriff's idea," he said.

"Okay. Whose was it?"

He glanced over at the trooper, who looked away quickly, as if the elephants were doing something. Erlanger leaned down into my window.

"What I heard, it was the governor."

I frowned.

"You don't believe me?" He raked his flashlight beam down the white rail fence following New Market Road. "This guy helped put the governor in office, throwing him the black vote. And now we're supposed to look the other way when Africans worship the god of grass."

A northern Virginian and graduate of Yale, the governor spoke without a trace of Southern accent. His millions were made as a personal injury lawyer and he promised to unite the state.

"Were you told the same thing?" I asked the trooper, still inspecting the elephants.

"Ma'am, I was told to inspect for explosives," he said.

I glanced at Erlanger.

"I'm just telling you what I heard," he said. "Don't go quoting me."

I drove down the long driveway. Three valets hovered around the lighted guardhouse. Young, almost too young for driver's licenses. When they got a good look at the K-Car, they stopped on the spot.

Finally, one walked over.

"Don't worry," I said. "I'll park it."

He pointed the flashlight east, to a field down by the river. Apparently, it was the automotive Siberia for hired help. I drove the K-Car over the terrain, listening to my shocks whimper, and parked facing the house. Checking my belt for cell phone, gun, cuffs, and flashlight, I locked the car and pulled on my long wool overcoat, walking back to the house. A column of translucent gray light circled the sky, bumping against clouds, and the white tent glowed from the lights inside. When I reached the house, I walked the red carpet from the drive to the tent. But a muscular man in a tuxedo held up his white-gloved hand, ordering me to stop. His frozen expectant smile was almost as good as my official smile.

"May I see your invitation?" The polite words clashed with his tone. And his voice, full of the Bronx.

"I'm with security," I said.

"Great, but only our security's getting inside," he said.

"I'm an FBI agent."

"Good for you, lady. But you're not getting into the tent. We got it under control."

I turned, walking back toward the house. The tuxedo called to my back, "Enjoy your evening, Miss FBI."

Somebody had parked the catering truck on the grass behind the house, right where the cross was. The evidence was taken, but I still felt annoyed. The truck's side panel was rolled up like a window blind and a rotund chef in white jacket and toque stood on the spot. The table in front of him held white plates with gold chargers.

"Get a-vay!" he was yelling. "Get a-vay from my table!"

His plump hands shooed at the confused waiters. All Hispanic, they wore black slacks and white jackets. The chef screamed some more and suddenly there was a sound like a flock of birds taking off. The tent flaps whipped open. A slim and elegant female was followed by a single-file column of waiters. She was black and the waiters were white, wearing all-white uniforms, each man so good-looking he looked fake, like Chippendales who planned to rip off their tuxes and start gyrating.

"Get them a-vay!" cried the chef.

The slender woman quietly told the chef to calm down. Then she turned to one of the Hispanic men. Holding one hand over the cordless microphone attached behind her ear, she said, "You're not to serve any of the food. Do you understand?"

The Hispanic man nodded. He turned, speaking rapid Spanish to the men behind him. They backed away from the serving table.

"Only the white waiters can serve the food," the black woman said. "You people are going to bus tables and clean up."

His dark eyes lingered on her a moment.

"Go on, tell them."

She turned to speak to the chef and slowly the man explained to his corps that a long-inflicted hierarchy wouldn't be changing tonight.

I continued around the side of the house, hoping to find the sheriff before the party started. He was on the other side of the garage. He wore his full uniform, including the brown cap with the county seal, and an expression of disappointment.

"How many men do you have out here tonight?" I asked.

"Two guys came in from Christmas vacation. That makes five. Four of us are going to walk the perimeter." He pointed his flashlight toward the woods behind the garage. "Where are you going to be?"

"I'll stay close to the tent," I said. "But I can't go inside."

"Welcome to the club."

I walked back to the tent. Four photographers now stood by the red carpet, setting up equipment, Wally among them. He wore a powder blue tuxedo, something left over from high school, and was testing his camera's light meter. When the canister light threw its beam, I saw his face. It looked fisted with fury.

The band cranked up inside the tent, and limousines began pulling into the keyhole drive, depositing partygoers on the red carpet. Two more security details were opening the limo doors, helping the women from the cars. Standing back, I watched from the side. I could tell who was a celebrity by how many pictures the photographers took—more famous, more pictures. The women wore short minks. The men wore long fur coats balanced on their shoulders like boxing robes. Moving down the red carpet, the couples formed a line. The Bronx bouncer took the invitations, wishing them a good night—and suddenly I froze.

Standing in line, waiting to get inside, Zennie was complaining to a man beside her. She turned her head, rolling her eyes in disgust, and caught sight of me. I jumped back, into the shadow of the tent. Moon was with her, wearing white tuxedo pants with a black stripe down the outer seam. Zennie's annoyed face had gone slack. Moon followed her gaze to the tent.

I stepped back again, feeling the vinyl tent against my back.

"What's the matter now?" Moon said.

"Nothing's wrong," Zennie said. "Why's something gotta be wrong?"

"Don't be like that tonight, baby. We came to party."

I heard the bouncer wish them a good evening, and Moon

wished one back. In the shadows, I counted to sixty before looking. They were gone. More limos were pulling up. I cut back
toward the catering truck, where the chef was now screaming
about missing truffles, and took out my cell phone.

"Something's come up," I told the sheriff. "I have to step
away for the evening. But if anything happens, I'll have my
phone on."

"That's a big help." He hung up.

I walked the long way to my car, down to the river, moving
along the soft sandy bank before circling up to the dark field. I
drove the K-Car without headlights to a stand of cypress trees,
both hands on the wheel to navigate the bumpy terrain. From
here, the tent was a vague white object through the trees. Sitting
in the cold car, I tried to decide which would be worse. Leaving,
and getting blamed by Phaup if something happened, or staying,
and having my undercover identity compromised, blowing the
task force.

It wasn't a tough choice. Phaup would blame me no matter
what.

I climbed out of the car, looking around. To the north, a roof
peaked in a shallow valley. Without turning on my flashlight, I
hiked across the field and wondered why Zennie was here. And
Moon. Where was XL? And if they saw me, RPM, Sid, Cujo—
they all knew who I was.

And Wally.

Would he keep my identity secret? I realized that once upon
a time, I wouldn't even have to ask that question.

The building was a horse barn. The doors rolled back on
steel rails. Hay bales were stacked against the paddocks, and
the scent of straw mingled with the odor of manure. I stood by
the first stall, taking out my cell phone, while a chestnut horse
pressed his muzzle through the bars. He had a white star on his

forehead. I dialed the cell phone number Milky had given me for Zennie, and the horse strained forward, pressing his nose toward me. Zennie's phone went to voice mail and the horse nuzzled my coat. I reached up, petting his white star, and told her that I desperately needed a haircut—it was an emergency, call back immediately.

I looked at my watch. It wasn't even 10 p.m. The chestnut horse pressed his face against my hand. I called Zennie once more. I told her my hair was on fire.

I stayed by the chestnut horse, hoping she would call. Then I walked the barn's length. There were six horses and they snorted and banged hooves idly against the wooden stalls. I found a ladder to the hayloft and climbed up. Bales leaned beside rusting farm equipment. And I felt a cold breeze coming from somewhere.

Crouch-walking under the eaves, I discovered a small window covered with iron bars. It looked out at the house and garage. From this height, the tent looked like a giant albatross. In the blackened woods beyond, I saw pinpricks of light raking the trees. The sheriff, patrolling with his men, just off the property line. And the gray strobe light continued to circle the sky. Suddenly I wished the Bat signal worked.

When my cell phone rang, I yanked it off my belt.

But it wasn't Zennie.

"I want to report a crime," Flynn Wellington said.

"What kind of crime?"

"Destruction of historic property," she said. "He cut down two trees over at Laurel. They both date back to the 1600s. I'm sure these trees were federally protected."

"Flynn, you need to call somebody else about this."

"I've contacted the National Preservation Society," she said. "They're outraged. Do you know Robert E. Lee tied his horses to those trees?"

"I can't help you, Flynn."

She hung up.

My second hang-up of the night. And Zennie wouldn't pick up.

Turning my face to the window, I drank in the crisp air, tasting the contrast with the musty scent of hay. I stared at the party tent, sensing trouble. It seemed to spin under my ribs. I felt responsible and helpless.

And it wasn't just this evening.

I came home to Richmond thinking that would make everything better. Yet here was my mother, turning into a pretty robot, and Wally, moving ahead in the world but angry all the time, and old friends inadvertently revealing how much my life had changed because theirs remained the same. DeMott, Flynn, life on the plantations. It was the same as ever, and it only highlighted my father's absence, our family's loss. My best companion these days was my overworked professional life, spent tracking down murderous bigots. And failing.

And tonight the task force almost blew up in my face. Again.

Taking a deep breath of cold air, I leaned forward, the hay pricking my hands. Outside, the circling column of light bumped against the clouds, striking again and again like a laser trying to carve through a gray ceiling. Watching the futility, I suddenly recalled something from a book that belonged to my father. It contained the writings of a medieval monk who called faith a "cloud of unknowing." The monk believed God was always with us, but we couldn't see him because of the thick veil separating us. Only during the briefest moments, mere slivers of time, did the clouds roll away, revealing for us the bright blue of eternity. And then, just as quickly, the clouds returned, leaving us to walk by faith, not by sight.

I leaned back, closing my eyes. There was so much I wanted to pray for. My mother, the children in the crack house, my work,

Wally. Even Phaup. I wanted to pray that she got her wish and moved back to headquarters. Please.

But in the end, it was all chatter. Those were things I wanted. Not what I needed.

Lifting my face to the cold, I offered up the words. Simple words, known by heart. But they carried the power of dynamite.

They were words about daily bread.

chapter twenty-six

Dawn came across the horizon like a yellow flame, burning off the night. I climbed down the ladder, picking hay from my hair, and walked outside. Crossing the field to the K-Car, my leg muscles ached from hours curled beside the window. I rummaged through my gym bag, searching for a baseball hat. I tucked my hair up into it and put on my sunglasses. I stared at my reflection in the window.

Not much of a disguise, but it would have to do.

I took the long route over to the pink stucco, searching for remaining partygoers. But all the limos were gone and the catering truck had carted off the angry chef, leaving ruts in the grass where the cross had been. When I came around the back of the tent, I saw the sheriff.

"You're just in time for nothing," he said. His voice sounded gravelly.

"I would have preferred to stay here," I said. "Any incidents?"

His blue eyes were glassy with fatigue, his skin drained of its red tones, leaving behind an unhealthy hue. He looked almost elderly.

"Far as we know, nobody died. Nobody fired a gun, nobody pulled a knife." He held a small box in his right hand. "I was doing a final sweep, just in case. The biggest problem is lost and found. I've picked up everything. Necklaces, bracelets, pins. You name it."

I glanced inside the box. It looked like bunches of costume jewelry. Enormous white zircons and simulates of diamond, the pieces badly made, the fake stones glimmering in the morning light.

"Lord have mercy," the sheriff muttered.

I looked up.

She was running toward the red carpet. The tent was empty, its white roof deflated, and right behind her was a man wearing a tweed jacket and newsboy cap.

Flynn Wellington.

She lifted the red carpet, searching the ground. The tweedy man held a small camera.

I walked over.

"Raleigh, I'm glad you're here," she said. "You're a witness. They were right here." Her face looked rigid, the fine bones in her neck brittle as glass rods.

The sheriff came up behind me. "What are you talking about?"

"Trees!" Flynn exclaimed. "He cut them down. For a party!"

"It's an abomination," the tweedy man said.

"I don't know what this is about," the sheriff said, "but y'all are on private land. You got ten seconds to turn around and get the heck out of here."

Flynn was already walking away, only she wasn't leaving. She dropped beside the red carpet once again, yanking it up. She pointed.

"Mulch! See? He turned them into mulch!"

The tweedy man snapped pictures.

The sheriff looked at me, his tired world slipping into the surreal, and the tweedy man took off his cap, throwing handfuls of bark into it. "We've got him now, Flynn."

"Maybe you didn't hear the sheriff," I said, walking over. "He asked you to leave. Now."

"Raleigh, a federal crime's been committed," Flynn said. "These trees were national treasures."

The man handed Flynn the cap of mulch and took out his camera again.

"Put it away," the sheriff said.

But the man didn't even hesitate at the words. He took three pictures in rapid succession, and the sheriff set the box of costume jewelry on the ground. He reached up, trying to grab the man's arm. He caught his sleeve by mistake and the man glanced down, as though something repulsive had touched the herringbone. Then he took another picture.

The sheriff's face contorted. With one hand he reached behind his own back, then grabbed the man's wrist and slapped handcuffs on him. When the camera fell to the ground, the sheriff kicked it away, grabbing the man's other arm.

"Tink!" Flynn cried.

"Don't test me, Flynn, you'll get the same."

Flynn's jaw dropped.

But the tweedy man smiled perversely. "What are you going to charge me with, Sheriff, revealing the truth?"

"Trespassing," the sheriff said. "Next, we have resisting arrest—"

Flynn looked at me. "Raleigh . . ."

"You said it yourself, Flynn. I'm a witness."

She spun toward the man. "Dr. Gordon, you have my apologies. I never thought—"

Behind us, the front door opened. RPM walked outside, then down the front stairs, moving with deliberate leisure. He wore a midnight blue silk bathrobe and white silk pajamas gathered on the tops of his slippers like snowdrifts. His liquid brown eyes fixed on the scene.

"Mrs. Wellington," he said. "How nice of you to stop by. However, I don't recall inviting you to my party."

"You killed those trees," Flynn said. "You sliced them to the ground."

RPM turned slowly, surveying the area. "Pardon me for saying, but I don't see any trees."

The tweedy man piped up. "We have photos of the mulch." He tried to straighten his back but the handcuffs hunched him forward. "We can prove those trees existed. The state arboreal records are extremely accurate."

RPM placed one hand on the man's shoulder, looking down at him.

"Now I remember," he said. "Are you referring to the trees they used for hanging misbehaving negroes?"

"You . . ." Flynn tried to summon the words, her voice shaking. "You are a hateful man."

"You're mistaken, Mrs. Wellington. I'm a man of peace. You're the one at war."

"These were native tulip poplars," the tweedy man said. "Planted in 1692 by Laurel's second owner. Nobody was ever hanged from them. The state records show nothing of the kind."

RPM kept his hand on the man's shoulder as a slow smile spread across his handsome face, a smile as patient as a glacier.

"I'm certain you don't have records of that," he said.

≈

I drove to the office, wrote up my notes from the evening, and placed them in my file on Rapland, then sent Pollard an FYI by e-mail, notifying him that at least one of the gangbangers from the crack house had attended the rap mogul's Christmas party.

Then I ran a background check on the tweedy man, Dr. James Gordon. According to state records, he worked as a "historic arborist." He lectured about trees at Monticello and Mount Vernon and listed among his associations the James River Preservation Society, headed by Flynn Wellington.

Just before noon, yearning for food and a nap before another night of KKK research, I drove home. When I came through the back gate, I was so hungry that even the gingerbread men in my mother's kitchen might taste good. Opening the kitchen door, I received a nice bark from Madame, and a shock.

DeMott Fielding sat at the kitchen table.

I stared at him. Down the hall, Andy Williams sang about the running of the deer.

"Raleigh," my mother said, standing at the stove, "look who's here."

I glanced at DeMott.

"I brought over some Christmas presents," he said. "Your mom invited me to lunch."

I glanced at the table. A large Virginia ham was resting on a silver platter. I could taste the salt from here. Closing the door, shucking off my coat, I sat down.

"I have candied yams too." She handed me a crowded plate. "DeMott, may I get you some more?"

"Please. It's delicious."

I said a silent grace and dug in. The yams were not delicious. They tasted like the can they came in. But a precooked Virginia ham was almost impossible to ruin. Smoked sweet, the ham's outside was blackened from caramelized basting and the inside was pink, tender as a good steak. I closed my eyes, chewing, giving thanks again.

When I opened them, Wally stood in the doorway.

"Wally dear," my mother said, "would you like some lunch?"

His face battened down in a deep frown. He looked at DeMott.

"Hi." DeMott lifted his hand.

"DeMutt, right?"

"DeMott."

"Right," Wally said, turning to my mother. "Where's the glue gun?"

"Oh, I'm making the most beautiful wreath. It has holly berries all around the—"

"I don't need to know that," he said, annoyed.

"I think it's in the den."

"You think?"

They walked down the hall, bantering back and forth while a version of "Jesu, Jesu" played on the stereo.

"What's up with him?" DeMott asked.

I looked back at my plate. Suddenly I'd lost my appetite. "My mother thinks it's the holiday. He's got no family, his parents are dead."

"What do you think?" he asked.

"I don't know." And I didn't, but I didn't want to talk about it either. "How often do you talk to Flynn?"

"Flynn? How did she get into this?"

"She was at the rapper's house this morning, protesting tree removal. How did she know the trees were gone?"

He cleaned his plate. A methodical eater, he worked his way through the food, never rushing. It was soothing to watch him.

"Flynn is like a beautiful bird with a broken wing," he said. "She looks fine, but then she tries to fly and you realize something's really wrong."

"How'd she know about the trees?"

"Spies."

"Pardon?"

"Flynn's got spies all over. She probably paid top dollar for that information."

"Who's spying for her? Not the hangers-on at his place?"

"I don't know. I've got my own problems," he said. "I've got to get Weyanoke ready for Mac's stupid wedding."

Topic closed, in other words. I decided not to push.

"You don't like him, do you?"

"Stuart?"

I nodded. "Your grandfather didn't seem thrilled with him either."

"This will be an amazing wedding and a bad marriage," he said. "I've known Stuart since grade school. He's the type who cheated on tests, then found another cheater to turn in."

"Have you told Mac how you feel?"

"She thinks I'm jealous."

"Jealous of what?"

He stared at the empty plate. His flannel shirtsleeves were rolled back, exposing forearms braided with muscles. Nice wrists. Really nice. And the right amount of hair.

He looked up. "What if I asked you . . ." But his voice trailed off.

"Asked me what?"

"What if . . ."

He didn't finish.

"DeMott, spit it out."

"If I asked you if you think—"

My cell phone rang. He dropped his head.

"You'd better get that."

I glanced down. Caller ID said it was the sheriff. More news about Flynn and the tweedy man. I walked over to the patio door, leaning against the cold glass, staring at DeMott's back. His wide shoulders tapered into a triangle, meeting his narrow hips. My heart thumped.

"Raleigh Harmon," I answered.

"Can you get out to the Chickahominy?" the sheriff said.

I waited, expecting him to explain. But he didn't.

"The swamp or the river?" I asked.

"The river," he said. "And wear boots."

chapter twenty-seven

At the river's edge, a county deputy waited inside an aluminum skiff. I climbed in, sitting on the middle bench, and he lifted a wooden oar, shoving the boat off the Chickahominy's muddy bank. Feculent and brown, the water smelled of decay as he rowed away from shore.

Dropping the outboard motor, he maneuvered the skiff around the swollen and knotted bases of cypress trees. We ducked under the leafless kudzu vines dripping from the limbs and when he finally cut the engine, we were approaching a humpback sandbar that stretched across the muddy river. Three skiffs were already pulled up into the sand. A man walked by carrying a toolbox. His black nylon jacket was emblazoned with white letters: ME.

Medical Examiner.

The boat's bottom scored through the sand and the deputy jumped out, splashing the shallow water, pulling it alongside the others. I climbed out and followed the ME's assistant down the sandbar until I found the sheriff. He stood under a canopy of trees, the bare limbs so twisted they needed no leaves to block the sun. Another skiff floated across the water. The motor was lifted, the propeller blades dangling ribbons of algae. The two officers wading beside it held the gunwales and skimmed fishing nets through the water. Erlanger was one of them, the officer stationed at Rapland's entrance last night. He glanced over his shoulder, as if expecting to bump into something. His partner was black and lifted his small net, allowing the water to drain before banging the handle against the gunwale, emptying the net's contents into the boat.

"Sheriff," I said.

"We got a call from a fisherman." His voice was as rough and dry as pumice.

"Yes, sir, but I'm still not clear on why you called me."

Like his officers, he wore rubber hip waders. They made him appear even shorter, truncated somehow, as he stepped into the river and pointed into the twisted trees.

My stomach lurched.

Hanging upside down, kudzu vines draping their flesh like veils, two men had been stripped to the waist. The bloated arms had been pulled open, the wrists secured to the sandbar with gray rope and steel pegs. Blood had dripped down their opalescent blue faces, drying in dark rivulets.

I looked away.

The medical examiner stood off to the right. A pristine woman with shiny blonde hair, Dr. Yardley Bauer exhibited little emotion, ever. It was difficult to say whether the job had changed her personality or whether her pared-down personality attracted her to the job. She stood with her hands on her hips, evaluating her staff.

"Who's going up?" she asked.

Before anyone could answer, the sheriff stepped forward. "Doc, excuse me. This is Agent Harmon, FBI. Can you show her what you showed me?"

The ME turned, passing her eyes over me. We'd met last summer. She nodded acknowledgment and stepped into the shallow water. The slow current caressed her rubber boots as she reached up, touching one man's bare chest with her gloved hands. She turned him, the ropes creaked.

"They were shot first," she said matter-of-factly. "Back of the head. One bullet each. Then strung up."

I must have winced, because she said, "That's not even the worst of it."

She pointed up, into the trees, just as the sheriff had, but I couldn't see what she meant. I walked into the water, looking upward from the base of the trunk, following the sight of their wet trousers, the blood, until I saw the bare feet. The toes looked broken, splayed like radiating stars.

"Somebody drove spikes through the feet," the ME said. "Do you have any idea how difficult it is to hammer into these trees?"

"Yes." I felt sick. "The trunks are petrified."

She seemed disappointed that I knew. But the sheriff rasped, "What do you mean, petrified?"

When I looked at him, he'd aged ten years in one day.

"The trees standing in the river soak up the water. It's full of minerals. Eventually the minerals colonize all the tree cells, turning wood into stone." I looked back up again. "The wood is probably softer the higher up you go, but not much softer."

One of the officers called from the water. "Sheriff, we found a shell."

The sheriff walked over to the boat.

I turned to the ME. "What do you make of it?"

"Agent Harmon, I'm sure you have your own theory."

"Symbolic," I said.

She made a noncommittal gesture with her head, a waggling motion that revealed all the beautiful highlights in her hair. "Why not just shoot them, is that it? Why go to so much trouble?"

The sheriff walked back from the boat. "Doc, can you show her the tattoos?"

Yardley Bauer reached up, twisting the body again. She

pointed to one bloated forearm. The tattoo's blue ink almost matched the color of the skin around it. Swollen with the accumulated fluid beneath the skin, the letters were still legible.

KKK.

I looked at the sheriff.

"It's on the other one too," he said.

I turned to Bauer, but she was speaking to her crew. "Pictures from every angle," she said. "Measure everything before we take them down. Torso, head circumference, you know the drill. But I still need to know, who's going up?"

An argument erupted among the assistants—who performed what duty at the last crime scene, who owed favors. I turned away, walking up the sandbar, the smell of the river like a tickle at the back of my throat. As I stepped into the water, silty sand give way under my feet, the cold temperature of the water seeping through the rubber of my boots. It soothed my nausea.

I took a pair of latex gloves and four empty film canisters from my short jacket. The Chickahominy was an ancient tributary, full of meanders and coves. I suspected its sluggish wake would carry only fine particulate as the water wormed its way across the coastal plain, down to the James River and the Chesapeake Bay beyond. Scooping soil into one of the canisters, I pinched some between my fingers, smearing it across my glove's pale latex. Greenish gray, full of clay. Glauconitic sand. I saw shiny platelets of mica, but I hoped this soil contained something more specific. A mineral uncovered by X-ray diffraction or chemical testing, a mineral persistent enough to cling to the clothing and shoes that touched this place, turning it into deadly ground.

Officer Erlanger pushed the boat like a shopping cart. His partner continued raking the murky water with his net.

"May I look?" I asked.

"Be my guest." Erlanger dragged the boat to the bank.

Between the aluminum benches, a rubber bin held three soaked street shoes. One white undershirt, river-stained the color of tea. Crushed beer cans, rusted fishing lures. I picked up one of the shoes, turning it over. The river had washed the fine-grained sediment from the rubber treads. At the bottom of the bin I saw the empty brass cartridge—what the deputy called a shell. I picked it up, rolling it across my gloved palm. There were no manufacturing marks. Not even caliber.

"Guns didn't go off at that party," Erlanger said. "But what about out here?"

I looked up at his wide face. He looked even angrier than last night.

The sheriff called my name. I dropped the cartridge case back in the rubber bin and walked back to where he stood with the ME.

"The doc has a question," the sheriff said.

In her green eyes, I saw the challenging expression. She enjoyed testing people, particularly other women. I assumed it was to make sure she was smarter.

"You're a Christian, isn't that right?" she said.

I nodded, bracing myself. That wasn't the question.

"How did they get your Savior off that cross?"

She said the word "savior" with inflected irony, and I chose my words carefully. "Given what they'd already done to him," I said, "they probably just tore him down."

She turned to an assistant. "You got pictures of the feet?"

"Zoomed in, tight focus," the assistant said.

"All right," said the ME. "Let's tear 'em down."

chapter twenty-eight

I drove north, away from the river, following the twists of county road until I saw the grassy driveway leading to the Airstream trailer.

The girl named Tina was standing outside, her face raised to the midday sun. In her small plump hands she clutched a gray cat, watching me wade through the piles of dead leaves.

"Is your mom home?" I asked.

"She's cleaning Poppy."

"Would you let her know I'm here to see her, please?"

Her brown hair flowed in long waves over skin white as refined sugar. With her bountiful figure, she looked like a maiden stepping out of a seventeenth-century canvas. Twisting her wrist, she turned the cat around, staring into its eyes. When the cat finally blinked, the girl laughed and tossed the animal into the leaves. It skittered and disappeared in the piles.

"It might be awhile," she said, opening the trailer door. "I guess you can wait inside."

The sewing room still smelled of stale cigarettes and chemical sizing, but the ceiling had been cleared of some satin. I could hear Angela Crell's husky voice coming from the next room.

"Don't let it go that long," she was saying. "I'm right here."

Tina picked up a pack of Salems next to the sewing machine. She shook a cigarette loose, flicked the lighter, and squinted one eye, ruining any resemblance to Rembrandt's beauties. Her mother was discussing scatological details of liquid diets.

"Maybe you should let her know I'm here," I said.

Tina took two more drags and left the cigarette burning in the ashtray. She shuffled into the next room and said, "Some lady's here for you."

There was a reply, unintelligible. But it prompted Tina to offer a brief description. "The one who drives that weird-lookin' car. What did you call it, a Mary Kay car?"

Another low reply.

"K-Car, whatever. She's here."

Shuffling back into the room, Tina headed straight for the cigarette. The ash was long, and in the next room the radio suddenly grew louder. Burl Ives reminded us to have a holly jolly Christmas; it was the best time of the year.

"How old is that car?" Tina asked.

"Old."

"But it's not a collector's, huh?"

I shook my head.

"So why drive it?" she asked.

"It was a gift."

"I'd give it back," she said.

When Angela Crell came into the room, she looked even more diminished than last time and completely incapable of having birthed this voluminous creature puffing her cigarettes with evident pleasure.

"Tina," she said. "Gimme a minute."

Tina shook a fresh smoke from the pack and walked into the next room. She passed by her grandfather without acknowledgment, even though Burl Ives insisted somebody waits for you.

"I'm mighty scared of getting old," Angela Crell said, lighting a cigarette. "You got kids?"

"No kids," I said.

"You married?" she asked.

"Nope."

"Boyfriend?"

I shook my head.

"You're single?"

I gave my official smile, not wanting to explain, not to some-body who was about to find out what paternal death felt like. The simple truth was, after my father died I never wanted to feel that sad again. Loneliness hurt less than lost love.

"Okay, you're not here for that." She took a drag, blowing it out. "What do you want to know?"

"Does the Klan get tattoos?"

"What kind?"

"Tattoos that say KKK."

"You must really think they're morons." She blew out the smoke, laughing bitterly. "Only a moron would do something like that. Besides, they're mostly Baptists. They think tattoos are a big sin. I had a guy tell me nobody was getting through the gates of heaven with ink on their body. So no tattoos with KKK. If you don't believe me, go check my daddy's body."

I let the goading jab pass. The damaged condition of the men in the trees made it difficult to guess their ages. But they weren't old.

"The new guys you mentioned," I said. "Do they get tattoos?"

"Where'd you see this?" she asked.

"I can't say."

"But you saw tattoos that said KKK?"

I didn't reply.

She shrugged. "Anything's possible. The young guys are different."

"How so?"

"For one, they don't drag God into the mix," she said.

"They just don't like black people."

"Or Jews or Catholics or Mexicans or the Chinese Commies. Did I leave anybody out? Oh yeah. Muslims," she said. "And they've got money. That's probably why they don't talk about God."

"How's that?" I asked.

"If you've got more money than God, who needs religion?"

"They're that rich?" I said.

She gave me a skeptical look, an expression that resembled her usual hard countenance, only mathematically squared. "I told you. If you want absolute facts, all I can give is measurements from shoulder to wrist. The rest just comes from what I hear, what I see, what I pick up."

"But you're certain they have money?"

"One of them does. I mean, he didn't come right out and say, 'I'm loaded,' but when I was taking his measurements he was talking with his buddy. After a while, they forget I'm there, like I'm the cleaning lady or something."

"What did he say?"

"He was talking about his honeymoon, listing all the places they were going. His buddy says, 'Man, that's a lot of places for one honeymoon.' And the guy says, 'Yeah, well, we've got three months.' I almost swallowed my pins. Three months—for a honeymoon! After that, I didn't hear nothing. All I could think was, 'You dummy, Angela. You should've married yourself a rich guy when you still had some looks.'"

≈

DeMott's pickup was parked beneath an oak tree on the plantation's side lawn. Both doors were open but nobody was inside;

as I came closer, I saw brown twine running from the steel cleats in the truck bed up into the old tree. The string bobbed and DeMott came around the side wearing a harness secured to the tree trunk, his spiked cleats biting into the bark. He was humming until he looked down.

"Everything all right?" he asked.

I shook my head.

He dropped the ball of twine, letting it bounce on the winter grass, and unbuckled the harness. With both hands he grabbed a tree limb and dangled, dropping himself into the truck bed, then hopped off the tailgate. He stared at me, the light in his blue eyes making me nervous. I thought he might open his arms. What scared me more was that I wanted to fall into them.

"What happened?" he said.

I glanced at the big house, waiting for words to speak. Thick clouds were blowing in from the bay, obscuring the sun. The mansion's wavy antique glass windows looked dark as slate.

"Where is everybody?" I asked.

"Let's see. Jillian and Mac went to some spa with the brigade of bridesmaids, my mom drove into Richmond to nag the wedding planner in person, and my dad's probably trying to find a loan to cover expenses." He pointed up to the tree. "And I'm hanging lanterns by order of the princess. It's her way of saving Dad money."

"Where are they going for their honeymoon?" I asked.

"Where aren't they going? Rome, Portugal, Paris. I think Tunisia's on the agenda."

"How long will they be gone?"

"A few months."

"Is Stuart around?" I asked.

He stared at me. "Stuart."

"Yes. Is he here?"

He pulled off his work gloves. The golden suede was worn, blackened around the fingers. "Why do you want to talk to Stuart?"

"Please don't make me say I can't tell you."

"He's not here. Mac ordered him gone until the wedding. She's superstitious."

"Where is he then?"

"Home, I suppose."

"In Richmond?"

DeMott brushed the work gloves against his jeans. He looked down and a section of his golden brown hair fell over his forehead. When he lifted his head, flicking the hair from his eyes, I couldn't read his expression.

"It's urgent, DeMott. Can you at least give me an address?"

"It won't do you any good," he said.

"I can find it."

"I'm sure you can," he said. "But you'd never get past the guards."

chapter twenty-nine

One of America's best-kept secrets was an hour east of Washington, two hours north of Richmond, and a world away from struggle.

Upperville, Virginia, looked like an English village on the cusp of the industrial revolution. The main road divided its painted clapboard stores with their quaint wooden signs. Beyond that, tender valleys rolled into horse country, disguising the ambitions of its residents. They were CEOs of multinational conglomerates and owners of NFL teams. Venture capitalists with computer systems raking in billions. In fact, Upperville had so many powerful residents that the late Paul Mellon managed to blend in on a horse farm that produced a Triple Crown winner.

Adding to the rarefied atmosphere, an evening gloaming filled the sky, casting the clouds into lavender gray. A light snow fell like sparkling ice.

"You've heard the poem?" DeMott said.

I looked over. I'd offered to follow his truck up here, but he insisted we needed to talk. I changed clothes at the carriage house and left the K-Car because civilians were banned from Bureau vehicles—and because his Ford truck was a much better ride. But after insisting we needed to talk, he was silent for most of the drive. And I didn't mind. I was busy mulling over facts and speculation.

"What poem?" I said.

"The one about Upperville," he said.

"You read poetry?" I said.

"Someday you're going to realize you don't know everything about me." He grinned. I looked out the window, unable to tell him I was already coming to that point.

He drove through the glittery snow to Delaplane Grade Road. The bare trees filamented darkening hills, the tangled limbs an amethyst felt.

"There it is," DeMott said.

Down in the valley, the white stone mansion with a copper roof looked airlifted from the British countryside and was encircled by a quarter-mile driveway. Another long spur linked the various outbuildings, each larger than my carriage house.

"Morgan Manor," he said. "When I say old money, think geologic time. This is Jurassic wealth."

He turned into a cleft of the hills and stopped at a gated house. The young man who stepped from the lower portion donned a black riding hat, the kind worn by English cabbies in the 1800s. It matched his black trousers and cape.

DeMott leaned out his window. "Hey, Barry," he said. "How you been?"

"Fine, Mr. Fielding," he said. "I don't see your name on the list. Was they expecting you tonight?"

"No, I'm just dropping in to say hi."

The sparkling snow dusted his top hat. With his simple face and clear eyes, he looked like a bit player in a Dickens drama. Some hardscrabble youth who worked long hours on the estate, then went to quaff an ale in the tavern before shuffling home to his grubby garret.

He also looked concerned, casting his eyes over DeMott's flannel shirt.

"You know it's dinnertime, right?" he said.

"I bet I can steal a biscuit off the table before they notice."

"Ah, Mr. Fielding." Barry restrained a grin.

"I just wanted to surprise Stuart." He leaned out a little farther. "You know, something before the wedding?"

Barry shifted his head, taking a quick glance at me. He looked back at DeMott, still doubtful.

"Promise not to get me in trouble?" Barry said.

"Promise."

He turned and walked inside the guardhouse. Moments later the black iron gates opened, dividing a double *M* soldered to the bars. Along the driveway, white Christmas lights blinked on, delicate pinpricks punctuating the hedges.

Waving to the guard, DeMott drove through the gate.

The Morgans were not, in fact, eating dinner. The butler escorted us from the imposing front entrance flanked with Greek statuary to a wood-paneled library where a fire blazed in the fieldstone hearth. Announcing our arrival, the dry wood crackling, the butler said, "Mr. Fielding and a Miss Harmon."

Like the guard at the gate, the butler wore antiquated formal clothing. Gray striped trousers, black waistcoat, tails, all of it ready for Grosvenor Square. The four people sitting in the library were also dressed formally. A middle-aged woman faced the fire from a deep red couch embroidered with gold fleur-de-lis. An elderly gentleman sat beside her, wearing a moth-eaten uniform, and the teenager who stood next to the fire squinted his eyes at DeMott, as if trying hard to remember something. Or to forget.

A middle-aged man, short, smiling, walked across the Persian rug and extended his hand. I suddenly remembered his face from Mac's party last week. He had stood next to the stage during the toast. His teeth were too large for his face.

"Marshall Morgan." He shook my hand, then turned to DeMott. "You're not dressed for dinner, but I can get you a jacket.

And I'm sure something for your friend." He glanced sidelong at my slacks. Nice slacks too.

"Thank you," DeMott said. "I just stopped by to see Stuart for a moment."

"He's not here." It was the woman, raising her voice. She was pretty and plump and large-breasted so that her lovely clothes gave her the trussed-up appearance of the Christmas bird. "He's gone hunting with his cousin Jackson."

"Hunting!" exclaimed the old man. "Bringing us some bear!"

She placed a dainty hand on his arm, where the gray uniform was worn thin. "Father, please."

"Indians, they like to eat the heart first," the old man continued, as though she'd begged him to continue. "Say it gives a soldier courage. That's why I don't mind fighting with this Injun." He nodded at the youth by the fire. "He's a brave one. More like him, and we might stop McClellan."

Mr. Morgan turned toward me, weighing my reaction to the old man and swirling the drink in his hand. It released the steeped scent of hundred-year-old casks. "As I was saying, they've gone hunting."

"When do you expect him back?" DeMott asked.

"I'm surprised he's not home already. They left yesterday and planned to spend the night in the woods. Stuart's usually home before dinner the next night. So he's late. Perhaps they're staying out longer because he's about to become an honest man." He showed his large teeth.

"Renegades!" the old man shouted.

"Father, stop," said the woman.

"Throw 'em in the brig!"

"You're upsetting Barky," she insisted.

Barky was apparently the young man, because they all turned to stare at him, including DeMott. His red hair was tangled in wiry nests of copper. His black tie showed Big Bird and Elmo from Sesame Street. And he was still squinting at DeMott as he said, "You are the brother of MacKenna."

"Oh, very good," said the woman, smiling. "That's very good."

He smiled, looking relieved. Only the left side of his freckled face moved. The right side was stiff, like molded plastic. "He was him before, I knew that."

"And he's going to be your brother-in-law," she said.

He looked confused. "My what?"

Mr. Morgan drew a deep breath. "DeMott, would you like me to tell Stuart you stopped by?"

"Thank you," he said. "Please have him call me, as soon as possible."

In the grand driveway, where a boxwood garden enclosed a marble fountain of maidens pouring pitchers into the pond, DeMott's truck looked like it belonged to the gardener.

"Sort of an odd bunch," I said, climbing into the truck. Snow dusted the windshield.

"Odd but not bad," he said, turning the key. "They're a little out of touch with the rest of the world."

"Wealth is a great insulator."

"Sure. But some other things keep them locked away."

He drove toward the gate, which opened on our approach, and waved at Barry. In the truck's side mirror, I watched the gate close behind us.

"Most people hate the rich," DeMott said. "What they don't realize is that money brings as much sorrow as joy."

I glanced over. In the dark, his perfectly proportioned profile resembled one of the Greek statues decorating the Morgan estate. As he stared out at the road, suddenly remote, I felt an urge to hear his every thought. I'd boxed him in all these years, placing him in the tidy category with the James River plantations. And I remembered how he saved my life last summer. How he wanted no credit for that.

"The older man's the grandfather?" I said, trying to draw him out.

He nodded, turning off Delaplane Grade Road.

"That Confederate uniform belonged to an ancestor, I forget who, some Morgan who fought alongside Stonewall Jackson. That's where the cousin gets his name—Jackson."

The Southern tradition. My first name was an ancestral last name. So was DeMott. And MacKenna. And perhaps Stuart . . .

"With Willis Barksdale, you can't exaggerate Southern senility. Bring him a drink, he tips you with Confederate bills. And poor Mrs. Morgan." He looked over, blue eyes full of emotion. "That's Stuart's older brother wearing the Sesame Street tie."

"Older?"

"Barksdale, named for the crazy grandfather in the uniform." He shook his head. "Strange how these things go. Now those two are so alike it's depressing."

"Did any Morgans fight in World War I?"

He frowned. "Why?"

"Just wondering."

"I wouldn't know."

The snowflakes twinkled like stars in his headlights.

"May I ask what's wrong with the brother?"

"Long story. I'll tell you over dinner. You're hungry, right?"

"Always."

He grinned. "I love that about you."

"What?"

"I mean, uh, I really like the way you eat—and I know a great place. You can't leave Upperville without going to the Hunter's Head."

But when he pulled into the Hunter's Head, I didn't immediately jump out of the truck. The painted sign had the same faux lettering that infected Colonial Williamsburg, a place where Ye Olde Corporate Moneymakers charged unwitting tourists twenty bucks for fish and chips served on a pewter plate.

DeMott waited. "What's wrong?"

"It looks like a tourist trap. At least with McDonald's, you know what to expect."

"C'mon, Raleigh. Live a little."

I started to protest.

"The shepherd's pie is out of this world."

That did it. I followed him through the stone wall that did nothing to decrease my expectation of historic theme park food. But when he opened the door, I was levitated by a luscious scent of braised meat and roasted potatoes, a winter-warm coziness that thumbed its nose at the cold. The walls were mortar and plank, an old cabin, and DeMott led me to a small room with farmhouse tables and mismatched chairs. I was taking off my coat when he let out a groan.

"What's wrong?"

"You got your wish." He picked up my coat. "I didn't, but you did."

Two men sat at a pine table across the room, hunkered over steins. They wore camouflage clothing, their faces reddened by the fire in the stone hearth and the beer in their mugs.

I recognized one of them.

"Don't tell me," Stuart Morgan said. "Mac wants to see if I'm behaving. She tell you to find me here?"

"You're supposed to be hunting," DeMott said with a tight smile. "If I'd known you were here, we might be eating Big Macs right now." He held out my chair. "I believe you've met Raleigh Harmon."

Stuart slid his eyes toward me. They were shiny as marbles. He stood, swaying a little, and shook my hand with just the right amount of pressure and dipped his head solicitously. "Well, well, Raleigh Harmon," he said.

But for all his manners, he didn't introduce his companion. I offered my hand. His companion barely shook it.

"Elliott," he said, leaving me to wonder, *first or last name?*

Stuart sat to my left, Elliott across the table. DeMott positioned himself at the table's end.

"We were just over at your place. Your dad said you were with Jackson." He turned to Elliott. "Are you a different cousin?"

"Cousin?" Elliott said.

"The story is I went hunting with my cousin," Stuart said. Elliott frowned.

"They're not exactly fans of yours." Stuart turned to DeMott. "And don't tell Mac. She's on the same page as my parents."

"You want me to lie to her?" DeMott said.

"No, I want you to keep your mouth shut." Then, remembering my presence, his face softened. "Please, I'd really appreciate it."

"What if I keep my mouth shut until they ask if there are any objections to this marriage?"

"Funny, Fielding."

"Funnier that you think I'm kidding."

I leaned forward. "Stuart."

"Raleigh Harmon," he said.

"May I ask where you went hunting?"

"You like to shoot?"

"She could pick both of you off at twenty paces," DeMott said.

Stuart laughed. Then suddenly stopped. "Oh. Yeah. You're an FBI agent."

"And I'm investigating the crimes over at Rapland. You know, that car bomb that killed a teenager? Maybe you heard about it."

From the corner of my eye, I saw Elliott's head snap toward Stuart, who didn't respond with so much as a glance at his companion.

"Of course I heard about it," he said. "You'd have to live in a cave not to, especially on the James." He looked at DeMott. "You and Mac were talking about that car bomb the very next day."

"This morning," I continued, "two guys were found dead in the Chickahominy."

"Sounds like a bad day on the river."

"How do you know it wasn't the swamp?"

He ran his tongue over his lips. "What?"

"I said the Chickahominy, but I didn't say whether it was the river or the swamp."

"I guessed."

"The guys had some interesting tattoos. You want to guess what they said?"

"The dead guys?"

"The tattoos."

"I can think of a few things." He smirked. "You really want to hear them?"

"Three letters."

"The word I was thinking of has four." He grinned at Elliot.

"They said KKK." I saw something pass behind his eyes.

"Why tell me?" He picked up his beer, sipping.

"Because I think you know who they are."

"Now how would I know a thing like that?"

"Because you're part of the new Klan," I said.

Elliott shot up, the chair tipping back. "I gotta work tomorrow."

He tossed a five-dollar bill on the table and hurried past the crowd reading the chalkboard menu.

"He's jumpy for a hunter," I said.

Stuart turned to DeMott. "Your girlfriend's not exactly making dinner conversation."

"Girlfriend?" I said, glancing at DeMott.

"Tell her to get to her point."

DeMott turned to me. "Raleigh, what *is* your point?"

"Stuart knows."

"You make a very weird couple. Did you tell my parents the FBI was looking for me?"

"No, she didn't," DeMott said.

"Why not?"

DeMott looked at me, waiting for the answer.

"It didn't seem appropriate," I said.

"Because you saw my retarded brother, is that it? You felt sorry for my parents? I've got news for you. My brother's not retarded. And he's not autistic. And he's not the result of over-breeding, which probably crossed your narrow mind."

"Hey, Stuart," DeMott said. "Cool it."

"Mac told me how you're in love with her. Man, if this is the girl you want to marry, you need your head examined."

I pulled back.

DeMott's throat colored. He refused to meet my eyes.

"Way to go, Stu," he said.

"My brother was at the top of his class at Georgetown," Stuart said, as though no atomic bomb had just detonated. "Double major, physics and astronomy. Straight A's. Brilliant. One night coming home from a lecture on nanoparticles he got off the Metro and some black guys jumped him. They had knives."

"I'm sorry," I said.

"Save it for somebody who believes you. He hands over his

wallet, his cell phone, his shoes, for crying out loud. They still stabbed him. Twenty-seven times. A nurse was coming home from her shift. She found him crawling down the street. He's bleeding to death and those guys were having a party, charging Cristal on his credit card. His brain's never coming back. The smartest, best—" His voice cracked.

"C'mon, Stu, I'll drive you home," DeMott said.

"And you!" he said. "You bring this chick Fed up here who thinks she knows how things are. But she's wrong. I know what happened to my brother. And I know that guy on the river is part of the problem."

"Wait—you're saying it's true?" DeMott said.

"He's made millions selling hate. Telling them to destroy, to kill. And now he sits around that ugly house counting his cash, whining that somebody's bothering him. You know what? My brother had to relearn the alphabet."

"Wait—" DeMott was still incredulous. "You're in the Klan?"

"I'm going to the restroom." Stuart stood, no longer swaying. "When I come back, you'll both be gone."

"I still have a few more questions," I said.

"Good. Call my lawyers." He gave me a hard smile. "My lawyers will bury the federal government."

chapter thirty

In the Hunter's Head parking lot, just beyond the quaint stone wall, I asked DeMott which truck belonged to Stuart. He shook his head.

I walked among the vehicles. Mercedes. Suburbans with trailer hitches. Audi TT. Infiniti sedan. More Suburbans with trailer hitches. None of them looked like Stuart Morgan. But at the farthest end, a new Chevy pickup sported a crust of mud on its dark green paint. And across the cab's back window, a high-powered rifle rested in its rack, complete with a 100-millimeter night scope.

I kneeled beside the driver's side.

"You're not," DeMott said. "Seriously, Raleigh."

I pulled out my keychain, opened my pocketknife, and spread a tavern napkin across my thigh. I slipped the two-inch blade into the wheel well, scraped, and carefully balanced the soil, depositing it on the napkin. Not exactly ideal evidence collection, but when it's fourth and long, punt.

"Here he comes," DeMott said, raising his voice. "Stuart, hey, listen, this seems like a big misunder—"

"She's slashing my tires?"

I put the napkin in my coat pocket and closed the knife.

In the cold night, he seemed taller, larger, as if the brisk air braced him for a fight. His eyes mineralized with anger.

"I didn't touch your tires," I said. Technically, that was true.

He spun around. "Fielding, you're out of the wedding. Don't even show up. And you can tell Mac why. Tell her how you and your girlfriend cornered me in public, slandered me, then tried to slash my wheels."

Slamming the truck door, he revved the engine and peeled out of the parking lot, spewing the gravel and ruining whatever evidence was in the tire treads. I watched his truck speeding down to Delaplane Grade Road, to the mansion, to the odd family dressed for dinner and awaiting his arrival.

Down the Mosby Highway, DeMott's headlights carved bright tunnels. But beyond the road's shoulder, snow-covered objects looked vague and threatening, like ghosts. By the time we reached the interstate, the snow was turning to rain and neither of us had spoken.

"I'm still hungry," DeMott said finally.

"I'm not."

He drove south on I-95, silently passing the exits for Burger King and Cracker Barrel and McDonald's. Just before the town of Ashland, when I was just fifteen miles from home and rest, the argument began.

"You should have told me you were ambushing Stuart," he said.

"Interesting word, *ambush*. That's exactly how I felt hearing that I was your girlfriend. No, wait, that we were getting married."

"It was stupid of me, seeing how you'll treat my brother-in-law."

"Oh, *now* he's family. This morning you didn't even want Mac to marry him."

When his truck came around General Lee rotary, the hero's bronze face was filled with a sad recognition, as if he understood too well the world's petty and profound battles. DeMott pulled up to the curb outside my mother's house and turned his face away, pretending to stare out the side mirror.

Neither of us bothered with "Good night."

In the front parlor, my mother was kneeling on the floor. A high-church choir was harmonizing about stars brightly shining, a world in sin and error pining, and my soul suddenly felt no worth. As the choir told us to fall on our knees, my mother stood. With her foot she shoved something under the sofa.

"I guess that present's for me," I said.

"Oh, Raleigh." She stamped her foot. "Can't you play along, just once?"

"Okay. That present you just hid must be for somebody else."

Her sigh caused the ornaments knit into her sweater to shudder. And my heart grew even more weighted.

"I'm sorry, Mom. Really, I didn't see anything."

She waved me off. But there was no music to her gesture. No bracelets. Just the blasted digital watch. I wondered why I yearned for home, when this was what it would be. Tilting her head, she offered me her quizzical expression. Her hair didn't move.

"You don't look happy," she said.

"I'm fine."

"Are you hungry? I made—"

"I'm not hungry."

She blinked. "You're not hungry?"

≈

The next morning was Wednesday, December 20, and I walked into the hair salon on Broad Street, my stomach growling.

Zennie's smile was like curdled milk.

"Could you touch up the sides?" I asked, because the manager with the purple hair was watching. "I love the cut," I added.

Zennie fastened the nylon smock as I sat in her chair. Our eyes met in the mirror. Behind us, the manager asked the old man in her chair about his plans for Christmas. In a tottery voice, he described his son's family in Chesterfield.

I kept my voice down. "You didn't call me back."

"I couldn't."

"Why not?"

Her amber eyes watched the manager. The woman was nodding at everything the old man said about pecan pie. But she glanced over suddenly and Zennie said, "I'll show you where it's at. Right this way."

"What?" I whispered.

"The bathroom," Zennie whispered into my ear.

I followed her past the bubble dryers all the way to the far back. She reached under her apron and yanked a cell phone from her jeans, clicking the buttons with acrylic nails. Before handing me the phone, she glanced back at the manager.

"The saved message," she said. "Listen to it."

The bathroom's toilet and sink were the color of Pepto-Bismol. Closing the door, I put the phone to my ear and heard noise. After several moments, I realized it was music. Live music. Closer to the phone, I heard bursts of words, exclamations. Ebonics. It seemed to continue with no perceivable point and I pulled the phone away, checking the time. When nothing meaningful was said, forty-nine seconds felt like eternity. After another twenty-two seconds I almost clicked it off but somebody mentioned fishing.

"Gonna make you fishers of men," a man said.

There was laughter.

"What we gonna catch?"

"Caviar. You know caviar?"

"Dawg, you got to bait a hook."

"Don't worry about the hook. This caviar be swimming around in the dark. When the light comes, you take 'em. Dig?"

There was silence.

Then somebody offered a vow of obedience, twisting Proverbs. The background noise dimmed and I heard one voice. It sounded amplified but far away, echoing as if coming through a microphone. The closer voices uttered quick responses—*"Yeah, that's right"*—and then the band started playing again.

Then: "Z-girl, what's wrong with you?"

The reply from Zennie was a mean mumble.

"When I get back here," the male voice said, "you be nice, or no fat man's coming down the chimney for you."

"Where you going?" Zennie's voice, close. "You leaving?"

"You just get ready to party."

Moments later, the recording ended.

I looked at the display. Six minutes forty-four seconds. I closed the phone, flushed the toilet, ran soap and water over my hands, and stepped out.

Zennie was dragging a broom across the salon's vinyl floor.

I sat in the chair and slid the phone onto her counter.

She touched my hair, glancing in the mirror.

"Think you're ready to even it out?" I asked.

She nodded.

I dropped my voice. "You recorded that at the party?"

She leaned down, as if inspecting the layers. "Moon and XL were talking in the limo on the way there. When I saw you, I thought y'all was busting in that night. I thought I'd buy me some protection."

Smart girl. "Where does RPM fit into this?"

"I don't know," she said.

"But they know him, or they wouldn't be there."

She nodded. "Everybody knows that man. He's the biggest thing in Richmond."

"Who went fishing?"

"Moon, XL, all of them."

"Did RPM have anything to do with it?"

She shook her head, glancing over her shoulder at the manager.

"When did they come back?" I asked.

"Late, past midnight."

"What did they say?"

"Nothing. But they had on different clothes." She stood up, speaking louder. "I think you're talking a quarter inch."

In the mirror, she watched the manager. The woman had finished with the elderly gentleman and now worked on a young mother holding a toddler in her lap. They talked about kids, naps, preschool.

When Zennie looked back at me, her round face looked tight. "He got away," she said.

"Who got away?"

"What?" she said.

"You said he got away."

"No. He's got a way of acting. After. I can always tell."

"I'm not following. Who—Moon?"

She nodded.

"After what?" I asked.

"You know."

"No, I don't know, Zennie."

She took the steel shears from her pocket and drove the blades forward, snipping the air in a sharp line, her small mouth twisted in torment. "I don't like saying it," she said.

I could see the contrasts in her face deepening, the wise eyes turning weary and despairing. She finally recognized the bitter end of it all.

I nodded. I knew what she meant.

And I didn't like saying it either.

chapter thirty-one

My first call was to Hannah Hamer at Aberdeen Proving Grounds. I asked for the information on lewisite.

"Didn't I send you that?" she said.

"No, you didn't."

"Are you sure?"

"Yes."

"Really?"

"Would I be calling you if you did?" I said.

"If you could just wait until after the holiday—"

"I can't wait."

There was a pause as she absorbed my tone of voice. Then the phone clanked as if set on a desk—or dropped to the floor—and I spent several minutes doodling on paper until she picked up the phone again. My notes were covered with polyhedron snowflakes.

"I've got to get into the archives," she said.

"When can you fax the information?" I asked.

"It's Christmas."

"The other side doesn't care. Can you please get me the information by this afternoon?"

She hung up and I checked my e-mail. Memos, interoffice reminders about the budget, no overtime pay. Requests for agents to move to Iraq and investigate missing antiquities. For a moment

I imagined life under a burka and considered whether it would be an improvement over things here.

I hit Delete and clicked on an e-mail from Pollard Durant. It was marked Urgent. I read it, then walked upstairs to his office.

Despite the dull winter light and soggy cattails leaning over the wetlands below, Pollard's office seemed cheerful. Opposite the windows, the wall was an exuberant quilt of children's finger paintings. Emerald Christmas trees and ruby Santas and gypsum-white snowmen.

"My Prozac," he said.

"Pardon?" I said, taking a seat.

"My antidepressant, pictures from my kids." He spread a dozen photographs over his desk. "Recognize any of them?"

I picked up the first black-and-white surveillance picture. It was enlarged to gray grains that made up Moon's shaved head. I picked up the next one. XL's horn-rims. Hooded Raiders.

"The guys running the house," I said.

"Phaup wants the task force to make one buy before the holiday," he said. "Can you work tonight?"

"Yes."

"She wants you wired."

"No way."

He hesitated, taken aback. "All we need is one decent transmission. SWAT will be out there with you."

"If you wire me, Pollard, I'm dead."

"Phaup's demanding it. I happen to agree with her."

"They'll kill me."

I told him about my visit to Zennie, what I heard on her phone, and how the sheriff found two guys strung up in trees. "Crucified upside down. We don't have IDs on the men yet; I'm heading to the morgue this afternoon. But this gang had something to do with those murders."

"Can we bring them in?"

I shook my head. "Right now it's not even circumstantial."

"Wear the wire, get something on tape."

"Pollard, they know somebody's snitching. They'll probably frisk me."

"We'll put it where they can't find it."

"But I'll still know it's there, and I haven't done enough undercover to pull it off. They see me acting differently, I'm dead. It's that simple."

He stacked the photos in a neat pile on the corner of his tidy desk. "I want you to feel confident going in. Let me see what I can do. We'll meet back here about seven and go over everything with SWAT."

Back at my desk, several bags of chocolate chip cookies whispered my name from the bottom drawer. I answered and drank a warm Coke from the can, sealing up the soil from Stuart Morgan's truck with the samples taken from the Chickahominy River. I wrote up the paperwork for Nettie Labelle in the mineralogy lab, asking her to identify each soil, then compare them for matching profiles.

I walked the evidence down to the processing room and pressed the small buzzer next to the Dutch door. Allene Carron greeted me with raised eyebrows, then gave me the pronouncement.

"You got the flu?"

"No."

"Then why do you keep pushing back the date?"

"I don't know. Isn't it December twentieth?"

"Yes, but you put the eighteenth on here." She corrected my documents, punching the pages with her red stamp. "You know what I think?"

"No. What do you think?"

She handed me the evidence's barcode. "Christmas is five days away, and you're not ready for it."

And with that, she closed the Dutch door.

Back at my desk, I found curling pages in the fax machine. They told of a chemist named Winford Lee Lewis who combined arsenic trichloride with acetylene in a hydrochloric solution of mercuric chloride. The result was lewisite, nicknamed "the dew of death."

And the United States wasn't the only country interested. Japan, Russia, and China stockpiled lewisite. It was particularly helpful because it lowered the freezing point of mustard gas, always useful in Siberian climates. Lewisite sometimes killed by drowning its victims, flooding the respiratory system with blood. Blisters erupted on the inside of eyelids, causing permanent blindness. But the U.S. military decided it was a second-rate weapon. It was unstable in humid atmospheres, and as I noticed that night at Rapland, the distinctive geranium odor warned an enemy of its presence.

The military deemed it obsolete. But they still had twenty thousand tons of the stuff. Some of the reserves were whittled away during World War II, when lewisite was used as an antifreeze for mustard gas. Some of it was even dumped in the ocean, back when we paid no attention to environmental damage. And some remained stockpiled at the Edgewood Area of Aberdeen Proving Grounds.

But in February 2005, the government built an on-site disposal unit and "neutralized" the last of the lewisite.

Not one drop of the dew of death was ever stolen.

None was missing.

And none was ever reported in any crime committed in the United States. Until now.

Worse, my employer, the United States government, was telling me lewisite no longer existed.

At the very bottom of the third page of information, Hannah Hamer had scrawled a note. With a happy face.

"Hope this helps," she wrote. "Merry Christmas."

≈

The late afternoon clouds looked hammered from a blacksmith's shop as I walked down East Leigh Street, the cold wind stinging the tops of my ears. I found Detective Nathan Greene in his office at the police annex, his brown skin dry and frangible as birch bark.

But his eyes . . . his eyes resembled the clouds outside.

"You ruined my source," he said.

"Sully lies, you know."

"Of course he lies, he's a snitch. But he won't even lie to me now."

"I understand. And I'm working on another source for you."

"You *understand*?" Heat roared into his voice. "Do you *understand* how hard it is for me to get informants?"

"Probably not."

"My cases aren't cold; they're frozen solid. I finally start to thaw something out and you come along to ice it up again."

"Sully will come back." I could sense the subterranean rumble rising up his throat. To avoid the eruption, I kept talking. "He's a born weasel. He won't make it a week on his own. Snitching is too easy. And he gets his drugs at the same time. He'll call you before Christmas."

The detective stared. It made me nervous.

"Look," I continued, "if you think it'll help, I'll grovel to him on the phone. I'll let him think he's got the advantage."

"He does."

"But after he's done whining, what's he going to do—get a job?"

"He's got a lawyer."

"Okay. But the lawyer is years from getting Sully money, if he even can."

The detective narrowed his eyes. "Why are you so eager to help?"

"Guess who the new undercover buyer is."

He nodded. "You earned it."

"And I'm ready to pay Sully out of my own pocket."

News of my punishment appeared to relax him. Reaching up, he massaged his jaw, loosening an ache, and I listened to the big wall clock. It ticked off three seconds. Four. Five. Six. A white analog face with large black numbers, the clock looked like it had been tossed out of a principal's office.

"Have you ever encountered any cold cases with unmarked cartridge cases?" I asked.

He shook his head. "I knew you didn't come here to apologize."

"I did. But there's more."

"There's always more with you. Always." He sighed. "All right. What do you mean, unmarked?"

"No stamps in the brass. No manufacturer, no caliber."

Like all good detectives, he was an expert at concealing his thoughts. He almost managed to hide the quick light sparking through his dark eyes. "If I find something like that," he said, "you're going to tell me what the connection is, right?"

"Of course. Don't you trust me?"

"Get out of my office," he said.

≈

The body only housed the soul, I knew that. The body was not the soul. But as I walked the windy streets from the police annex to the city morgue on South Jackson, I needed reminding. Dead bodies, I told myself, were nothing more than broken shells on a beach. It was just that in the morgue, that beach so often looked like a bad stretch of the Jersey shore.

I showed my credentials to the receptionist at the front counter, clipped a temporary ID to my coat, and walked down the hall. My mortal weakness sensed spiritual mist in the atmosphere, tangible as the condensation entrails produced by high-altitude airplanes. I pushed through the swinging double doors.

Two stainless steel gurneys waited, each draped with a white sheet. Across the room, Dr. Yardley Bauer came through another set of double doors connected to the back offices. She wore clean turquoise scrubs, looking as peaceful as somebody returning from vacation. She hit a light switch on the wall to spotlight the first gurney. Under the pendant light, her blonde hair sparkled like faceted citrine.

The dead man's wrists and arms were bruised deep violet.

"We ran fingerprints," she said in her sandy contralto. "So far nothing's come up, locally or nationally. And we found some more tattoos, but the images aren't all that clear due to the pronounced swelling."

She placed both gloved hands under the man's shoulder and lifted, nodding at the image on the back of his shoulder.

The blue-and-yellow ink was as pearlescent as the contusions. But I saw faces and halos over the heads.

"The other guy's got one just like it." She rested the shoulder back on the gurney. She walked to the end of the table, where his feet tented the sheet.

"Madonna and child," I said.

"Mm, something like that," she said dismissively. She lifted the clipboard hanging on the end of the table. "They ate borscht."

"Pardon?"

"Stomach contents. At first I thought it was blood. But it was beets. Last meal: borscht."

"May I see their faces?" I asked.

Even without the inflicted damage and swelling, these were homely men. Rough-featured, almost grotesque noses. I moved my eyes down the neck, the chest. An archipelago of blisters had scabbed over, stretching across the sternum.

"Friction?" I pointed to the injury.

"Some kind of burn, but not abrasion. I sent tissue samples to the lab. It's on both of them."

I leaned down, recalling the photos Nettie Labelle gave me. Compared to what lewisite was supposed to do, this looked minor. "When do you expect the tissue samples to come back?"

"With the holiday?" She walked over to a stainless steel sink stretching along one wall. She yanked off the gloves and hit the soap dispenser with the back of her wrist, lathering to her elbows. "I wouldn't expect anything until after New Year's."

"I can give you a prediction," I said. "If you're interested."

"Oh, I'm always interested in your guesses, Agent Harmon."

Hard to tell with her—sarcastic, authentic?—but I offered a brief summary of lewisite's blistering capabilities, along with mustard gas. "Somebody around here got hold of these chemicals," I said, "although our government insists they destroyed all of it."

"These guys don't look like chemists." She dried her hands, moving the paper towel between each finger. "Send me what you have. I'll alert the lab."

For one brief moment, she seemed taken aback by not knowing. But with my next question she reverted back to her old self.

"May I see the bullets?" I asked.

She reached under the sheet draping the first body, offering me a steel bedpan. When she tilted it, the two copper-jacketed bullets and one cartridge case rolled across the metal, a dull piti-less sound.

"One bullet went all the way through," she said. "The cartridge was stuck in a shirt collar."

"May I borrow the case and one bullet?"

"I don't see how much good they'll do. They're unmarked."

"That's exactly why I want them," I said.

chapter thirty-two

One of fashion's all-time worsts ravaged my years at Mount Holyoke College: pegged jeans.

They fit tight, so tight it looked like we showered in them. But as a teenager far from my Southern home, hoping to fit in with my stylish New England peers, I wore a pair to a mixer down the road at Amherst College. I spent the entire evening standing with my back to the wall, too self-conscious to dance.

I never wore the jeans again, but I was a squirrel who rarely threw things out. Wednesday afternoon, dredging through my closet, I found the jeans next to the flowing white dress worn in Mount Holyoke's laurel parade, the graduating seniors linked together by botany representing classical wisdom.

Now, feeling stupid, I lay flat on my bed trying to squeeze into the jeans. When I stood, I was one Big Mac from bursting the zipper. Pulling on a fire-engine red sweater, purloined from my mother's closet, I slipped my bare feet into my three-inch black heels and wiggled over to the mirror on the back of my bedroom door.

I still looked too healthy.

Wiggling down the hall to the bathroom, I dampened my hair and applied way too much gel, scrunching Zennie's cut into a dysfunctional shape. I traced my lower lashes with a blue eye pencil and applied too much mascara. Throwing on my overcoat,

I carefully made my way down the carriage house stairs. The alley cobblestones were already coated with frost, but I tried to run anyway, jumping into the icebox K-Car because if my mother saw me like this, there would be no explaining how it connected to geology.

I drove out to Parham Road, parked, and went directly to Pollard's office. He had dressed down for the occasion too—the Virginia gentleman's version. Dark jeans with perfect creases, pristine tennis shoes, blue sweater. If Pollard saw what passed for casual in Seattle, he'd have a heart attack.

"I talked to Phaup about the wire," he said. "She agreed to take it off."

"But . . . ?"

"How do you know there's more?"

"When it comes to Phaup, I'm like Pavlov's dog."

"She's giving you ten minutes."

"Excuse me?"

"Get in there, Raleigh, make the buy, get out."

"And what if they don't do the deal in ten minutes? I'm supposed to say, 'Sorry, guys, but my boss at the FBI says I have to go now.'"

"That's her compromise."

"That's not a compromise, Pollard. That's a death sentence. You know these buys. They're rarely clockwork."

"It was the best I could do. Come out that door nine minutes fifty-five seconds after you go in, or SWAT comes in."

"They've got assault rifles, Pollard."

He gave a tight nod. "I want you to brief SWAT on the layout of the house; we want to know about everything you saw in there."

"How many SWAT?"

"All six."

"It could be a bloodbath."

He didn't bother nodding. "Ten minutes," he said.

≈

When I pulled up in the K-Car, the Raiders were in jovial moods, laughing about something, and through the cold night they tossed a football, the pigskin arcing under the only streetlight that wasn't shot out.

Pretending to watch the football, I climbed out of the K-Car and let my eyes roam the street. Somewhere, in the dark recesses of abandoned houses and overgrown lots full of dead cars and broken glass, six SWAT guys waited for me to walk through that door so they could start their stopwatches.

"Hey, that ride still going?" one of the Raiders called out.

I smiled with annoyance and wiggled toward the front steps. Taking hold of the icy metal handrail, I heard nylon friction. The ball getting tossed. I climbed the stairs and heard the *thwuck* of a football getting caught. But then it got quiet. Too quiet. I felt their eyes on my back. Or maybe the jeans. Just like that night with Sully, I sensed something slipping out of sync. The happy mood, the casual atmosphere. But I opened the front door, clinging to the foolish hope that uncertain success could repeat itself.

In the amethyst living room where Linus had witnessed to the two children, half-naked women danced around the modular couch. Moon sat front and center with three other men lounging on the other sections. The ceiling projector beamed a rap video— more dancing, more women wearing less clothing.

Moon glanced over as I closed the front door. He nodded and a girl dropped on his lap. She wore a leather miniskirt and a white tube top that was losing its battle with gravity. Running her eyes over me, she made me feel invisible and known at the same time.

"XL's in the kitchen," Moon said.

I walked down the hall. The front door opened behind me, but I didn't immediately turn around. I waited two counts, then casually glanced back. A Raider stepped inside, pushing back his hood. He followed me down the hall and I tightened my grip on my clutch purse. Cell phone, money. The Glock.

"Right on time," XL said as I came into the kitchen. "I like a lady who knows when to show up."

I could barely breathe. The stench of scorched microwave popcorn was so thick I could taste it. Outside, the dogs woofed, clawing at the back door.

"I hope it's ready this time," I said, annoyed.

He smiled in a way that never reached the sloe and languid eyes. "Make yourself a drink. It'll be ready in about fifteen minutes."

"You said it would be ready."

"Chill, girl. Hang with the party."

"I've got an appointment."

It was the last word. Even as it left my mouth, I knew it was wrong. But it had already passed over my lips and when XL's eyes shifted, a quiver of adrenaline shot across my shoulders. I turned around. The Raider held a gun to my head. Nine-millimeter Beretta. With silencer.

"Gimme the purse." The Raider held out his free hand. His mustache looked like grime.

I glanced over at XL. "You've got to be kidding. You're gonna pull this crap?"

"Precautions, baby."

"You play too many games." I shook my head, disgusted. "Forget it, keep your stuff. I'm outta here."

I was two steps across the filthy kitchen floor when the wall exploded, spitting chunks. I dove, trained to instinct. Hitting the floor, I rolled left and shoved my right hand inside the clutch. My hand came up, index finger beside the Glock's trigger.

But nobody had moved.

XL wasn't even looking in my direction. Staring into the aluminum pans, he poked the white slop with his knife. The Raider poised the Beretta at my forehead.

"What I thought," XL said. "You know exactly what you're doing."

A second Raider stepped into the room. He held a .45 and grabbed my right wrist, squeezing the gun from my hand. He tossed my purse to XL. The little man with the horn-rimmed glasses caught it effortlessly. I looked down, shaking my head, and stole a glance at my watch. Three minutes something.

"If you're not a cop," XL said, "what're you carrying a piece for?"

"I live two blocks from Gilpin Court. I sell product. You think I'm stupid?"

He flipped open my cell phone. "No name?"

"Yeah, Nadine." Agent phones had no identifying names, and our names didn't come up on other people's caller ID.

He smiled. This time, his eyes went along with it and my blood ran cold.

He pushed the buttons on the phone, searching. My heart bumped a pulse into my neck and I took a breath of stench. I inhaled four beats, held it four beats, and released it on another four. Then I started over again.

The phone rang. I assumed he hit something accidentally.

But he looked up, his grin bigger than ever.

"Let's see who this is," he said, as if this was a fun game.

He stared at the LCD display. But his grin disappeared. He looked at the second Raider with a face like granite. "Tell Moon to get in here."

The Raider stepped over the blasted pieces of drywall.

"Now!" XL yelled.

Moon came running down the hall, heavy feet like thunder. XL lifted the ringing phone, holding it out.

"It's Zennie," he said. "Why is Zennie calling her?"

Moon shifted his eyes toward me, unfazed by the gun at my head. Taking the phone from XL, he hit the talk button. "Zennie?"

In the quiet, my pulse pounded. Too hard, too fast. Down the hall a girl laughed. It sounded like a scream.

"Yeah, it's me," Moon said.

Another pause.

"She's right here."

I rolled my eyes, glancing at the windows. Moisture dripped on the dark glass. And the dogs were quiet. My pulse kicked up.

"Talk fast. XL's got a piece pointed at her head."

There was a long pause while he listened. Moon's eyes shifted around the kitchen, calculating her words. I tried another four-count breath, but adrenaline killed it at two.

Moon grunted and handed the phone to XL. "She wants to talk to you."

XL held the phone away from his ear, as though it carried a disease. Zennie's voice sounded like a malicious bee. XL reached into the purse, throwing the wad of bills to Moon.

Moon counted out hundreds. I reached up, scratching my neck, glancing at my watch. Seven minutes something. My neck was damp.

"One G." Moon rolled up the bills.

On the phone the high buzz took off again.

"Watch that mouth, Zennie." XL snapped the phone shut. "You buying for her?"

"Why, is that a problem?" I said.

XL looked at Moon.

"Zennie's running her own deal here," Moon said.

"You believe her?" XL asked.

"It's Zennie. She cuts us out, that surprises you?" He shrugged. "I ain't that surprised."

Down the hall, the girl laughed again. No dogs barked. I imagined SWAT approaching, hitting the animals with tranquilizer guns.

"How do you know Zennie?" XL asked.

"She's my hairdresser. I told her what Sully did. When I said I was buying, she put in some money."

"And Sully . . . ?"

"From school, that's how I know him. Look, if I'm a cop, why did I drive back here with Sully? That's insane." I opened my hand, my fingertips numb. "Gimme my money."

XL glanced at Moon.

Moon said, "Zennie's mean, but she ain't stupid."

I rolled my fingers, one thought slamming against my skull: *Hurry, hurry, hurry.*

XL put the phone back in my purse. "No hard feelings."

"Maybe not for you. I want my money and my gun."

He gave a smile that turned my stomach, placing the roll of bills in the purse. "My associate will walk you out," he said. "You can have the gun outside."

I turned for the front door, clicking down the hallway. The heels and tight pants felt like lead on my ankles and I begged time to stop, stop, please, stop. But it was like racing down an endless tunnel. The faster I walked, the more the front door receded. I no longer heard music, only blood rushing through my ears, my pulse pounding.

But another pounding told me time was up.

Glass shattered in the kitchen behind me.

"FBI, on the floor! Down! Down!"

The front door burst open. I threw my hands in the air, holding the purse away from my body. I made eye contact with the masked SWAT agent, diving in the direction he indicated. I rolled across the floor. Two grenades passed over my head. I squeezed my eyes, clamped hands to my ears. And red fireballs ignited my eyelids. Shock waves punched my bones.

On the floor, I felt footsteps running past. When I squinted, trying to get my position, the walls spun. The living room was already filled with smoke. And screaming.

I scrambled for the open front door, falling across the threshold. Cold air stung my burning throat. I stood, but suddenly doubled over. My stomach convulsed with dry heaves, eyes watering. I pressed one hand against my solar plexus, trying to stop the spasms, and looked at the street. Green spots swam everywhere. I blinked.

Two Raiders.

I blinked again. They sat on the curb. More blinks revealed they were cuffed, headlights beaming into their faces. Pollard stood over them, holding a shotgun.

I stumbled down the stairs.

"Guns," I gasped.

"We took the kitchen first."

Pollard's face swirled with colors. I tried to read his expression.

"One more minute, that's all I needed. I was coming out the door—"

He kept his eyes on the Raiders. He said nothing.

I turned, shielding my face and wiping away the tears.

chapter thirty-three

The following morning I sat by the carriage house window with a yellow legal pad and a pot of coffee.

In the courtyard below, Madame sniffed the garden perimeter, inspecting the dormant foliage and leftover autumn leaves for intruders. Her paws melted the frost on the blue slate, leaving small dark prints until the courtyard looked like a connect-the-dots image.

I glanced back at the yellow legal pad.

My head still foggy from last night's flash-bang grenades, I made my first list simple.

Across the top of the page, I wrote *Christmas Presents*.

I listed my mother, Aunt Charlotte, Wally, and DeMott, since he'd brought gifts for us. I left my sister Helen off the list because she preferred to ignore Christmas. I stared at the list. It didn't seem possible. What happened to all my friends? My mother's friends? So many people came to my father's service, the overflow covered the sidewalk outside. Now I had four people to buy gifts for. Counting Madame, five. No wonder she wanted to return to St. John's. We built a protective fortress in the aftermath, and it worked all too well. Suddenly I heard DeMott's words, ringing in my ears that day on the croquet lawn. *"I know you. If some purpose isn't attached, you won't come."*

I made a second list. *People to Call on Christmas Day.* I was eleven names into it when Madame barked.

I looked down. She stood at the garden wall, tail stiffened. A gray squirrel darted back and forth on the flat brick ledge. It gripped an acorn in its mouth.

Madame barked again.

I poured another cup of coffee and started my third list. It was based on my dad's advice for dealing with worry. Face the worst. Look it in the eye. Write down every worst-case scenario you can think of, then plan your strategy.

At the top of the page, I wrote *What Will Phaup Do Now?*

Toxic memos in my personnel file.

Formal reprimands.

Suspension.

Transfer.

Under the word *transfer*, I made a sublist of field offices far away from Richmond, followed by resident agencies, the Bureau holes that didn't even qualify as field offices, and when Madame barked again, sounding furious, I looked outside.

The squirrel jumped from the wall to the bare maple, still clutching the acorn.

Bismarck, North Dakota.

Selma, Alabama.

Provo, Utah.

The next page began with *How to Survive.*

But nothing came to mind.

I looked out the window again. The squirrel realized Madame was out of reach. Standing on the branch, it removed the acorn from its mouth and nickered at the dog.

Madame barked and barked and barked, losing her cool.

The French door opened, my mother called her into the

kitchen. Madame threw one last bark, letting the squirrel know the war wasn't over.

When the door closed, the squirrel put the acorn back in its mouth and dashed back across the garden wall.

≈

After autumn flamed red, orange, and yellow, one of the most beautiful sights in Virginia was the clear winter sky. An endless dome, it began the morning with a faint color, deepening throughout the day until by evening the luscious lapis ceiling brought thoughts of heaven.

On Thursday morning, after the scouring Atlantic wind pushed the clouds west, I drove north to Hanover County under that winter sky, arriving at the town of Beaverdam with an icy halo still on my windshield. The 1840s train depot looked like an heirloom photograph. I followed back roads to a farmhouse that had witnessed two detonations of that train depot, both by Yankees, including one by General Custer. The air around the farmhouse was filled with incendiary smoke and the percussive boom of a rifle.

I came around the side of the house calling, "Hold fire!"

But the man with the rifle couldn't hear me. He wore headset ear protection and pointed the gun downfield, toward a tin target shaped like a deer. I stuck my fingers in my ears. He fired. When the smoke cleared, the deer was down.

"Hold fire!" I yelled, coming closer.

Tolliver Lambert pointed the rifle at the ground, turned, and squirted tobacco juice into the tall grass.

My father had other good advice besides worst-case scenario lists. He believed a woman should have certain skills. She should be able to drive in reverse with the same degree of skill that she drove forward. She should know how to sew on a button. Cook a steak, change a flat. Shoot a gun.

The day after I turned thirteen, my dad drove me to Beaverdam for firearms lessons with Tolliver Lambert. Known as Tolly, he belonged to a long line of Lambert gunsmiths that stretched back to the Revolutionary War. One of those Lamberts got off a round at Custer when he blew up the train depot. A family hero.

"It's good to see you, Tolly." I meant it. His was one of the names that came up on my list this morning.

"Been awhile." He lifted the rifle. "Look what I got. Winchester Yellow Boy."

Polished brass gleamed along the firing mechanism, so well tended it looked like gold.

"Very nice," I said.

"And rare as good sense coming from a politician." He squirted another stream of tobacco juice and launched into lesson mode, telling me how the Winchester gun company ran out of iron after the Civil War. For several years they used brass instead.

"You want a shot?" He looked at me through his pale eyelashes.

"Yes, badly. But right now I need your help." I held up a clear plastic baggie with the blank cartridge case and bullet. "What is this?"

Tolly's white lashes fluttered. Cradling the uncocked gun in the crook of his arm, he took the baggie in his gun oil–stained fingers. He left fingerprints on the clear plastic.

"Unmarked," he said.

"Yes."

He walked to a small wooden bench, picked up a chamois cloth, and wrapped it around the gun's gleaming brass, setting it on the bench. He turned, putting the sun over his shoulder, and held the baggie inches from his eyes.

"Nine millimeter." He squeezed the bag around the bullet. "And see this star?"

I peered down. On the bullet's brass bottom, a star. So small I felt cross-eyed looking at it.

"I see it."

"That's a five-pointed star at three o'clock," he said.

"Three o'clock?"

"Think of a clock face. Noon, three o'clock, six o'clock, nine o'clock. Got it?"

"Okay."

"Three o'clock." He handed me the baggie. "Soviets."

"Soviets? You mean in Russia?"

He batted the eyelashes. "You went to the fancy college, but the only Soviets I know of were in Russia."

"Sorry, Tolly. That's not what I meant. Soviets are way, way out of the ballpark here. This isn't some Cold War crime."

"You asked. I'm telling you. That is a five-pointed Communist star. Stamped on the bullet at three o'clock. That mark means it's Red Army ammo."

"What if I said this ammo came from the Chickahominy River?"

He looked up, squinting into the sun. "Those dead guys hangin' upside down?"

"How—"

"Guy who found 'em called the sheriff on his CB. Word got around, especially with the truckers." He picked up the chamois, gently wiping the rifle's brass. "What else do you want to know?"

"Who's selling Russian arms around here?"

"That's not the right question," he said. "The question is, who wants to buy that junk? Go read *Tent Life in Siberia*. There's a section on how to kill a bear with a Russian gun. You'll laugh your head off."

"Tolly."

"Yes?"

"I'm serious."

"So am I. *Tent Life in Siberia*. By George Kennan. Just don't get him confused with the second George Kennan. He was ambassador to Russia during the Cold War. Uncle and nephew. Actually, great-uncle. But they both wound up in—"

"Tolly!" I held up the baggie.

"There's Commie stuff all over the black market," he said. "When the USSR busted up—and by the way, it was the second George Kennan who came up with the idea of containment—"

"Tolly . . ."

"I'm getting to it. Listen. When that whole experiment in spreading the wealth around failed, like it always does, the Russians had tons of unmarked ammo from the Cold War. The Soviets did tons of covert operations. They didn't put regular marks on their cartridges and bullets, thinking we wouldn't be able to trace them. Then the Soviet Union collapsed and renegade KGB agents flooded the black market with stuff. I hear you can get an AK-47 for five cows in Somalia. And those Kalashnikovs can last fifty years. Not that the guy who invented the only decent Russian gun ever saw one dime. Or ruble. I guess that's what he'd get, rubles."

I rubbed my forehead. "Tolly, focus. Please."

"Fine. How were these guys shot?"

"What?"

"Did it take the face off?"

I shook my head.

"That bullet looks to me like a nine millimeter. So possibly something like a Makarov."

"Makarov—that's Russian?"

"Russian, and let me tell you why I don't like that gun . . ."

The file on Phaup's desk contained my FD-302, the factual account of the various ways I almost died last night. Pollard's FD-302 covered his apprehension of the Raiders. SWAT laid out their siege on the crack house. Three reports. They presented the information in the most accurate terms. Three reports forming a triangulation of facts, and a hole for Phaup to throw me into.

Sitting in her office, preparing for her lecture, I glanced out the window. There were no washboard clouds to count. Only that beautiful winter-blue sky. The color seemed to mock the worry that was cinching around my rib cage. To distract myself from panic, I tried to name all the planets in the solar system in order. Something simple, I thought, something I could repeat over and over while she berated me.

But it wasn't working. Maybe I was too tired, but I couldn't remember the right order. I fell back on a mnemonic device learned as a girl. It began, *My very excellent mother just served us . . .*

Phaup closed the file. "This is certainly not what I expected."

My very excellent mother, I thought.

My stood for Mercury. *Very* for Venus, *excellent* for Earth, *mother* for Mars. Four planets down.

"Raleigh, have you nothing to say?"

"Everything's in my report, ma'am."

"Yes, your report. Your report where you claim the problem last night was the time constraint."

My very excellent mother just served . . . Just stood for Jupiter. *Served* meant Saturn. Phaup stared at me, waiting. Her eyes were like scoured gray rocks. Waiting.

"I was coming out the door when SWAT threw in the flash-bangs."

"You *think* you were coming out the door. I seriously doubt you would have gotten that far."

My very excellent mother just served us . . . us for Uranus. Seven down.

She took a moment, shaking her head, showing her profound disappointment in me. "Once again you're leaving me with no choice but to take formal action. You compulsively disobey my orders. You go out of your way to make a fool of me."

My very excellent mother just served us . . . I went blank.

"What do you expect me to do?" she said.

What did she serve us? I knew it started with *N*. Whatever my very excellent mother just served us was *N* for . . . "Nothing?" I said.

"Nothing? You expect me to do nothing?" She looked appalled, the gray eyes enlarging.

I shook my head. No, that wasn't right. *N* was something else. *Nine*, that was it. *Nine* for Neptune. *My very excellent mother just served us nine . . .*

"Expect to hear from OPM after the holiday," she said.

I went blank again. The Office of Professional Management. The Bureau people deciding who was right and who was wrong and what the consequences should be. I drew a deep breath. *My very excellent mother just served us nine . . .* It started with *P*. The last planet was Pluto. Or used to be. That meant *P* for . . . *professionals?* No, that wasn't right.

"As you probably know," Phaup said, tugging at her blouse, "second offenses bring terrible consequences. Perhaps it's time for you to consider another career."

Sure, I thought, *I can deliver pizzas.*

Pizzas. That's the word.

My very excellent mother just served us nine pizzas. I felt a wave of relief.

"Have you considered what you would do if you didn't work for the Bureau?"

"No, ma'am, I haven't. And I won't."

"You won't?"

"I won't consider leaving until we hear from OPM. I respectfully defend my actions last night. You gave me a time limit that placed undue burden on—"

"Undue burden?" she said. "I was trying to keep an agent alive."

"That might be true, ma'am. But the time limit made my work more dangerous. That was something both Pollard and I pointed out to you beforehand."

"You wouldn't wear the wire, I had no choice," she said. "And you admit that they took your weapon. You're lucky to be alive."

"It wasn't luck."

"You claim credit for everything good."

"No, ma'am. I just don't believe in luck."

"You shouldn't. Your suspension will be effective after the first of the year. I don't have time to write up the paperwork with this silly holiday bearing down on me. But if OPM allows you to return, expect another disciplinary transfer. I cannot tolerate rogue agents in this organization, and you—"

She didn't stop there, she kept going, steamrolling over my work, my life, my future. But I stopped listening. I went back to thinking about the planets, wondering why Pluto got dropped and what took its place and what my very excellent mother would serve now instead of pizza. And Phaup's voice receded to hostile white noise.

But suddenly she demanded: "Are you listening?"

I didn't want to lie. So I said, "I can hear you."

~

After my pleasant visit with Phaup, I walked down the hall and poked my head into Pollard's office. His characteristically tidy desk was covered with paperwork. He held the phone in one hand, as if about to make a call.

"I wanted to apologize, again," I said. "I'm truly, deeply sorry."

He hung up the phone and motioned me inside. I closed the door but stayed there, leaning my back against it, feeling unworthy of taking a seat. I stared at all the paperwork on his desk. He was calling the task force team, letting them know the investigation had closed. I tried to imagine Detective Greene's face when he heard.

"Do you have anything to work with?" I asked.

Shrugging wasn't in Pollard's DNA. He cleared his throat instead. "The crack house is hard evidence," he said. "There was plenty of product. But everybody denies making or selling. Everybody was just visiting. You'll be called to testify. You're our only credible witness."

"Where are they, downtown?"

"They were, but everybody posted bail early this morning."

"What?"

"Thirty grand apiece for the girls. Hundred grand for the guys."

I whistled.

"Yes," he said. "They've got money, and some hotshot defense attorney flew down from New York. They even sprang the girls, so we lost that angle."

Girls.

I grabbed the doorknob. Zennie.

"What's wrong?" Pollard said.

"My source. She called my cell, inside that house, they know—"

chapter thirty-four

I raced down the stairwell, leaping over the steps.

"Zennie, pick up!" I listened to her cell phone ring. And ring and ring. "Pick up!"

At the third-floor landing, I threw open the steel door and ran to my desk. I ducked under the heat vent, wondering at my selfishness, and grabbed my briefcase. I was running back to the stairwell, considering a call to 911, when Zennie picked up.

"We busted the house last night; they know I'm an agent—"

"I wasn't born yesterday."

"Listen to me, Zennie. They posted bail. They're out. They'll come looking for you."

"And if I was born at night, it wasn't last night," she said. "When I called you last night, I was already packing up. Something was wrong with Moon; I could tell it was about to get ugly. I called to tell you and when I heard him on your cell phone, I hit the road."

I dropped my head. The relief I felt was visceral. "Zennie," I said, "you did great. Where are you now?"

"At Granny's with my boy."

"Does Moon know how to find you?"

"He'll figure it out."

"What do you have for protection?"

"Don't sweat it. Granny called her church boys. They all came out here. All of them. If you ask me, these Christians are just busting for a fight."

"Okay, but if Moon or anybody who's related to that gang contacts you, call me. Immediately. I promise, Zennie, I'll be there to help you."

"Uh-huh," she said. "I've seen how that goes."

≈

I parked the K-Car in the alley behind my mother's house and walked through the courtyard to the kitchen. The windows in the French door were opaque, white. I rubbed my finger on the glass. Sodium polyacrylate, otherwise known as fake snow. But this wasn't low drifts gathering on the lower panes. The entire window was smothered.

Inside, the kitchen felt as suffocating as a small tent. I looked around. Nothing baking. Nothing on the counter. Down the hallway, Rosemary Clooney was singing about frosted window panes that looked nothing like ours and I found my mother on the couch in the parlor. She was staring at the Christmas tree like it was a television.

Madame, curled at her feet, wagged her tail.

"Hi," I said.

She didn't respond. She didn't even turn to look at me.

"Are you all right?"

She turned. "What could possibly be wrong?" she said in a voice that said the opposite. "Did you just get home?"

"Yes. But I have to go out again."

"They're calling for snow."

"When?"

"Tomorrow."

I nodded, hesitating, hoping my next question sounded casual. "Is Wally home?"

Her skin looked drained, the eyes distant and troubled. "He hasn't come out of his room all day."

I walked upstairs, leaving behind a song in three-quarter time, and knocked on Wally's door. His rap didn't play as loudly as before, but I could still hear the lyrics. Pigs, guns, whores. And a hollered response from a monosyllabic choir.

I knocked again, but he didn't answer.

I stood at the door, wanting to believe he was working.

But later, I could never say for sure.

≈

After a glass of sweet tea and some cold ham, hoping to cheer up my mother—to no avail—I drove south out of town. Dusk was settling its luscious blue on the horizon, and when I crossed the dual-span bridge, dropping down into the town of Hopewell, I could see heavy clouds blowing in from the Atlantic, cumulus shapes darkening toward violet.

Hopewell was America's second-oldest city, second only to Williamsburg. It sat on a point of land where the James River met the Appomattox River. During the Civil War, General Ulysses S Grant commandeered a cabin built on the point, supervising his nearly yearlong siege of Petersburg.

But these days Hopewell was the town under siege. From the bridge above the James River, I watched weak steam rise from declining factories. The city's main drag of East Broadway presented a historic downtown that was little more than antique shops. One Chinese restaurant was open for dinner and an elderly couple sat in the window, staring out at the empty street like grandparents of the people in Hopper's *Nighthawks*.

There was plenty of parking behind St. Nicholas Orthodox Church. I walked around to the front, where a cracked plastic sign greeted parishioners in both English and Russian. The small vestibule inside smelled like incense and a sandbox held votive candles, the flames flickering as I passed, casting light on the gilded portrait above, the eponymous saint with two fingers raised.

Two people sat in the dark pews, a black-robed priest and a woman wearing a head scarf. But somehow the church still felt overpopulated. On three walls, life-sized portraits of saints stared out, their melancholy eyes like onyx, faces gold above jewel-toned robes. And at the front of the room, a spotless white cloth draped the altar.

The church, circa AD 400.

I watched the priest make the sign of the cross and then touch the woman's shoulder. But she remained curled around her concern, and the priest walked down the red-carpeted aisle. He came toward me with measured steps, a tall man covered in black vestments from collar to ankle except for his long beard. It foamed white from his face, touching his chest.

"I am Father Dmitri." His accent was Slavic, his dark eyes storing heat like coal. "You have need?"

"Yes, Father."

The woman stood, crossing herself before the white altar, and came down the aisle like a bowl of porridge. Tears bathed her doughy face.

"*Dobry,*" she said, stopping beside the priest. "*Dobry.*"

The priest nodded. "Yes, my child. It is good."

She pulled on her coat, kissed her fingers, and touched the portrait of St. Nicholas before walking outside. The candle flames fluttered.

The priest turned to me. "What is need?"

"Are we alone, Father?"

"For time being."

I opened my credentials. The black eyes stared down at my ID. When I showed him photographs of the tattoos, he stared even longer.

"We found two men, killed. These were their tattoos."

He reached a bony hand into the seamed pocket of his robe, pulling out wire-rimmed glasses. The oily lenses were flaked with dust.

"This mark is for men who kill and ask God to forgive," he said. "It is Holy Mother and Child."

After my meeting with Phaup, I searched our database for information on tattoos and gang insignias. Using Tolly's information, I scanned for Russian mob information. The priest was right. Among the favorite tattoos was the Madonna and child.

He handed back the photos. But his black eyes continued to drill into me. Gathering his white fingers, he swung his hand toward the pews. "Come, sit," he said. "Tell me of these men."

The hard wood of the pew pressed against my spine. The priest sat beside me but faced forward, his eyes on the altar as I told him that the men were crucified upside down.

"It looks like some kind of retribution and torture," I said. "But there was another tattoo, Father, on both of them. Have you heard of the Ku Klux Klan?"

I showed him the photos of the KKK tattoos. He nodded slowly, the white beard scratching his robe.

"Why would the Russian mob join the KKK?" I asked.

"Mob of Russia wants money. Drugs, diamonds, guns. All black market. Even women are for sale."

"What kind of guns?" I asked.

"I should know from guns?" He looked over, white brows dropping.

"If you saw pictures, could you identify the type of guns they're selling?"

"*Nyet.*" He shook his head. "I do not see these men often. One came to me last year, offering a great jewel, to give it for the church. For forgiveness. I told him there is but one rock, and he is life everlasting. But his ears were closed. He could not hear."

"Do you know where I could find these men?"

"I do not see them often. Every other year at best." He turned suddenly, evaluating me for a long moment. "You saw?"

"Pardon?"

"You saw these men crucified?"

I nodded.

The black eyes glittered. "You bear it on your soul."

"It's my job."

"Ah, you refuse to admit weakness. There is problem. Do you not know that it is weakness that brings us into God's presence?"

"Yes, but—"

"I think it is not these wicked men you should find. It is God."

I continued to protest, explaining my work. But he faced forward, raising his chin, silencing me. I stared at the Slavic structure of his face, cheekbones like chiseled rock. Behind him, the saints bore expressions of millennia, of a church unswayed by time and trend, whose glorious peak occurred just before the plummet of Constantinople. And still it stood, centuries endured, making its way in this struggling town in an unimaginable country, as if to testify for what was and what is and what will be. I began speaking, keeping my eyes on the veiled white altar, and told him about the men strung in the trees. It was a simple dictation of facts, the description of wounds almost clinical. I thought that was all.

But he waited.

He waited until the authentic poured forth, until I told him what it was like to see skin stretched so tight it was ready to burst, eyes bulging like poisoned fish, shattered toes twisted with pain. And I told him how the winter vines seemed to yearn for the tortured bodies, hoping to caress the grotesque, and how the silt seemed to drink in the blood, thirsting for death.

When I drew in a ragged breath, I believed I was done. But the priest still did not turn to look at me. Staring at his hard posture, I told him about the two children who heard the good news from a cartoon in a crack house, and how I drove away.

I felt light-headed, dizzy, and grabbed the pew, bracing myself. The back of my hand was wet.

The priest turned. His black eyes glittered.

"You carry too much," he said. "God detests it."

"Yes, Father."

He gave a quick and decisive gesture with his head, causing the beard to jump. "What I find, I find. But I will not betray a man's trust if he comes to confess. My vows are to God alone."

"I understand, Father. Thank you."

His pale hand touched my shoulder, and he spoke over me in the ancient and unwavering tongue, saying things I didn't understand.

And things I did.

chapter thirty-five

Later that night I walked through a forest so dark, so deep that the green trees turned black and the white snow looked blue on the ground. Behind me, bells jingled and I turned to see a chestnut horse with a white star on its forehead. The horse I petted in RPM's barn the night of the party. Shaking its mane, the horse pulled a black sleigh. The iron runners sliced like lances through the snow, and I felt a sudden stab of fear.

Running deeper into the woods, I hid behind a tree. But as I touched the bark, it turned to mulch. The harsh bells came closer and I heard women singing. The sleigh was full of women waving mottled brown arms, their voices rising in that old spiritual about flying away.

I saw the sleigh driver. He flicked the reins over the chestnut horse, wearing the black hat and topcoat from Morgan Manor. He turned his face toward the women, singing with them. I saw his face.

It was my father.

I ran out, calling. But the sleigh zipped past, disappearing in the dark and venal forest. I stood, watching it go, wondering why the bells sounded even louder.

I opened my eyes. Ringing.

The phone.

I slapped my hand across the nightstand, searching for the receiver. I was too late. The answering machine picked up.

The message was delivered twice, a recording from the Virginia Department of Transportation. All "inessential" state and federal workers were being asked to stay home until a winter storm front passed over central Virginia. Roads were closed, travel advisories were issued, treacherous . . .

I shifted the curtain beside my bed.

White flakes big as quarters spilled from the low clouds. I watched it fall, a weightless December gift.

Then I sat up. It wasn't snowing.

It was dumping. Inches.

I looked out at the courtyard. It was smothered with white. I glanced at the clock. Just past 7 a.m. No wonder they sent out the message. Richmonders were notoriously fearful of snow, even the lightest flurries. Here were buckets of snow. The city would screech to a halt.

Picking up the phone, I called Zennie. She answered on the fifth ring and yelled at me. She was fine, don't ever call this early, get a life.

I pulled on sweats, gloves, and a knit cap, then clipped my cell phone to my waistband. I stuck my Glock in the hip holster, covered it with a windbreaker, and kicked through four inches of snow crossing the courtyard. Madame, prescient as ever, had scratched the fake snow from the bottom panes of the French door. When I opened it, she shot out like a cannonball and we ran down Monument Avenue. No footprints on the sidewalk, no car tracks on the road. In the muffled quiet, the only sounds were my running steps and my breathing, both as methodical as a metronome.

At Monroe Park, the dog and I traced separate paths through the undisturbed white landscape. My thoughts drifted back to last night, to the church and the priest and the silent offer of confession. This morning, there was no mistaking the sensation.

It wasn't the snow. It wasn't the city's standstill. It was the feeling of a burden lifted, a relationship restored, a promise kept.

If I thought it felt good to come home to the place I loved and find that it waited for me, it was nothing compared to the feeling of returning to a God who loved me and who waited for me. That was home, true home.

At Oregon Hill, I slowed to a walk, Madame falling in beside me. The blue-collar neighborhood overlooked the James River, and my sister Helen lived here in creative squalor with her partner, Sebastian Woodlief. Their row house was close enough to VCU that Helen could walk to classes and humble enough that Sebastian could pretend he was a working-class guy.

I stretched my calves, standing outside their house, kissing my endorphins good-bye. The clapboards were painted a blue leaning toward purple—what I considered fluorite—while the windowpanes were pink—or poor-quality rubies. The colors were especially striking since next door the porch had a dented freezer on it with an orange extension cord running through a conveniently cracked window. I kicked the snow off the stairs, knowing Sebastian would never shovel it, then knocked on the front door.

"What's wrong?" Sebastian said.

He had aqueous blue eyes and his paisley pajamas appeared to be missing their ascot. Descended from some sort of nobility, Sebastian Woodlief was that curious spur of modern Britain, the self-loathing privileged class. I never doubted his tales of land holdings in Scotland or Wales or wherever, but these days even gentry scrabbled for cash and my guess was that Sebastian opted out of hard work and good accounting in order to come to the New World and impress us with his elegant accent and barely veiled condescension.

"Is Helen home?" I said.

He looked down at Madame. She was panting happily, the snow dusting her black nose.

"I'm allergic to canines," he said. "She can't come in."

He turned, leaving the door open. Since British schools drilled etiquette, there was no doubting when Sebastian was insulting. I told Madame she deserved better—but so did my sister—and asked her to sit on the doormat. She obeyed. I left the door cracked a few inches and made my way down the tight hallway to the living room. It was filled with gigantic contemporary masks. Spooky things. Empty eye sockets. Encephalitic foreheads.

They were Sebastian's "art."

"Helen," he called up the narrow staircase. "It's your sister." The last word sounded like an affliction.

Helen clomped down the stairs wearing flannel pajamas and wooden clogs.

"What's wrong?" she said.

"Woodchip asked the same thing."

"Wood*lief*," he said. "My name is Woodlief."

"And Sebastian asked because you only come around when something's wrong," she said.

"You don't come around at all," I pointed out.

"Excuse me." Sebastian allowed a sardonic smile to tug at his pasty face. "I'll leave you *ladies* to your conversation." Pecking Helen on the cheek, he stepped around a papier-mâché footstool shaped like a turtle. More art. He left the room.

Even at eight in the morning, wearing wrinkled flannel pajamas, Helen looked beautiful. It was too bad she had the temperament of a fishwife.

"What's wrong?" she demanded again.

"Mom wants you to go to Weyanoke for Christmas," I said.

"Weyanoke—the Fielding plantation?"

"Yes."

"Oh, please." She brushed a loose auburn curl from her perfect face. "Tell her I can't; tell her I made other plans."

"Helen, how about some effort here? This is all Mom is asking for for Christmas."

She twisted her mouth and frowned petulantly, yet only managed to look even better. My sister was a living, breathing example of the color wheel, where opposites created some kind of artistic perfection. Helen was gorgeous, and she was rotten.

"You can even bring Woodshed," I said.

"Wood*lief*."

"Right. Bring him." And then I wouldn't have to face DeMott again. They could take my mom and I could . . . I was still trying to think up a reason for not going.

"Sebastian would never set foot on a plantation. It's a matter of principle."

"Oh, I'm sure. But why not ask him? It's free food."

"Fine." She lifted her swanlike neck, calling out, "Sebastian, darling?"

He hovered into view. "Yes, darling?"

"Some old friends of my parents are having an open house. A Christmas tradition here in Virginia. Mother would like us to go with her. But, well, I'm afraid these people live on a plantation."

"A plantation?" His watery eyes filled with the assumed indignities of British colonialism. "Are you mad, Helen?"

My cell phone went off. They swiveled their heads, glaring at me.

"Excuse me."

I stepped down the narrow hall. Madame waited patiently on the doormat. "Good girl," I said, opening the phone.

Once again, the sheriff from Charles City County.

"I'm afraid to ask," I said.

"You should be," he said. "Think you can get out to Rapland somehow?"

"Is it urgent?"

"It was," he said. "The medical examiner's on her way, if she can get through the snow."

"I'll be there." I closed the phone.

They were still in the living room, discussing Christmas.

"Actually, darling," Helen was saying, "you know who might be there? Collectors and curators. The art patron crowd. You would have a chance to discuss your work, perhaps even sell a piece."

Indignity drained from his eyes. It was replaced by an expression I liked even less.

"I have to go," I said. "Call the house when you decide."

≈

Madame and I raced through the Fan District, cutting down Park Avenue and into the alley. When I opened the patio door, letting her jump inside, I was already figuring on wrapping chains on my mother's car. I closed the door.

But I opened the door again.

My mother's sleepy face turned to DeMott like a morning blossom seeking sunshine. He stopped talking midsentence and my mother sat up.

"Raleigh, look who came to see if you're okay!" she exclaimed.

I looked at DeMott. "How did you get here?"

"Is that the only question you can think to ask?" she demanded.

"We keep a bunch of plows on the farm." He moved his hands, showing my mother. "The blade just hooks to the front of my truck, ready to go."

She touched his arm. "But it was still very, very difficult to get here, wasn't it?"

"Oh, yes, ma'am."

She threw me a look, insinuating his white horse waited at the curb.

"I need a ride," I said.

"Raleigh, sit down," she said. "There's nowhere to go on a day like this."

"I got a call from work."

"That office, what is wrong with that office?" She touched his arm again. "They call her at all hours. As if the rocks are in a hurry."

"Five minutes?" I asked DeMott.

He nodded and I was closing the patio door when I heard my mother attempt a whisper.

"Don't let Raleigh fool you," she was saying. "She's actually quite lonely."

≈

DeMott plowed a path to Stonewall Jackson and said, "I'm really sorry about the other night."

The tire chains chinked down the road, the rubber wipers stuttered across the windshield, sweeping away fresh snow. The words I wanted to speak were stuck in my throat, but I forced them out.

"I was wrong, DeMott, not you. I put my job ahead of everything else, including family and friends. It wasn't fair to put you in that situation. I'm sorry."

He stopped at the light on the Boulevard and Broad Street. "So we accept our mutual apologies?"

I nodded.

"Excellent." He smiled. "Which way to your office?"

"I'm headed to Rapland."

"What?"

I stared at the CVS drugstore across the street. The windows were shuttered and dark.

"Oh," he said. "Something else I'm not supposed to know about."

"It doesn't involve you," I said. Then, remembering Stuart Morgan, I added, "At this point, I can't see that it involves you."

He ignored all the other traffic lights, slowing down just long enough to glance both ways. But the streets were empty and white, the snow falling in thick bundled flakes. His truck chugged up the overpass by the baseball stadium, then down the other side to the interstate. In the haze of snow, a bright red garland of brake lights carved the highway's middle lane. We joined the procession, inching toward I-64.

"You're still coming for Christmas, right?" he asked.

"If I can get there."

"I'll pick you up."

After several minutes of silence, I took out my phone and called Zennie. She sounded only slightly less cranky than earlier, but still nobody had contacted her.

When I hung up, DeMott was taking the exit for Williamsburg Road. He asked, "How long have we known each other, Raleigh?"

"Since sixth grade."

"It was the first spring dance, to be exact," he said. "St. Catherine's girls and St. Christopher's boys. You were wearing white pants before Memorial Day. I think I fell in love with you right there."

He stopped at the light for Williamsburg Road. I didn't dare turn to look at him. I watched an army of jacked-up pickups with snow blades scraping the road to Varina, refusing to wait for help.

"Do you remember that dance?" he asked.

"You wore a shark's tooth on a leather string around your neck."

"Raleigh, look at me."

All of the reflected light from the snow seemed to gather in his blue eyes.

"If I thought it would convince you, I'd climb out of this truck right now and get down on one knee in the snow."

"DeMott—"

"No, listen. The whole time you were in Seattle, all I could think about was you meeting somebody else. When I heard you were back, I knew it was time to tell you how I really feel. No more playing games and acting cool. I've always felt this way about you. But you don't like surprises—"

"Yes."

"Yes?" he said.

"Yes, I don't like surprises."

"Oh."

"The light's green."

The truck's back wheels spun, then the chains caught, carrying us through Varina. The streets were clear, the sidewalks shoveled, even though more snow was falling.

Inside the truck, there was more silence.

Finally he said, "I had all these romantic ideas how I would ask you. Then I realized it would just push you away. So here's the deal. I'm asking if you would consider getting engaged, maybe at some point in the near future?"

I stared at the falling snow, unable to look at him.

But I nodded.

We drove in silence. When we reached New Market Road, the stone elephants looked like white hummocks. At the keyhole at the other end, two county cruisers and the sheriff's vehicle were parked in the driveway, chains on the back wheels, snow packed into the undercarriages.

By the front door, an officer bounced on his feet, trying to keep warm. No Cujo. No Sid.

"When should I pick you up?" DeMott asked.

"I'll call you." I held the door handle, hesitating. "Thanks, DeMott."

"For what?"

Once again the words stuck in my throat. It wasn't just the place that waited for me, but the people. The people who made room for my flaws.

"Just, thanks," I managed.

"Be careful."

I walked toward the front door, and behind me his truck made its way down the melting slush. The chains were chinking rhythmically, metallically, and a deep and unspeakable ache was squeezing at my heart.

chapter thirty-six

The county officer bouncing from foot to foot was a large man, and his nose was crimson from the cold. He followed me into the house, although the temperature inside felt no warmer. Checking my credentials, he slapped his arms across his chest, bouncing again.

"Down the hall," he said. "Turn at that room with all the pictures. You won't believe it."

The room with all the pictures was where I'd spoken to RPM after he returned from Liberia, where pictures of celebrities hung near pictures of wounded Africans. But the room looked even more surreal now. Like an optical illusion, the back wall had rotated thirty degrees. Stepping into the opening, I smelled a damp odor of mildew rising from below. Gray marble stairs led down to a cellar, and centuries of dripping humidity had dimpled the stones and rounded off their edges, shortening the steps so much that I had to walk sideways and keep one hand on the wall for balance. The wall felt slimy.

I knew how these old plantation houses nested around secret passages. The most famous ones were at Monticello, designed by Thomas Jefferson. But I'd been in the one at Weyanoke, when Mac hosted our debutante party, and I remembered playing hide-and-seek as a child at Belle Grove, discovering Flynn tucked behind a swiveling bookcase.

But as I made my way down the dim curvature of stairs,

hearing voices echo from below, I began to realize this passage was different.

I counted three dead bodies on the floor.

Glancing away, pressing back a wave of nausea, I saw the sheriff on the other side of the cellar. Two officers stood with him. Behind them RPM leaned against the stone wall. His elongated posture was broken, his face slack with shock.

I walked around the bodies, glancing down only to avoid stepping on body parts and the puddle of blood. I went to RPM first.

"What happened?" I asked.

He swallowed hard enough that the Adam's apple bobbed in his neck. "I don't know."

"You don't know?"

He shifted his head. His eyes were moist, the long eyelashes flat. "I was in there." He pointed to a short door disguised by the gray rock wall around it. A passage within a passage.

Unlike the rest of the cellar, the ten-by-twenty room was sleek with modern technology. Poured concrete covered the floor and the walls. Track lighting ran along the ceiling, and stainless steel appliances gleamed from a corner, providing a kitchen. One couch was positioned in front of a flat-screen TV. The air was dry. Holding my breath, listening, I heard the faint hum of a dehumidifier.

"It's called a safe room," the sheriff said, coming in behind me. "You know what that is?"

I nodded. It was a human vault. The wealthy built safe rooms to secure themselves against intruders and kidnappers.

"Bulletproof," the sheriff continued. "Lock yourself in and wait for the bad guys to leave."

"Or die," I said.

He glanced over his shoulder, making sure RPM hadn't followed us.

"He heard shots fired," the sheriff said. "Somebody broke in, his bodyguard fought them off. RPM called 911. They sliced the phone line, but he keeps a cell phone charged down here." He pointed to a small desk next to the kitchen area.

After a moment I said, "Where is everybody?"

"You mean all his buddies?" The sheriff flipped the pages in his small notebook. "They went to New York for a shopping trip."

I stepped back through the stone door. RPM was bent at the waist, vomiting in the corner of the cellar. Bracing myself, I looked at the dead men and resisted the same reaction.

The bottom jaw remained on two of them, above a now-useless neck, but the heads were cored like melons. They were black. Across from those two, Sid lay with his mouth parted as though saying something. His gold tooth glinted, the diamond shining persistently. He gripped an assault rifle in his right hand, apparently used to blow away the other two. But not before somebody got off a round. The blood under his body formed a maroon-colored lake.

I glanced back at the other two. One of them held a small black pistol.

RPM spat discreetly. I waited for him to wipe his chin.

"Can you take me through it?" I said.

He shook his head. The confident millionaire was gone. He dragged a wrist over his mouth, the midnight blue jogging suit clean except for that right sleeve.

"Nobody else was home?" I asked. "Just you and Sid?"

"I sent my family to the city. I do it every year. They stay at The Plaza. My kids go to FAO Schwarz . . . I couldn't say no. Not after the kids heard that bomb go off."

"So you and Sid stayed, knowing what had already happened?"

"We always stay." He opened his arms plaintively. "Sid insisted I sleep down here, with the door locked. I woke up hearing gunfire. And Sid—" He pressed the sleeve to his mouth. "They killed my best friend. They *killed* him."

The sheriff walked up beside me. He nodded, as if to say the story matched what he'd heard too.

"Do you know these guys?" I indicated the other two bodies.

RPM opened his arms again, pleading. "They don't even have faces."

The officer guarding the front door suddenly appeared on the stone stairs.

"Coroner's here," he said.

The medical examiner stepped into the basement wearing an all-black outfit. She looked ready for Aspen, her snow pants clinging to every fit curve of her body. She glanced at the sheriff and I could sense the shift in the room. She was a woman who studied death but carried a live electrical charge, like a downed cable in search of grounding.

"Just these three bodies?" she asked. "No more anywhere else?"

"That's correct," the sheriff said.

I glanced at RPM. Tears hovered in his dark eyes. He turned his head, coughing.

"I need everyone to clear out," she said. "There's not even room for us to think in here."

Her crew stood to the side as the sheriff's officers went up the stairs first, followed by the sheriff, then RPM. I looked back, taking in the crime scene one more time. The brutality bothered me, the violent slaughter of it. But something else nagged at my mind as I made my way up the steps, balancing myself with one hand on the mildewed wall. I listened to the ME giving orders.

"I want this done right," she was saying. "Bag the hands on

those two. Forget dental records. We need fingerprints, DNA matches. Otherwise, identification's going to be a nightmare."

In the foyer, the sheriff was telling RPM how his officers would guard the property 24/7. RPM stood at the base of the stairs, leaning on the dark banister.

"When will they clean this up?" RPM asked.

"It's a crime scene. I want it sealed," the sheriff said.

"My kids come back tomorrow, and they like to go play down there. I don't want them to see it."

"Then keep them out," the sheriff said. "It's evidence."

RPM nodded, turning. He shuffled up the stairs, holding the rail for support.

The sheriff posted the large officer at the door, with another patrolling the grounds outside. As he gave them instructions, telling them that if nobody was available to relieve them he'd come out himself, I stepped outside. I called DeMott, asking him to come pick me up.

I watched the snow fall. Two fresh inches rested on the roofs of the cruisers. I stepped off the porch, looking for footwear impressions. The ground had been trampled by officers and the ME's staff. The white vans her staff drove were parked all over the lawn.

The sheriff stepped outside.

"Something's not right," I said.

"No kidding."

"Those guys are not with the KKK."

"Not unless the Klan's trying for diversity." He took out his cell phone, punching in a number. "Erlanger," he said, "can you work today?"

I walked over to the guardhouse. There were no footprints in the snow.

I walked back to the sheriff. "Do you believe his story?"

"About being in that safe room?"

I nodded.

"The front door lock was busted," he said. "I checked. Door was wide open when we got here. Our dispatcher said he was panicking when he called." The sheriff kept his flickering eyes on the falling snow. "So right now," he said, "there's nothing else to believe, is there?"

≈

When DeMott drove me home, I stared out the windshield feeling as if I was adding two and two and getting five. In my mind I saw the cellar, the bodies, the blood on the stone floor. I would never forget the sight of missing faces. And I would never forget seeing the famous RPM spitting up fear.

Cranking the window three inches, I let the cold air brush my forehead. I felt feverish, dizzy. Maybe I was coming down with the detective's flu. But when DeMott's truck made the slow turn around General Lee, I was still going over the facts in my mind.

I looked over.

And he nodded, as though we'd been having a long conversation, even though I hadn't spoken one word.

chapter thirty-seven

When my grandmother passed away, I overheard grown-ups saying she had a good death. I was nine. I'd already heard about people in high cotton, people who chewed the fat, people who got on like a house afire.

People enjoying a good death joined the list.

But later, when life sifted out its elemental truths, I realized that climbing into bed after seventy-nine years of living and reading yourself into eternal sleep was a pretty fine way to go.

To use another Southernism, that was a whole heap better than what happened to those guys at Rapland.

Saturday morning, with another five inches of snow on the ground, I shoveled my way to the garage and found chains for my mother's old Mercedes. An hour later I was heading west out of town, the big German auto relishing the challenge, chewing up the white drifts like a Prussian attack on Mother Nature. It still took almost two hours to get to Chopping Road, and from there I had to walk down a packed foot trail. Outside the chicken shack, a lopsided snowman grinned a copper-penny smile.

"She won't come out of her bedroom," Granny Lew said, answering my knock on her front door. A cameo brooch clasped the lace collar of her wool dress. Nylon hose turned her ankles into sandstone pillars. "I'm trying to celebrate Jesus' birthday and she's busted up over a man who's not worth the salt in her tears."

She took my coat. In the next room somebody was playing a piano, the notes that described the little town of Bethlehem.

"We're keeping the boy occupied," she said. "Go on and talk some sense into her."

Upstairs, Zennie was lying on a twin bed with her back to the door. Her straightened hair spiked around her head like an onyx crown. Hearing my approach, she rolled over.

"What'd Moon do now?" she asked.

I sat down on the bed parallel to hers. It was decorated with Star Wars pillows and a stuffed rabbit. The boy's bed.

"Zennie, I need to ask you a favor."

"I already did you a favor. Look what it got me. I'm hiding for my life."

"Has Moon tried to contact you?" I asked.

She raised her chin, injured but proud. Her small hands toyed with a black velvet box, turning it over and over. "He will soon enough. I expect today."

"Did Moon have any distinguishing marks? Moles, scars, maybe some tattoos?"

Her hands squeezed the velvet box. "He got himself killed?"

"I don't even know if—"

Before the words were out, she threw the box across the room, covering her face with her hands. She let out a wail.

The box hit the wall, exploding its contents. The pieces scattered across the floor as she sobbed. Feeling useless, I walked across the room and began picking up the pieces, putting them back inside the velvet box.

"What'd they do to him?" she asked.

"I don't even know if it's him," I said, dropping the stuff into the box. They were pale objects, like rock chips. "That's what I need you for."

"Oh, my Moon!" she cried. "It's all my fault."

I picked up another piece, turning it back and forth. It was a tiny rock.

"I killed my boy's daddy!"

I lifted one of the rocks, holding it to the light. It looked like a pallid quartz chip, the kind that settled on sandy river bottoms. Far from pretty, a rust-colored soil covered the stippled surface. I picked up another. This one was octahedral. Eight-sided. Like two pyramids glued at the base.

"I got his blood all over my hands," Zennie said, whispering.

I walked over to the window. A light was on in the chicken shack, and I dragged the octahedral stone across the corner of the glass, right next to the wooden pane. I ran my finger over the scratch.

"What do I tell my boy?" Zennie looked at me. "What do I say, 'Merry Christmas, Daddy's dead'?"

I touched my hand to the radiator under the window. The painted iron was hot, so I held the stone against it, counting to sixty. Zennie was plucking at her comforter, rocking almost catatonically, and when I lifted the stone, it felt cool. Not even warm.

"Zennie." I held up the stone. "Do you know what this is?"

She had tears in her eyes. "Moon's idea of a joke. He's getting the last laugh now."

"I don't understand."

"I asked him for a ring every single Christmas," she said. "And every year it was the same stupid joke. He'd say, 'I got you a box of rocks.'"

"Do you know what these rocks are?"

"Ugly. Look at 'em."

"How many boxes did he give you?"

"Four. I would've thrown them out, but he was always checking to see if I did."

I walked over to the bed and sat down. The box was in my hands. "Zennie, I need you to come down to the morgue."

"Uh-uh, no way. I ain't looking at him like that."

"It might not even be Moon," I said. "But if it is, and you don't go identify him, he'll stay on that cold metal cart for weeks."

"My last look at Moon is not going to be that way."

"Then I'll get a court order. You want your son to see you get served with papers?"

She looked at me with rage and despair. Her next breath was long and bumpy, as if the air was rippling over the jagged pieces of her broken heart.

≈

The drive into the city was punctuated by the sound of Zennie sipping from a silver flask, and by the time I turned onto Jackson Street two hours later, her words were so slurred I decided to park at the snow-packed curb and leave the hazard lights blinking on the Benz's big tail.

Taking her elbow, I guided her across the snow and into the medical examiner's building. The front desk receptionist wore silver bell earrings. When she turned to look at us, the earrings produced shimmery music. I showed my credentials and signed us in.

"You got my man," Zennie said, leaning over the counter. Her breath smelled like butane.

The receptionist pulled back. The bells made a sound like a question.

"She's here to identify," I said.

"My Moon," Zennie breathed.

I clipped a temporary ID to my coat and another to Zennie's jacket. But I sat her down in a seat in the corner of the waiting room.

"Stay here." I wanted to make sure everything was ready for her.

She pulled a second silver flask from her purse. I was about to say something but instead walked down the hall to the double swinging doors. The room smelled of death and dissection, that weird stench peculiar to pathology. Isopropyl putrification. The ME was standing at the head of a steel gurney, her rubber apron and gloves bloody. She glanced up, staring at me through the clear plastic face shield, then went back to her work.

"We've got two more bullets for you."

I moved my eyes to the body's face. Sid, the gold tooth.

"Two," she said, "both in the chest. I sent one to firearms. I saved one for you."

"Unmarked?"

She nodded.

"What about the other guys?"

"The faceless wonders," she said. "They have something else."

She stepped down from the riser giving her height over the gurney. Jabbing her elbow into a button on the wall, she called in an assistant.

The ME described the autopsies in medicolegal terms, making them almost sound like cars. I walked over to the gurney across from Sid. A sterile evidence sheet draped the entire figure. But it was shaped like a mountain. I decided there must be a body block under his upper back, the rubber brick that caused the neck, head, and arms to fall back, making it easier for the ME to carve her Y-shaped incision down the chest.

The assistant was a young woman with large brown eyes. She lifted the evidence sheet.

"Look at the skin," the ME said.

The brown arms and belly were covered with blisters weeping with pus and blood. I turned to look at Sid, under her knife. "Is that on all three?"

"Not like that," she said. "This guy with the pretty tooth has a very mild case. It looks like what was on those guys at the river. Only fresher."

"He's the bodyguard," I told her. "His name was Sid."

"Well, Sid died of two gunshot wounds to the chest," she said. "Probably from the handgun this nice fellow was holding." She nodded at the body before me, and then at the other white mound. "But these two didn't die in that cellar."

"Pardon?"

"The faceless wonders. They were dead when their faces were shot off."

"How can you tell?"

She looked at me through the protective shield. I rephrased it.

"I'm not challenging your expertise, Dr. Bauer. But can you explain it to me?"

"The circulatory systems were already down."

I thought back to the cellar. "But I saw blood."

"Under this guy, the bodyguard. He died down there, no doubt about it. But these two died somewhere else, and of something else. They were probably dragged down there. One leg's broken, heels are damaged."

"When will you have something definitive?" I asked.

"I'm working as fast as I can. Every year this happens. People like to shoot each other over the holidays."

I looked back at the swollen mounds, that elusive element from the cellar coming to me. It wasn't just the brutality. I recalled walking down the gray stones, my hand on the wall.

The wall.

"Humidity," I said.

The ME didn't look up from Sid's open chest cavity. "What about humidity?"

"Down in the cellar, the walls were damp."

"It's underground," she said dismissively.

"Yes, but the injuries we're seeing look like reactions to lewisite, possibly mustard gas. Lewisite doesn't work in humid atmospheres. It's one reason our military stopped using it. Which means you're right. If these guys were gassed first, it was somewhere other than a damp cellar."

For once, I saw appreciation in her eyes.

It increased when I said, "I have somebody here to identify one of the faceless bodies."

"I'll cover this guy up," she said. "Bring her on back."

I dragged Zennie down the hall, her rubber-soled boots squealing protests on the linoleum.

"He ain't in bits and pieces, is he?"

I tightened my grip on her elbow, her butane breath mingling with the putrid antiseptic scents. When I pushed through the door, the lights had been turned down, obscuring everything except the two swollen shapes under the white sheets. The ME and her bloody apron were gone, leaving the female assistant to supervise. She stood between the two gurneys. She did not look happy.

Zennie stopped just inside the door. "I can tell you right now," she said. "That's not his shape."

I pulled her forward. "He has a tattoo?"

"But I don't need to look. It ain't him."

I glanced at the assistant. Her expression said patience had left the building.

"Right ankle," I said. "The letter Z."

"For my name," Zennie said, staggering to a stop beside me.

"You're identifying," the assistant said. "You have to look."

"Fine, I'll look," Zennie snapped. "Because it ain't him."

The assistant lifted the bottom edge of the first sheet, exposing a brown right ankle.

"I told you," Zennie said.

The assistant dropped the sheet and pulled back the second one.

Zennie stared.

She didn't gasp. She didn't cry. Standing like a post, she stared. Her eyes traveled up his leg, moving over the mounded sheet to where his face would have been. "Oh, baby," she whispered, leaning down. "What they done to you?"

"Don't touch him," the assistant said.

"I ain't about to." She turned to me. "I saw that on him before." She pointed to the oozing blisters on his shin. "He had that when I was pregnant."

I looked at the dark leg. "You're sure it's the same rash?"

"I ain't but so drunk."

It was true. When the sheet was pulled back, it was as if the sight of him hit her like cold water. The tragic romance was gone. Now she looked resigned and sad, even angry at the waste. And I finally saw her grandmother in her.

"I thought maybe it was some STD," she said. "Something he picked up over there."

"Over where?"

"Africa."

I gazed at her, trying to gauge her sobriety. "When was Moon in Africa?"

"Back when Zeke was in my belly. Five, six years ago. He went over on some mercy mission. He came back oozing like a leper. I told him, 'If that's some sex disease, you are gonna need mercy.'"

"Was he sick?"

"Yeah. But it went away."

The assistant gave the sheet a little shake, looking at me.

"Thank you," I said.

Dropping it over the ankle and foot, she lifted a clipboard off the stainless steel counter, checking off boxes. She glanced once at Zennie, her eyes dismissing her. I guessed it was a long assembly line of gang death in here.

When she held out the pen, she said to me, "You're going to help her with the paperwork, right?"

chapter thirty-eight

That night, Broad Street's deserted lanes sparkled, crystallized with ice. Rather than attempt the drive back to Chopping Road, I took Zennie to the Lucky Strike building and explained to Milky what happened. I told him to keep her safe and he wrapped his arms around her, cradling her like a child, telling her this was gang life. And gang death.

I drove slowly through downtown and parked in the alley. When I opened the patio door, the kitchen smelled amazing. My mother was in the den watching television.

"What are you cooking?" I asked.

"Roasted turkey. I found your grandmother's cookbook." She lifted the book on her lap. *Housekeeping in Virginia.* "Don't you think roasted turkey is the best thing on Christmas Eve?"

She was watching *A Christmas Carol.* The good one, with Alastair Sim, but I excused myself. Walking upstairs, I headed for the percussive assault of sound behind Wally's bedroom door. I knocked loudly. There was no reply. I tried the knob. It was locked.

I could have walked away.

But I didn't.

Stepping back, I drove my foot into the door. The old iron lock cracked and the door hit the wall with a bang.

White smoke curled inside the glass pipe. He gasped, inhaling like a man going underwater.

When he tried to stand, I pushed him back down in the chair.

A cold breeze blew through his open window, but the unctuous odor of crack was unmistakable. Words pounded from the sound system, lyrics of hate. I twisted down the volume and held out my hand.

"Give me the pipe."

His eyes were molten. "You barge into a man's room?"

"I knocked, plenty." I grabbed his wrist, twisting until his fingers released the pipe. The glass felt warm, sticky with saliva. "Your new friends hook you up with this garbage?"

"Something to help me work." He gave a dopey grin. "It's not like I'm a junkie. My pictures are in *Newsweek*. Big time."

"You're a pipehead."

"You're crazy."

"You need help."

"I don't need nothin'."

"You need another place to live."

"Say *what*?"

"The lease says no drugs."

His jaw fell open and I realized how emaciated he'd become. Cheekbones protruding like elbows, eye sockets cavernous, hollow.

"You're kicking me out—at Christmas?"

"Or jail. Which one?"

"You call yourself a Christian." He hissed the last word. "You know what you are? A cop, a stupid white cop who—"

I held out my hand. "Give me the drugs."

His bloodshot eyes darted, wondering if this was a bluff, whether he could keep his precious drugs. But he guessed right. He slapped a baggie in my palm.

"Is that all of it?" I asked.

"You want my wallet?" he said. "How about my cameras, my computer?"

"Call me when you're ready to get help. But I want you out of here. Tonight."

I turned, walking for the door.

"Merry Christmas, you—"

I closed the door on his last word.

In the half-bath downstairs, my hands shaking, I opened the plastic baggie and dumped the white rocks into the toilet. I wrapped the glass pipe in layers of toilet paper, set it on the porcelain rim, and crushed it with the seat. I threw that in the small wicker trash bin, then flushed, washed my hands, and carried the trash out as though performing a helpful chore.

My mother looked up as I walked through the den to the kitchen.

"Did I hear something upstairs?" she asked. "It sounded like a door slamming."

"The wind. Wally's window was open, so the wind slammed the door."

"You talked to him?"

I nodded and she returned to her show.

In the kitchen, I lifted the discarded Butterball wrapper and stuffed the broken pipe into the garbage can. I washed my hands again and was carrying the trash can back when I saw Wally coming down the hall. Shifting the trash can to my left side, I stood behind my mother's chair, reaching under my bulky sweater, placing my palm on the Glock.

"Don't touch anything," he said. "I don't know when, but I'll be back."

"Are you going out?" my mother said. "You could use the fresh air, Wally. You've been cooped up in that room for days."

His molten eyes fixed on me. He didn't seem able to look at her.

"Do you need Raleigh to drive you somewhere?" she asked. "She put chains on my car."

He turned without a word. I followed him down the hall. He opened the front door and stepped outside. I latched the dead bolt behind him, parting the curtain over the leaded glass sidelight. He walked across Monument Avenue, passing by General Lee, his head down against the cold. His new car was snowbound at the curb.

In the front parlor and living room, I checked the window locks. I put the wastebasket back in the bathroom and was coming through the den when my mother said, "I just don't know. Wally seems like a different person. Do you think he's all right?"

I nodded, pretending to look outside at the snow, checking the den's window locks. Then the kitchen, where I took the phone book from under the rotary-dial phone and carried it into the front parlor. Using my cell phone, I called down the list of locksmiths until one of them agreed to come tonight after midnight, charging double his usual rate to change the door locks.

When I hung up, my phone rang.

The sheriff. He wanted to inform me that RPM just kicked the officers off his property. "And there's nothing I can do about it," the sheriff drawled. "But maybe you got a federal law regarding stupidity."

When I hung up, I stared at the Christmas tree. Ornaments smothered the fir's pale green limbs. My mother's overdone Christmas. And yet the house felt so empty. When something brushed against my leg, I looked down. Madame stared up at me.

"Do me a favor," I said. "Don't bark when the locksmith shows up."

I pretended to watch TV with my mother, wondering whether I should notify the Bureau. I tried to imagine how Phaup would twist the whole thing. I rented a room to a crackhead, who lived in the house with my mother. Then I considered calling the Richmond police. But it would sound ridiculous. Wally had no priors. Not even a traffic ticket. He wasn't violent—yet. And I'd flushed the evidence.

"Did you hear me?" my mother asked.

"I'm sorry, what did you say?"

"Can you drive me to the Christmas Eve service tomorrow?"

"Where?" I asked.

"St. John's."

"It's probably canceled."

"Oh no, I called. Remember how your father never missed one?"

I stared at the television. Scrooge realized he was alive, really alive. Throwing open the bedroom window, he yelled to the boy in the street to go buy the biggest goose in the butcher's shop.

"I just love this part," my mother said.

When the movie ended, she said she was turning in for the night. I promised not to forget tomorrow night's service.

"Do you mind if I keep Madame down here?" I asked. "I'm going to stay up awhile."

"My goodness, what a refreshing night. First, Wally comes out of his room. And here you are, relaxing for a change."

I channel-surfed with Madame on the couch, listening to my mother's feet pad across the bedroom floor upstairs. When she finished her beauty routine and climbed into bed, I waited another forty-five minutes, until just after 11 p.m. The house was dead silent. The security lights were on over the back patio, and I raced over the glittery snow to the carriage house, grabbing my toothbrush, geology kit, and briefcase with T-III notes.

I was back in the big house in less than five minutes, and when I opened the kitchen door, panting, Madame was standing right where I left her, staring out the bottom pane cleared of fake snow. She was one of those dogs with the intelligence to understand certain things had greater meaning. Things like suitcases and sudden phone calls and surreptitious behavior.

I set my geology kit on the kitchen table. She didn't lie down at my feet.

She stood beside my chair, watching.

No bigger than a book, the mineral testing kit was a gift from my father on my sixteenth birthday. I plugged in the power cord, changed the backup AA batteries, and waited for the instrument to warm up. Under the kitchen sink, I took out my mother's jewelry cleaning machine. The best ionic cleaner on the market. I should know. It was the same one we used in the FBI's mineralogy lab.

I took one of the octahedral double pyramids from Zennie's box of rocks and placed it inside the cleaner's basket, adding the diluted solution. While electrolysis and bubbles did their work—weakening the surface tension between mineral and debris—I petted Madame, trying to soothe her. Sixty seconds later, the machine beeped. I rinsed and dried the stone, checking it with my loupe, the small magnifier jewelers use. The loupe looked like a tiny top hat and magnified the growth artifacts covering the flat surfaces. Tiny triangles like frost, the atomic replication of the mineral's crystal structure.

Next, I held the stone in front of my mouth and breathed. I tried to fog it. But it refused condensation, immediately dispersing the heat from my breath just as it dispersed the heat from Zennie's radiator.

I chose a stone from my test collection, placing it on the testing machine. Also octahedral, to the naked eye it looked identical to Zennie's rock. Only I'd collected it from Sunset Beach, New Jersey, on a field trip with my dad, right after he gave me the test kit. We rode the ferry over from Delaware, hunting the famous Cape May "diamonds," and he told me the difference between real and fake. I touched the testing stylus to the Cape May diamond, measuring the stone's thermal conductivity and reflectivity. The needle on the gauge swung up then down. When the machine beeped, the needle pointed to the correct answer: quartz.

I performed the same procedure on samples of cubic zirconia and moissanite, a mineral simulate. Each time, the machine answered correctly. There was no doubt about calibration and accuracy.

Finally I placed Zennie's clean rock on the testing pad, touching it with the stylus, watching the needle go wild.

The rock wasn't quartz. It wasn't cubic zirconia. And it wasn't a counterfeit.

What Zennie had was a diamond.

Lots and lots of diamonds.

~

Christmas Eve dawned with more snow, every inch bringing palpable relief. Every inch meant Wally was less likely to trudge back to the house today.

At the kitchen table, I wrote a note for my mother, informing her that Wally had called very late last night after losing his wallet and keys. He recommended we change the locks immediately, in case somebody linked the address on his license with his keys. But he was fine, I added, no need to worry.

I stared at my boldfaced lies.

They were getting easier to tell.

That's what bothered me.

I locked the door with one of the keys and jogged through the snow to the carriage house. I showered, changed into fresh clothes, and made coffee. Then I called Zennie.

My eyes felt grainy from four hours of sleep on the couch in the den, and I prepared myself for her cranky morning attitude. But she sounded relaxed for once. The voice of someone who had cried a long time and was finished with it.

"If you're asking me to go back to that cold storage," she said, "you can forget it."

"No, I wanted to ask you about some things the gang said."

"Like what?"

I looked down at the list. After the locksmith came and went, I pulled out my T-III notes and the transcripts that Stan gave me. I went over the wiretap conversations again and again, trying to fit the pieces together.

"They used the word 'blowflies,'" I said.

"Something stinks," Zennie said. "Something's not right."

Sully was a blowfly; that made sense.

"How about PeeWees?" I asked.

"Guys in the gang they don't care about. Like, if they get killed, it's no big deal."

"How about Minks?"

"What?"

"Minks. Somebody's name. XL called him a couple times. You've never heard of Minks?"

"No. I need breakfast."

"One more," I said. "Greens." It was on the transcript Stan gave me. I thought it meant money, but the context didn't work. "It sounds like it's a person's name."

"It's that Jew down on Broad Street."

"Excuse me?"

"Greenstreet, Greenberg. Somebody like that."

"Greenbaum?"

"That's him, the green bomb. Only XL wouldn't let Moon say it that way."

"Why not?"

"Because it's who they were talking about!" She gave a snort, something a mean bull emits before charging. "Moon bought my jewelry down there. Only I never did get my ring."

She said it without pity. It was a sad fact, that was all.

"You sound better, Zennie."

"I'm seeing clear, if that's what you mean. Guess who called me last night?"

I froze. "Who?"

"RPM."

My mind shifted the pieces, scrambling the jigsaw again. "How did he get your number?"

"I don't know."

My heart accelerated. "Did you tell him where you were?"

"You still think I was born last night."

I started writing notes on my pad. "What did he want?"

"Said he wanted to tell me how sorry he was Moon was dead." She gave another snort. "And I'm supposed to go crazy because he's the big superstar."

"He knew Moon was dead?"

"I told him, 'You can be sorry all you want, it won't bring my man back.'"

I scribbled madly. "What did he say?"

"He felt sorry for me, wanted me to spend Christmas with him. So I wouldn't be all alone."

"But—"

"I'm not going," she interrupted. "Can you see me coming back, looking like a leper?"

I waited a moment. "Pardon?"

"He said he's sick of the snow and wants to go somewhere warm. He said he'd fly me over to Africa," she said. "But I hung up before he got it all out."

chapter thirty-nine

In a city whose best strategy for snow was always hope, the roads looked as bad as I'd ever seen. Richmond always hoped the snow didn't come. Then it hoped the snow didn't stay. And when that didn't work, residents hoped to ignore the whole thing by staying inside with hot chocolate and good liquor.

From the looks of traffic, most people were doing just that. But I drove the mighty Benz out the interstate, heading west into a shifting white curtain that dangled from the gray clouds. Visibility was beyond ten feet, and I followed the eighteen-wheelers driving in first gear.

And I dialed Phaup's cell number.

"Victoria Phaup speaking."

I heard several quick puffs of air, as if she were running. I identified myself, since for security reasons agent names never appeared on caller ID.

There was no reply. Only more puffing.

"We have a situation with RPM, the rap musician on the James River," I said.

"What kind of *situation*?"

I started telling her about the triple homicide at his estate, but she interrupted.

"Does the media know about this?"

"Not yet. The snow's shut things down and unless he released the news, the sheriff won't be talking to reporters."

That seemed to open her ears, and I explained how the

sheriff offered twenty-four-hour protection, since his bodyguard was among those killed. "But RPM kicked the officers off his property. Additionally, I have solid information suggesting that he intends to leave the area, perhaps the country. I think it would be wise to place him on the no-fly list."

"What—you're accusing him of *terrorism*?"

"No, ma'am. Not exactly. But his behavior is highly suspicious. It looks like his trips to Africa are—"

"His trips to help the poor? Those trips to Africa?"

"His trips to Africa are somehow tied to the gangbangers on Southside. He called my source—"

"Oh, now I get it," she said. "This is about your screwup."

"Excuse me?"

She was not puffing anymore. "You screwed up the task force and you tried to blame me. When that didn't work, you started reaching for straws. Is this some way of trying to kill two birds with one stone?"

"Ma'am, it's nothing—"

"Raleigh, he's the victim of hate crimes. But you're assuming he's a criminal because he's black and works in rap music."

"No, I—"

"Three different magazines called me this week. Do you have any idea what this man has done with his life? He adopts orphans from Liberia. Kids whose parents get killed fighting over those blood diamonds. And do you know what every single one of those reporters wanted to know?"

I waited. I was thinking of the blood diamonds. The black market in white stones that grow in abundance in West Africa.

"Every one of those reporters wanted to know why the FBI can't find the bigots who are trying to kill this man. And I couldn't tell them. How do you think that makes the Bureau look, Raleigh?"

"Ma'am, the men who allegedly broke into his house were black. One of them has been identified. He was a member of the gang on Southside, and my instinct tells me—"

"Your instinct?" she said. "You mean your gut. The same gut feeling that wound up ruining the task force. And here you have the gall to ask that we place this man on the no-fly list, based on this same gut of yours."

I took a deep, deep breath, staring at the truck in front of me. There was an 800 number on the mud flaps, followed by the question, "How's my driving?" Right above that, on the back door, was an ichthus. The fish symbol. There were people who considered faith sentimental, a harmless exercise for the simple-minded. As if Christianity meant cherubs playing harps and angels in the clouds. But the truth was gritty. The truth hurt. It stung. And obedience to it sometimes showed the hallmarks of torture—you could cry out in pain, but there was no guarantee that would stop the agony.

"Ma'am, with all due respect, this is more than a gut feeling. If you'll let me explain."

"All right. Is the investigative file opened? I presume you have all the necessary documentation—the subpoenas? I'll send them to HQ for approval and we'll place this man on the no-fly list."

I counted to five. I had nothing, and she knew it.

She was puffing again. "Why are you calling me, Raleigh?"

"Because his statements and actions don't line up with the facts. And if he leaves the United States for Africa, extradition will be almost impossible. Could we at least assign twenty-four-hour surveillance?"

"On Christmas Eve? Sure, why not. I'll call SOG, tell them to throw something together."

SOG, the Special Operations Group.

"We are under the microscope with every single civil rights

case. And this man, who is a victim, has a direct line to the national media." She puffed, puffed. "But if you're sure, I'll take this straight up the chain of command."

The chain of command. The chain that linked Phaup to headquarters and the oversight committees. I stared at the mud flaps. Nothing sentimental about it. Just the opposite. My chain of command told me to respect authority, even when that authority painted a giant bull's-eye on my forehead and locked me in its crosshairs. I had to obey. And right now, that felt like toothpicks were being shoved under my fingernails. And I knew that pain was nothing compared to what was endured for me by one who remained sinless.

"I apologize for bothering you, ma'am," I said. "It sounds like I caught you at a bad time."

"Raleigh, it's Christmas Eve. I'm in the middle of the Arizona desert. And because of you, I've lost my group. Is there something else, or can we hang up now?"

≈

Like most of the city, Richmond's airport was connected to the War of Northern Aggression. As part of the flat area east of town, the land was originally used by Confederates floating tethered reconnaissance balloons to spy on the enemy in Petersburg. Later it became an airport named Byrd Field, after the Virginia aviator and explorer Admiral Richard Evelyn Byrd. But more recently civic leaders suffering from a case of prosaic mercantilism changed the name to Richmond International Airport.

Folks still called it Byrd Field.

On Christmas Eve, stranded passengers filled the terminal. They flopped in the plastic chairs and slept on the carpet, and their faces carried that peculiar shade of pale that was produced by travel combined with deprivation. I took the main escalator to the atrium mezzanine and saw more weary travelers waiting out the storm, including one little girl who was twirling her wrinkled Christmas dress and imploring her bleary-eyed mother to watch, watch, watch.

The FBI's airport liaison waited at the security checkpoint.

Known as Sonny, Special Agent Carson McCauley guided me around the X-ray machines monitored by bored-looking TSA agents. He was a fast walker, so fast that strands of his hair lifted as he walked, like masts in search of sails. His white dress shirt was wrinkled; his tie swung from a loosened knot.

"Tough day?" I asked.

His short, thick legs chafed against his slacks, raising the cuffs.

"We started diverting flights yesterday when this storm came in," he said. "We had emergency staff on the ground, and everything was going pretty well until I got radioed about a flight from Miami. Three Arab guys on board, sitting in back. They were taking fifteen-minute turns in the can, with their cell phones. The stewardesses are freaking out because these guys keep talking about Allah, and I'm heading down to the gate when an elderly passenger comes off a flight from Atlanta and drops dead of a heart attack. And next gate over, some woman's screaming she's going to blow up the airport if we don't get her to Pittsburgh for Christmas. While I'm putting out those fires, these Arab guys slip out on the last flight leaving for LaGuardia."

He stopped at a metal door, keyed the code into the touchpad, and held the door for me. The phone was ringing on his desk. He ran over and picked it up.

Turning to the window to give him privacy, I watched the plows on the tarmac, churning through the whiteout, the yellow lights blinking on their cabs.

"Not Kennedy, LaGuardia," Sonny was saying.

The visitor's chair was under a bulletin board glaciated with white paper. New regulations, laws, official standards, all of it sending shivers of despair down my spine. Crimes committed on aircrafts were no different than those on the ground—theft, robbery, sexual assault, extortion, concealed weapons, murder. But when the plane door closed, every one of those crimes turned federal. And they fell on guys like Sonny, our agents monitoring the unfriendly skies.

"Three of them, yeah," Sonny was saying. "Lemme look . . . aisle 25."

I've heard people wonder aloud how nineteen foreigners managed to hijack airplanes and tear a hole through America. I've heard all the conspiracy theories. But the truth began with a July 2001 memo from an FBI agent in Phoenix. He noticed an alarming pattern of Arab men taking aviation training classes, and by August the Bureau had counted six hundred Middle Eastern men taking aviation lessons. Most of them turned out to be commercial and military pilots, sent by their governments for official training. But the FBI still had to run background checks on all six hundred, conduct at least twice that many interviews, and scale the college wall—a good portion of these six hundred subjects attended universities where professors and fellow students were openly hostile to law enforcement. To complicate matters further, there was the politically sensitive issue of racial profiling. They were all Middle Eastern men, but we weren't supposed to say that.

All this was known by August 2001.

September came next.

Boom.

Boom.

Boom.

It's always easy to connect the dots later, that 20/20 of

hindsight. And maybe things should have moved more quickly. But Western justice is a very slow grind. Unlike our enemies, we can't just behead suspects.

Now, on Christmas Eve, I was looking at a guy sweating bullets over three Arab men. We needed to be right every single time; the terrorists only needed one decent shot.

"Call me soon as you know anything." Sonny hung up the phone, drawing a hand over his hair. "Now, Raleigh, what do you need?"

"Quick check on a private plane registered out here. The owner is a guy who goes by the name RPM."

"Him?" Sonny said.

"You know about him."

"I've wanted to slap a search on that plane for years," he said. "What do you got?"

"I don't know," I said. "Can I look at his plane?"

chapter forty

I walked from the terminal to the private hangars beside the tarmac. A spiteful wind blew across my face, and by the time I got to the corrugated metal structure housing RPM's private plane, snow clung to my jeans and I couldn't feel my lips. Moments later a four-wheeled cart, the kind used for towing luggage carts, pulled up. A man jumped out wearing an insulated snowsuit. Tearing off a thick glove, he inserted a key into the hangar's lock. We hurried inside, stomping feet on a rubber mat, as he brushed his hand along the wall, turning on the lights.

It was a cavernous hangar, and he looked like a teenager. Long hair. Gray-blue eyes bright with adrenaline.

Extending my hand, I introduced myself.

"Jimmy Gint," he said.

"Thanks for coming out in this weather, Jimmy."

"Hey, no problem."

I walked toward the plane. It was a sleek white jet parked diagonally across the poured concrete floor. Not much more than six feet in height, the plane's narrow body tapered fifty feet from tip to tail in aerodynamic perfection.

"What is it you do out here, Jimmy?"

He followed me like a puppy.

"I'm a mechanic." He caught himself, suddenly bashful. "Well, almost a mechanic. Maintenance apprentice. But this summer I get my degree from J. Sergeant Reynolds. I love planes, all planes."

I smiled. This was good. "What can you tell me about this plane?"

"This one?" He walked toward it like a man approaching an altar. "This is one hot machine. They hate it next door."

"Who's that?"

"The Billion Air people, private charter guys? This sweet baby makes their planes look dumpy. They're not, but you know rich folks. They gotta have more. Know what I'm saying?"

"I know exactly what you're saying." I smiled again.

Jimmy Gint was eager, alive, and pumped, the antithesis of studied cool. I watched more adrenaline flash through his eyes. The big storm, right in the thick of it, and he was an expert. I was suddenly very happy to have him here.

"So, Jimmy, what makes this plane so special?"

"This is a Gulfstream V-SP," he said, taking on the tone of authority. "It can cover seven thousand miles at Mach eight, nonstop."

"That sounds fast."

"Six hundred miles an hour? Yeah, that's fast. And it's totally decked out inside. Leather, white carpet, the whole bit."

"Sounds nice."

"Don't even get me started," he said. "The pillows? They're zebra. Fur. From the animal."

"You really know this plane."

"I get to look," he said, boasting. "The pilot likes me."

"Who's the pilot?"

"He lives in New York. Victor Minsky."

I stopped walking. I tried to give a nice smile. "Is Mr. Minsky around, by any chance?"

"He flew in right before the storm. But where he goes after he lands, I don't know."

"So he lives in New York but flies out of Richmond?"

Jimmy nodded. Minsky, he explained with boasting knowledge, flew down in his Cessna, which Jimmy went into some detail about, once again proving his expertise. "He just flew some people to Africa."

"Really. When was that?"

"Couple days ago. He took a whole bunch of people over."

"Does he do that often?" I was wondering if he meant the trip Wally went on.

"This time, yeah. Second trip in a week. But this other group didn't come back with him. I think maybe they live there. Anyway, he flew back by himself."

I smiled again. "You keep your eyes open."

We were standing near the jet's tires, which looked much too small for a machine that could fly close to the speed of sound. Small bits of stone were embedded in the rubber treads and I took a pen from my pocket, prying one loose. Underneath, sandy red soil was lodged deep inside.

"Whatcha doing?" Jimmy asked.

I turned around. "I've got this bad habit. I like things to look perfect. That rock in that beautiful tire, it bugged me."

I smiled again.

But Jimmy Gint didn't smile back.

I walked slowly around the plane, admiring it, letting several significant moments pass. "Can you keep a secret?" I asked.

He nodded, wary.

"I mean, *really* keep a secret. Not tell anyone?"

Another nod.

"Some people are trying to make life very difficult for the man who owns this plane. The FBI was called in to find out who's behind it. But this is all top secret. You cannot repeat this to anybody."

"Making life hard, how?"

"I can't reveal that."

"Like death threats?"

"Why do you say that?"

"Because of something Mr. Minsky once said."

"About death threats?"

He nodded. "I asked him one time why he lived in New York City. He said it was safer. I said no way can that place be safer than Richmond. But he just laughed. I always wondered about that."

"You know Mr. Minsky pretty well."

"He—" But then he stopped.

"I gave you my secret, Jimmy."

"It's not a big deal. Some other pilots do it too," he said. "You know, pay me a little extra, to take extra good care of his plane?"

I held the small stone in my hand, knowing that if I pulled out the clear plastic evidence bags from my coat pocket, I would rip the helpful attitude right off Jimmy Gint. I wasn't paying him; Minsky was.

"I hate to ask this, Jimmy, but is there a restroom in here?"

He pointed across the hangar. "The door with the Cessna sticker."

In the small bathroom, where I briefly wondered about how much time I spent in places that made me want to compulsively wash my hands, I took out the evidence bag, depositing the stone. Then I called Sonny.

"Thanks for sending Jimmy," I said.

"I thought he'd be a good choice."

"Now find something else for him to do."

"You don't want a ride back?" Sonny asked.

"I'm okay."

I flushed, washed my hands, and found Jimmy walking around the plane with the top half of his snowsuit unzipped and peeled down to his waist. When his radio suddenly squawked, he reached under the empty arms.

"Yeah?" he said into the radio.

"Need you back at the shop."

It wasn't Sonny's voice, so it was somebody he had called.

"Something happen?" Jimmy said.

"If it does, nobody's here," the man said.

"Got it." Jimmy clicked off the radio and gave me a cool expression. "You ready?"

The radio squawked again.

"Leave her there," the man said. "She's going to lock up when she's done."

"Yeah, sure," he said into the radio.

But I watched several thoughts float across Jimmy's brow, none of them good. He didn't have his degree from the community college yet, but he had a master's in common sense.

And as he left the hangar, I knew time was running out.

≈

Sixteen minutes later, I shrugged off my snow-smothered coat and waited for Sonny to finish his phone calls—two at the same time. Cell phone to one ear, desk phone to the other. I lifted our Most Wanted flyers from the ring on the bulletin board and became acquainted with the seven dangerous men and three equally hazardous women, reading until Sonny hung up.

"We found 'em," he said.

"Congratulations." I replaced the flyers.

"They're staying near Columbia University. With a physics professor. He's from Algeria."

"Physics?"

"Yeah, New York had the same thought. Bomb-making smarts. They've been watching this prof since 2002 when his brothers started flying over. Guy has more brothers than John Boy Walton." He leaned back. His relief was palpable. "So what's with the plane?"

"I'm not sure."

"You keep saying. But you've got nothing better to do than drive out here in a blizzard. On Christmas Eve."

"I'm working a case that involves him. If he leaves in that plane, I'm concerned he won't come back. Did he file any flight plans for upcoming trips?"

Sonny laughed.

"What's so funny?"

"Flight plans are optional, Raleigh."

"Since when?"

"Since always. The FAA strongly encourages pilots to file them, especially for travel that air traffic control can't track. But nothing's compulsory. The pilot files one, great. If not, we can't force him. And that pilot of his isn't about to clue us in on his travel plans."

"Victor Minsky."

He smiled. "Jimmy told you. I thought he might talk. Jimmy likes to impress pretty girls."

"Minsky pays him to keep an eye on things?"

"Yes, and then I have lunch with Jimmy." Sonny smiled again. "But Minsky's a slick character. Ever hear of a flag of convenience?"

I shook my head.

"Pilots claim Liberia is their country of origin, even if they're not citizens. No taxes, no inspections."

"And he flies there with RPM, doing humanitarian missions?"

"Maybe. But if he's hooked up with Minsky, the guy's not Mother Teresa. What else you got?"

I thought about RPM's estate and the crack house on Southside. They had one thing in common: guns.

"I saw some assault rifles. They looked like AK-47s but with some modifications. Beat-up wooden stocks. Old guns, heavily used."

"You see a lot of them, or just a couple?"

"Dozens."

He spun his cell phone on the desk. "Rumor is Minsky once flew for the Soviets. He's a creepy dude. Comes in and out of here like a cipher. We can't get anything on him."

"You think he's gun running?" I asked.

"If you're a crook, there's good money in it. But Minsky's careful. Like I said, I'm dying to slap a search warrant on that Gulfstream."

I stood up. "I'll let you know if I come up with something solid." I shrugged back into my coat. It felt heavy with melted snow. "Phaup shot down my idea of putting RPM on the no-fly list. But maybe this weather will keep him grounded."

"The storm's supposed to be gone by tomorrow," Sonny said. "Blue skies for Christmas."

The expression on my face must have revealed my thoughts because he immediately tried to cheer me up.

"Hey," he said, "you ever hear the saying about those old Kalashnikovs?"

"No." I buttoned my coat.

"The Russian mob loves those guns. Their saying is, 'Kalashnikovs Cut Clean.' Only they spell it with all Ks. Don't ask me why. Maybe it's a Russian spelling."

"What did you say?"

He repeated the phrase.

"The acronym," I said. "KKK."

"Well, yeah," Sonny said, in a tone that said I was missing the point. "But not our KKK. That's the Russian mob's KKK."

chapter forty-one

It was 12:22 p.m. on Christmas Eve when I walked into Greenbaum's Jewelry Emporium at the corner of Fourth and Broad. The store's owner, Reuben Greenbaum, stood behind the counter and as I turned to close the door, I heard him tell a customer, "You want to knock her socks off, this'll do the trick."

The gray granite building was among the few structures that survived the fires of 1863, and the store smelled fusty and parched, as if the old plaster walls had been sifting their limestone into the crimson rug. Aside from the four guys at the counter, the place felt dead.

"Be with you in a minute," Greenbaum said to me.

He stood behind the counter near a brass register that looked original. I knew of his store, and of him by sight, because his niece Lydia went to St. Catherine's. A beautiful girl who lowered her eyelashes as we read through the Gospels, she did almost the same thing when her uncle showed up at fund-raising events, passing out inexpensive green pens advertising his store. In the ten years since I saw him last, the large man's posture had only worsened. The weight of his large stomach pulled his shoulders forward, yet he walked on tiptoes, like a man perpetually on the verge of saying, "Boo."

"Is it gorgeous or is it gorgeous?" he asked the youths at the counter.

One held a gold ring. Diamonds smothered the surface like

white coral. All four of them wore black parkas and black jeans and black tennis shoes.

"Still not big enough," the guy told Greenbaum.

"That's four carats."

"Yo, Greens," the guy said, "it's all broken up. My lady wants her diamond *big.*"

Snatching the ring from the guy's hand, Greenbaum snagged his fingernail under a gold chain, lifting it from a velvet display. He dangled the necklace like a hypnotist.

"This has been known to cause temporary blindness. And she doesn't even lift a hand."

The pendant was made to look like a nest of gold woven around a large diamond egg. Mostly, it looked like the jeweler was in a hurry. But as Greenbaum turned his wrist, light ricocheted from the stone.

"You're getting warm, Greens." He closed his hand around the pendant.

Greenbaum turned to me. "What can I do for you?"

"I can wait," I said.

He nodded then looked back at the buyer. "You want a second opinion?" He tossed his head toward me. "Ask a woman."

The guy glanced over with a dubious expression.

"They're all the same," Greenbaum said, reading his thoughts. "Go ahead, ask her."

He lifted the necklace.

"Wow," I said.

"What'd I tell you?" Greenbaum chuckled, his shoulders inching up with mirth.

The guy said, "Sold. On the tab."

Sweeping the necklace from the guy's hand, Greenbaum walked it down to the old register. The brass had tarnished to a dull brown, but he opened a drawer under the counter instead.

Taking out a white box, some cotton fluff, and a red ribbon, he dumped it all in a green bag advertising his store. He handed the bag to the guy. "Happy holidays."

"Back at ya, Greens."

When all four guys cleared the door, I reached into my coat and took out Zennie's box of rocks.

"I'm not sure what these are," I said, setting the box on the glass counter. "My friend gave them to me. All rocks sorta look the same to me."

Because of his tense shoulders, when he looked down, his chin touched his chest.

"A friend gave you these?" he said.

"Uh-huh."

He picked up the box, tipping it to one side. A jeweler's loupe hung on a black cord around his nonexistent neck. The cord was frayed, apparently from his habit of running the lens back and forth, which he did several times before pinching a stone out of the box. The ocular muscles around his right eye cinched around the loupe as he moved the stone forward and back, then dropped it into the box, plucking another.

"This friend just handed these to you?"

I kept my hands on the counter, the glass warm from the lights shining below. But the surface was so scratched I couldn't see what was on the shelves.

"To tell you the truth," I said, "she's fallen on hard times. I thought maybe these were worth something. You know, to help her out?"

He lifted his eyebrows, letting the loupe fall on the frayed cord. "You need a gemologist," he said.

"A what?"

"Gemologist—expert on gems."

"So you think these rocks are worth something?"

"I didn't say that."

"But, boy, that would be some good news."

"Give me your name and number. I'll take these over to him. He'll call you."

"Oh."

"Something wrong?"

"Well, I'm not sure . . ."

"I got insurance," he said. "And I'd like to help your friend." He grabbed a pen but searched for paper, finally ripping a piece off the receipt roll. "Name?"

I bit my bottom lip. "I need to think about this."

He smiled, dark eyes flattening, and pushed the box toward me. "You change your mind, I'm open tomorrow."

"Really, on Christmas Day?"

"Not my holiday," he said.

≈

The female guard at the front desk of the Richmond police annex was singing along with a jazzy version of "Jingle Bell Rock." As she checked my credentials, her head bopped to the beat in the frosty air and I walked down the hall, hoping it was the right time to knock on the pebble glass door.

Detective Greene's eyes still looked jaundiced. "How'd you know I was here?"

"I'm a trained investigator."

A simple deduction, really. I guessed he was the kind of cop who probably couldn't enjoy the holiday unless he got work done first. He'd missed almost a week because of the flu. Coming in Christmas Eve meant nobody would interrupt. So he thought. The detective's work ethic was among the reasons I believed my dad's killer would one day be caught. One day. Someday. Just not today.

"I'm sorry about the task force," I said. "I take full responsibility."

The sound in his throat wasn't good. "You want to apologize, help me close some cases. I found six murders with blank ammo."

"Six? That wasn't a red flag?"

"You think we keep track of these on spreadsheets? These are inner-city murders, years old. I've got hundreds."

"You're right. I'm sorry. And I might as well apologize now for what I'm about—"

The mustache twitched. "What?"

"It seems things are a little more complicated than I thought," I said.

He glared. "Now you don't need this?"

I laid out the facts about the men in the swamp and what I heard on Zennie's cell phone. I told him about the break-in at Rapland and what Sonny said KKK stood for. The detective held up his hand, stopping me. He reached over, turning down the volume on a police radio at the edge of his desk.

"Make it quick," he said. "I've got two bikes and a Ping-Pong table to put together by tomorrow morning."

I pulled out Zennie's box of rocks, opening the top. "I was just over at Greenbaum's Jewelry. He claims he doesn't know what these are."

The detective looked inside the box, shaking it. "What are they?"

"Diamonds."

He looked up. "They don't look like diamonds."

"These are rough diamonds, what they sometimes look like coming out of kimberlite pipes in Africa. I tested them; they're real."

"So maybe Greenbaum didn't know," he said.

"Sure. Except every jeweler knows the scratch test. By the looks of his counter, he's scratched a thousand times. I watched a posse shopping in there. They left with a three-carat diamond and Greenbaum didn't charge them."

"The cold medicine's still in my system," he said. "Tell me nice and slow."

"I thought I was."

"Slower."

"I think the gang on Southside is money laundering through RPM. They give him drug money; he takes it over to Africa. He does some humanitarian aid, but he also buys black market diamonds and guns and ammo, bringing the merchandise back to Richmond on his private plane. The gangs give the diamonds to Greenbaum. He cuts and polishes, then sells them to unsuspecting buyers, funneling most of the money back to the gang. On the wiretap they talked about 'the fat man coming down the chimney.' That's probably Greenbaum."

The detective pawed his mustache. "You tell the task force all this?"

"Not yet. It's still a theory."

"You mean she didn't buy it," he said, referring to Phaup.

I nodded. "Shot me down before I could explain."

"And you expect me to jump in?"

"You just found six cold cases linked to blank ammo," I said. "Do you remember when I first asked you about these gangbangers?"

"I'm trying to forget."

"You said they had big money suddenly. The idea was they were going national, hooking up with a gang in Chicago."

"I still think that," he said.

"Okay, but there's more. And this guy RPM is involved, somewhere between the locals and the Russian mob."

I waited while the detective stared at some middle distance between us. The big analog clock on the wall ticked eight times. When his brown eyes shifted toward me, I couldn't read his expression.

"They already shipped you to Oregon," he said.

"Washington."

"The point is, you're out on a limb again. And I can hear the branch cracking."

"That's odd, because I hear cases closing."

He grunted.

"Look, I'm not going to get you in trouble. But I can't play it safe right now. My source said RPM talked about leaving for Africa. He already shipped his family over there, his house is empty, and he killed the main guys running the gang, the guys who knew what was going on. He's literally cleaning house and if he gets to Liberia, we'll never get him back."

"What do you want from me?"

"Hard evidence. I need a warrant to hold him. Please, can you check your cold cases again? Blank ammo *and* victims wearing a substantial amount of diamonds. If there are any heavy rashes—"

"You want me to match up elementary schools?"

"Thank you."

"Don't thank me," he said. "I haven't got anything. And you might wind up in Oregon again."

"Wash—" I stopped. "Whatever."

chapter forty-two

At six o'clock on Christmas Eve, I held a flickering candle in the darkened church and thought the priest should hurry up. We sat in back—closer to the exit, I decided, as my mind went over dilemmas and theories and evidence. Time was running out.

"Peace be with you," my mother replied to the priest's recitation.

Her eyes were closed and in the candlelight her tears were golden, slipping down her cheeks. Her weeping began the moment we arrived—late. My fault. I'd spent the afternoon rushing through the snow to track down the sheriff. But I didn't find him and he didn't call back. When I finally got my mother into the church, my mind filled with chattering thoughts. *What if—*

"Listen." She placed her hand on mine.

I looked up. The priest's white vestments glowed in the candlelight. Hundreds of candles, the valiant worshippers who made it here tonight. Standing in the elevated pulpit, the priest looked down on our flickering flames and said, "God does nothing by accident. We know that. So why did he choose an inn with no vacancies?"

Not now, I thought, inwardly groaning. *Not now. Just give us the blessing and let me out of here.* My mind bounced with images of RPM getting on that plane, taking off forever. And me, explaining to Phaup what was really going on. How I would take the fall for her mistake. I checked my phone again, turned to silent ring. I kept hoping the detective would call. Or the sheriff. Just not Sonny. I didn't want Sonny telling me the guy was leaving. I wondered again about getting this warrant on Christmas Eve, whether I'd have enough evidence and how much—

"Are you listening?" she whispered.

"God could have sent them anywhere. But he chose that inn. Two thousand years later, it's still true. That inn is symbolic. It represents our hearts."

I stared at the candle flame.

"We fill up our lives with work and concerns and lists of things to do. We go, go, go. We shop, we buy things. We wrap presents. But take a look at your heart. Is it so full of stuff that there's no room for the Savior?"

White wax dripped down the side of the candle.

The church smelled of paraffin and my mother's tears and my own shame. Closing my eyes, I felt something wash over my shoulders. I saw Wally, staring at me with hate. *You call yourself a Christian . . ."* I sent up a prayer for his protection. And a second petition, almost contrary, asking that rock bottom came fast, so fast he asked for help. I prayed for my mother, and for myself, for mercy. I'd thrown Wally out at Christmas, in the icy cold. The list went on but when I heard feet shuffling, I opened my eyes.

The congregation was standing. Above the flickering flames, each face looked tender and expectant as the organ released its tonal notes. The voices lifted, rising, singing of angels heard on high, a sweet singing over the plains. And our echoed reply: "Gloria, Gloria, Gloria."

~

When we walked inside the big house with its new locks, I felt spent and exhausted. It was as if weeks of worry and failure caught up with me all at once. Slowly I unraveled the scarf around my neck and wondered about this night. What would happen now?

"Oh, look." My mother peered at the blinking red light on the answering machine. "Aunt Charlotte, I'll bet. She misses us."

She hit Play. I tugged off my boots; my socks felt damp. In the background of the message I heard sounds like traffic, cars. I could see my aunt standing outside her New Age store in Seattle, calling from the sidewalk because cell phone microwaves interfered with the vibrations coming from her crystals. She was loony and I loved her.

"It's me," the voice said.

I whipped around, staring at the machine.

"Oh, it's Wally," my mother said.

In the background I heard something metallic scraping, a long scar of sound. It was followed by a rhythmic rattle and clatter. Trains.

"I thought about what you said."

She turned to me. "Raleigh, what did you say?"

I couldn't look at her. I stared at the answering machine. His voice. What was that I heard?

"You're right, I'm not okay. I need help."

Not defeat. Despair.

"Why—" My mother's voice was rising. "Why does he need help?"

"I'm so cold," he said. "I'm so cold and tired and—"

"He's crying!" she exclaimed. "Why is he crying?"

"I'm on the Lee Bridge. Help me. I want to kill myself, I—"

My mother screamed. The line went dead.

I threw on my boots and ran out the door.

≈

Richmond's bridges crossed over the river like shuttles in a giant loom. As I raced the Benz down Cary Street, I counted them off.

I turned south at Fifth Street, fishtailing into the parking lot at Tredegar Iron Works. The parking lot was empty and I left the car where it stopped, jumping out. I ran, boots slipping, and raked the beam of my flashlight across the footbridge. The concrete path was suspended high over the city falls.

"Wally!"

I aimed the beam with my left hand. In my right, I held my Glock. Pitch black, ice cold, not the best part of town, I ran down the span, pointing the light at the water below. It was black, except where it fulminated around the boulders. I pointed the light up and saw him.

He stood on the handrail facing west, his arms outstretched, fingers curled around the steel suspension cables.

I walked forward, slowly. The crust on the snow crunched under my boots. "Wally."

His body swayed like a diver about to launch.

"Don't do it," I said. "Don't."

He stared down, transfixed by the rushing water below.

"You'll kill Nadine."

"Nadine." His voice sounded even more broken. "I didn't mean to get like this. I didn't."

"I know that." I pressed the flashlight into the snow, holstered my gun, and grabbed the cables, pulling myself up. My stomach lurched. "She's really worried about you." I slid my feet sideways across the bar. He was three feet away. "She loves you and she's scared and she—"

"Raleigh." His arms were shaking.

"Take it easy." I moved hand-over-hand on the cables. Two feet away.

"Don't," he said. "Don't come any closer."

One foot away. The braided cable felt cold against my clammy skin.

He let go with his left hand, windmilling his arm across the dark.

"Wally—no!"

He let go of the other hand.

I swung my right arm, connecting with his chest, and kicked my right leg out, extending like a trapeze artist. His falling weight ripped the cable from my left hand. I dove back for the bridge, throwing both arms around his body, tackling him, and for a long, quiet moment, we fell. We fell one centimeter at a time, ticking down through the dark with no purchase, all air. I held his coat and squeezed my eyes shut.

The bridge punched the air out of my lungs. My eyes flew open. Thick steam clouded the cold air. My breath. His breath. Snow on my face. My arms wrapped around him. I stared at the back of his head, relief pouring through me.

"Let me die, let me die!" he sobbed.

"I can't."

I waited. He said nothing.

"We love you."

Still nothing. My arm ached under his body. And my left hip. I wondered if anything was broken. Turning my head, I searched for the flashlight, wondering if we landed on it. Above us, the city lights shimmered.

Another light, a single beam, was coming toward us. It pointed directly at my eyes. I yanked my arm out from under Wally, patting down my right side. I came up with my Glock.

"I'll take that," said the man with the flashlight.

I moved my finger to the trigger, but yellow tracers ripped through the dark. His bullets pinged the steel cables with deadly speed, ricocheting into the river.

Then silence.

I could see the shooter, his shape outlined by the city light behind him. Another man stepped from behind him, holding the flashlight. His shoes crunched over the cold snow. Taking my Glock, he pointed the barrel at my left temple and drew back his foot. He kicked snow at Wally.

Wally continued to lie on the ground, inert.

"I was certain you would make every effort to save your friend," RPM said. "My associate had doubts. But I was right, Minsk."

"You win," said the man with the assault rifle. He pronounced the word "vin."

I looked over at Wally. RPM had the flashlight pointed at the side of his face.

"Wall-Ace feels bad. He likes you. Really, he does. The problem is, he likes crack more."

My voice scratched up my throat. I felt ragged with adrenaline and strain and cold. And fury was packing itself down like gunpowder inside my chest. "You set this up," I said. "You watched."

"With an appropriate night scope, we can see this entire bridge from the iron works. We began our walk over after you pulled up in that rather attractive Mercedes. And I must say, Wall-Ace, you did an admirable job. You must give him some credit, Miss Harmon. We had the scope on you both. He didn't want you shot."

The famous man once more planted the toe of his polished black boot in the snow, sending another spray of snow into Wally's face. I looked down. Wally had closed his eyes, ice clinging to his lashes.

"But for a moment there," RPM told him, "I thought you might actually jump."

chapter forty-three

The Hummer trounced out of downtown, smashing every bundle of snow in its path. RPM sat in the passenger seat, his body turned sideways. He kept the assault rifle pointed at me in the backseat. Wally sat listless, leaning against the back door. RPM followed the cello music on the stereo. He swung the rifle's barrel like a conducting baton, following the tune about angels near the earth, touching harps of gold.

"Quite nice on the cello, don't you think?" RPM asked.

Victor Minsky drove like a man in a hurry.

"Miss Harmon?" RPM asked.

I nodded and counted the days. Tomorrow was Christmas, a Monday. Maybe by Tuesday someone would trace the Mercedes abandoned at the iron works, linking it to a woman who would be shattered by then, paralyzed with fear inside her big empty house on Monument Avenue, her fragile mind a kaleidoscope of fractured images. Wally's suicide. Her daughter following him off the bridge.

They might even comb the river for our bodies.

But none of it would lead them to Rapland.

And when the Hummer finally zoomed around Rapland's keyhole drive, Wally slid across the seat. Bumping into me, he pushed off and opened his back door, falling on the snow.

Minsky opened my door, reaching in. He grabbed me by the wrists, squeezing the wire that held my hands together. He shoved me toward the house.

The night air smelled fibrous with cold and somewhere in the woods beyond, a bird pierced the darkness, its winter whistle ascending in silvery mercy. Minsky walked behind me, holding the barrel of the rifle against my back. Ahead of me, RPM hummed about glad hours and grace.

Wally stumbled inside the foyer.

"Keep going-k," Minsky said.

We walked down the dark hall to the room with all the pictures. Dank mildew rose from the cellar and I wondered whether I would smell the geraniums, whether it would matter. When I slipped on the marble steps, Minsky grabbed the back of my coat, yanking me up.

The basement had not been cleaned. RPM walked around Sid's bloodstain, opening the door to the safe room.

"Please, have a seat."

Wally stayed near the door. "Where's my hit?" he said. "I need a hit. You promised."

Minsky shoved me through the door, pushing me onto the couch.

"You promised," Wally whined.

With one hand the Russian yanked my coat, pulling it over my head and forward. My sleeves turned inside out, covering my wired-up hands. Another layer of restraint.

"I need it and you said—"

"Wall-Ace," RPM said quietly. "Don't ever tell me what I said."

The couch was set low, my knees rising above my chest. Minsky looked over at RPM, his cold blue eyes dancing.

"Geev him the drug," he said.

RPM held my Glock and glanced at Wally, considering him with a detached expression. Wally's neck quivered, his head twitching. Under a track light, a scrim of perspiration shone on his skin.

"I am a man of my word," RPM said. "You will find a pipe in the living room on the mantel. I believe the goods are stored in the cigar box."

Wally stumbled away. I listened to his shoes slap the damp stones. Then his steps faded away.

RPM shook his head. "Poor Wall-Ace. He just can't help himself." He smiled, lifting his eyes to Minsky. The Russian stood behind me. "Are you ready, Minsk?"

"Ray-dee," he said.

I turned my head. But the Russian stayed out of view.

"You were asking questions about my airplane." RPM stood in front of me. "I would like to know how much information you've gathered."

Jimmy. But I stalled. "Who told you?"

RPM had not taken off his cashmere overcoat and when he brushed back one side, leaning against the kitchen counter, he was ten feet from my chair. "You'll be answering the questions, Miss Harmon."

I held my mouth closed.

He nodded at Minsky.

A bolt of lightning shot through my shoulders. My back arched, rigid. I thought my spine would snap. But just as suddenly my body dropped, my head falling forward.

"You also took something down to Mr. Greenbaum," RPM said. "I need to know how those stones came into your possession."

I tried to hold my head up. "I don't know what you're talking—"

Minsky hit me with the Taser again. My shoulder twisted, torquing my body. I heard vertebrae popping and clenched my teeth. Count, count, counting to nine. When he pulled it off, I stared down at my coat. It was wet. Drool. I lifted my arms, they felt weighted. I wiped my chin. I couldn't feel it.

"My friend from Russia is more than happy to continue. But I sense a certain stubbornness about you. I'd rather not extend this time together. What will it take to convince you, Miss Harmon?"

"Answer my questions first." My lips felt numb.

He considered the idea.

"Nyet." It was Minsky.

But the proud man across from me wanted to tell me where I went wrong.

"Blood diamonds," I said. "That's what this has been about?"

"She knows," Minsky said.

"Miss Harmon knows more than she's telling." He smiled again. "When you came here that first day with that empty paint can, I told Sid we needed to do a background check. In case you didn't succumb to our story. And lo and behold, we discover that Wall-Ace lives with your mother. I decided we had an insurance policy. Look how that policy paid off. You're here. And I'm leaving."

"The chemicals, they're coming from Liberia?"

"Yes, the chemicals. When you found lewisite and mustard gas, not once but twice, I told Minsk we had to hurry up."

"But why?"

"Why?" he asked.

"Why all the killing?"

"You're referring to the gentlemen in the river?"

"The kid in the car, Moon. I'm guessing that was XL with him. And Sid—"

"Sid was a mistake," he said. "Sid was supposed to come with us."

"Nyet," replied the Russian.

"Mr. Minsky does not agree. He killed Sid. Seemed rather unfair after Sid took care of those two groveling gangsters. I will miss him terribly."

"But what, what was it all for?"

"You have an unfortunate need to know, Miss Harmon. All you were supposed to do was go after the Klan. Or that silly Wellington woman. But you had to keep digging, didn't you? And you sit here, minutes from death, asking why. I'll satisfy your curiosity. People became greedy. We had a profitable enterprise. Everyone received their portion."

"The gang was laundering money through you?"

"Those petty thugs received pretty guns and diamonds for their cheap women, and they made me a tidy sum of money."

"You need it?"

"Record sales are not what they used to be, particularly in my line of music. But money draws flies. The Russian mob wanted in, along with a national gang, and the local thugs decided they were something important. This was no different than a hostile takeover of any business. Although very hostile." He smiled again. "Mr. Minsky and I decided the best strategy was to allow the competition to take out each other."

"So the Russian mob lights the cross—"

"No, no." He wagged the Glock. "This is where you're wrong. Sid lit the cross. Mr. Minsky planted the car bomb and lured his fellow Russians to the river. The gang thought the Russians were coming after their enterprise." He opened his hands, smiling. "We just sat back and let it play out."

I tasted blood on my tongue. "And now you leave."

"Well, that's your fault. If you hadn't stuck your nose into this, I could remain here, a clear victim of hate crimes."

"Time," Minsky said.

RPM glanced at his beautiful diamond watch. "Yes, you're correct. We have to go."

"Liberia?"

"I'm treated like a king there. But I will miss this home. I've rather enjoyed my time in Virginia."

In the silence that followed, I heard the hum of the dehumidifier. The air was drying out for the gas. Seal the room tight. Fly away. I felt dizzy and nauseous. There was a ringing sound in my head. I thought the Taser had done it, but Minsky was tugging at my coat.

"It is phone," he said.

He fumbled with the folds and for one split second I considered an uppercut. And then? RPM held my Glock. The assault rifle was on the counter behind him. And Minsky, he would come back, even more venomous.

The Russian flipped open my cell phone and read the caller ID aloud.

"Detective Greene."

"You've spoken to the police?" RPM said. "About what?"

I shook my head. "I was meeting him tonight, to tell him. I'm late. He's probably wondering."

"You will tell him something's come up. Tell him you will call tomorrow. If you say anything else, I will make sure your mother suffers. Do you understand?"

I nodded.

Minsky held the phone to my mouth and pressed the button.

"Hi, Nate," I said. "Look, I can't make dinner tonight. Something's come up."

He paused. I never called him Nate. Ever.

"I found what you're looking for," he said.

RPM looked at Minsky. The Russian frowned.

"Nate, do me a favor. There's been a change in plans."

"Not again," he groaned.

"Get over to my mother's house right away, her address is—"

Minsky slammed the phone shut. He dropped it on the floor,

grinding it under his heel. The third electric shock roared down my spine. Deep inside my head I heard a scream.

When he pulled the Taser off, the room was spinning. I leaned forward, preparing to throw up.

"Tell me what the detective found, Miss Harmon." RPM stood directly in front of me now. "Tell me or I'll kill your mother."

My tongue was almost useless, the words slurred. "Ammo, no marks. Homicides."

"Call Jimmy," RPM told Minsky. "Tell him to get the plane de-iced. We'll be there in twenty minutes."

Minsky nodded, walking toward the cellar.

Wally stepped into the doorway. "Might be longer than twenty." He held an assault rifle in his hands, pointed at the Russian.

"Wall-Ace, what are you doing?" RPM looked over coolly. "You're compelling me to shoot you."

"Untie her," Wally said.

"I have a gun."

"And if I pull this trigger, you're dead." His eyes looked too large for his emaciated face. "Untie her."

Minsky didn't move.

"I already died on that bridge. I'm not worried about dying again."

RPM looked annoyed. "Go ahead," he told Minsky. "Untie her."

The Russian stood between me and RPM. He pulled the coat sleeves, revealing my wrists.

"Hurry up!" Wally shook sweat from his eyes.

Blood stained my coat where the wire was cutting into my skin. I couldn't feel my hands. I stared down at the wounds and saw RPM's fine leather boot. The toe was pivoting, inching side-ways. Moving for the assault rifle on the counter.

I looked at Minsky. He was watching the floor, gazing back at his partner's foot. I drew a slow breath and gave a one-word prayer. Flexing every muscle in my legs, I came up off the couch, ramming my head into Minsky's chin. With my fingers, I grabbed the front of his shirt, pulling him close, turning him like a shield. I heard my Glock fire. One. Two. On the third round, the assault rifle released. I drove deep my fists into Minsky's solar plexus, pressing him forward.

But RPM wasn't there.

Minsky's legs hit the counter. He crumpled. I let go, diving for the floor, rolling under the desk. My Glock fired a steady *pow-pow-pow*. I tucked my body into a ball.

And it was quiet.

I waited, ears ringing. Then I stole a glance.

Victor Minsky lay on the concrete floor, blood pillowing his head. His blue eyes were open. But he didn't move.

I waited, then leaned out farther.

RPM was crawling for the door. An intermittent fountain of blood spurted from his neck.

I climbed out from under the desk.

My Glock was in RPM's hand, scraping along the concrete. I walked over and reached down, my wrists still tied. But he barely kept a grip, crawling toward the doorway.

I stepped over him and squatted beside Wally, pressing two fingers into his neck. He stared up at nothing, his face almost young again. My eyes stung and I moved my hands, ready to close his eyes, when I remembered why I couldn't. He was my friend, but he was part of a crime scene.

I looked at RPM.

Behind him, his body left a red smear on the concrete floor.

His eyes were fixed on the door and for a long moment I watched him, feeling an emotion as tangible as thirst.

I walked back to the desk and picked up the charging cell phone and dialed 911. Holding the phone with both hands, I gave the operator the address and told her to call the sheriff immediately. And state Hazmat, for the chemicals.

A wet rattle filled the room. RPM rolled on his back. His cashmere coat was soaked. His legs shook. I watched the heels of his boots knock against the floor and heard a voice as clear as somebody standing beside me. It told me to leave him, let him taste this for himself.

"Are you all right?" the operator asked.

His eyes roamed the room, searching. Beyond him Wally's body lay, his arms spread out.

I struggled to get the words out. "Send an ambulance, right away. It's an emergency."

I hung up, walking over to where he lay. His eyes shifted. He stared into my face and I beat back the impulse, smothering that imploring voice that thirsted for revenge.

Sitting on the floor, I picked up his head with my hand and placed it in my lap. My lip curled with hate and revulsion and his eyes shifted once more, locking on mine. He took a breath and opened his mouth.

And then he was gone.

chapter forty-four

Christmas arrived as a pale blue glory. I watched it come, looking out the open window in Wally's bedroom. Dawn spread itself across the dome of Virginia, the sky chasing away the snow and gray winter light. When the sun rose, I closed the window. My mother was singing in the shower. We had a party to attend.

I walked downstairs, crossing the courtyard under the bright sun, tramping through the snow. I got dressed in the carriage house.

Twice. I dressed twice.

When my mother was ready, I drove the Benz over to Helen's house, silently wondering what to tell my mother. And when.

I glanced over.

"What a glorious day!" she exclaimed. "Look at this sun!"

Last night I came home from Rapland and found her asleep in the den, too scared to go upstairs to bed. An officer had knocked at the front door, asking if she was all right. And where was Wally, my mother wanted to know. I told her he went to stay with a friend. Leading her upstairs, I put her to bed, assuring her Wally was fine now, really. Closing her bedroom door, I walked down the hall.

I opened his closet and stared at his clothing, hoping to forget the shape hefted from the cellar in a body bag. The surfaces of his desk felt oily, grimy, the way everything gets with junkies. I tried dozens of passwords on his computer. What finally opened his files: NADINE.

"I'm so glad we're spending Christmas together," my mother said as I drove toward Oregon Hill. "If only Wally could come with us. Maybe we'll see him tonight. You're sure he's all right?"

I nodded.

There were plenty of incriminating photos. Shots taken on his trip to Africa. Victor Minsky next to the Gulfstream wearing aviator sunglasses. Behind him stacks of Kalashnikovs, RPM holding a rock that looked like a small potato spud. When Zennie's rocks were run through the lab's scanning electron microscope, I was certain the soil would show magnetite and ferrous nickel alloys and upper mantle ilmenite—all the detrital elements of African kimberlite pipes. It was even possible I would match it to the soil in the Gulfstream's treads.

I printed Wally's photos. Nobody remained to back up my story. I would need proof that my last trip to Rapland wasn't voluntary. It wasn't even for the sake of the Bureau.

I stopped outside Helen's house. My mother stared at the paint colors, the sun reflecting off the white snow. The place looked like a garish dollhouse.

"Do you suppose these two need extra attention?" she asked. "Maybe we should call them more often."

I would tell her one day that Wally had saved my life. One day, I would tell her. I would. She needed to hear that he finally figured out who loved him.

And who didn't.

There were other photos on Wally's computer, images that played no part in the case I was mounting. But I spent as much time looking at them. In one, my mother stared into the dead man's camera, her eyes sparkling with love and generosity and confusion.

"I'm glad you changed," she said.

"Pardon?"

"I'm glad you decided to wear the dress."

"Even if it's thirty-eight degrees outside."

"Raleigh, with legs like yours, you should throw away all your slacks."

I could throw away his clothing. I could donate it. But I still had my father's clothing, four years later, his shirts still piercing my heart with the specificity of a hypodermic needle.

"Is that a poncho?" my mother asked, looking out the window. "She can't be serious."

But she was. Helen's lithe figure was draped by an elaborately woven garment. It looked like a horse blanket. Above it, her beautiful face seemed small, out of proportion.

"Maybe she'll take it off when we get there," I said, hoping to ease the distress in my mother's face.

The green front door opened again and Sebastian stepped out. My mother cried, "Heavens!"

He wore a three-piece suit, yellow hound's-tooth. With brown spats. And like the English gentleman he portrayed, Sebastian helped my sister down the icy steps, opening the back door of the Benz. Helen lifted the poncho's copious wool and scooted across the red leather seat. Sebastian slid in behind her, slamming the door.

I jumped.

"You all right?" he asked.

It sounded like gunfire.

Too many shots fired. It would take forensics days to figure out the trajectories and targets, and we might never know why I was spared. But it wasn't luck. RPM fired at Wally, again and again. And Wally fired back, one round straight through RPM's torso, severing his spine. The Russian was dead when his head hit the floor.

"This is just the nicest Christmas," my mother chirped. "I was just saying how I wished Wally was with us."

"He's staying home, alone?" Helen asked.

My mother turned in the passenger seat, facing her. "We came home from the candlelight service and there was the most desperate message from him on the answering machine."

"Desperate?" Helen said, as though combing my mother's statement for literary accuracy. "What do you mean by desperate?"

"He sounded terrible. He begged Raleigh to come get him. He was on the Lee Bridge, can you imagine? At night. Saying he wanted to kill himself. Raleigh drove down there and do you know what time she got home? Two a.m. And he still wasn't with her."

I glanced in the rearview mirror. My sister met my eyes, holding the glance. I raised an eyebrow.

"He's all right?" she asked.

"Raleigh says he's fine."

Helen glanced at me again. "Well, you know kids these days. They get dramatic about nothing. I see it all the time." She immediately changed the subject, blathering about Sebastian and his masks, and the puffed-up creation beside her pretended to be offended by the flattery.

I stared out at the sunshine. The snow was beginning to melt, making everything glisten. It made me want to shield my eyes and never stop looking all at the same time. When we turned into Weyanoke's drive, the melted snow splashed against the car, the bare trees raised their arms to the blue sky, and the river flowed like a ribbon of gold.

I parked near the icehouse. Sebastian escorted Helen up the front steps. I took my mother's arm. She teetered on spike heels, her skirt was too short, and a sudden hope sparked across my heart. Maybe she would be all right after all. I looked into her eyes. I saw joy.

"It's perfect for you," she whispered.

I looked down at my hand. My still-sore wrists were discreetly covered by the long sleeves, but my left hand was shining brightly. The ring was citrine and peridot, alternating gold and green. When I opened DeMott's present this morning, I realized he had chosen the colors of spring. And no diamonds. I felt a wave of gratitude.

Lifting my hand, I watched the gems light up with the sun, radiating their colors of life. New life.

At the top of the steps, the big door opened.

DeMott stood there, smiling.

Waiting for me.

acknowledgments

This book forced me to examine things I would've preferred to ignore. Namely, the condition of the human heart.

Above all, it reminded me that our struggles with race come not from our skin color but from our souls. White, black, or other, we are made of strange stuff inside. And for that reason, my first thanks goes to the one who sat with the Samaritan and the sinner and the tax collector; the one who knows what we're like inside and whose empty tomb continues to free the slave, and the slaveholder, within each of our fallen souls.

From Him, thanks proceed accordingly.

Retired special agent and novelist Wayne Smith provided his usual expert knowledge but also prayed with me through wordless valleys. The redoubtable Katie Land, special agent and special girl, spoke candidly about her life, generously allowing this pesky novelist to pry. And Bruce Hall, retired special agent, shared his geologic and forensic expertise, tossing in bonus rounds.

This book benefited immensely from interviews with Gary J. Clore, manager of the gang management unit of the Virginia Department of Corrections. He knows more about gangs in America than anybody should have to, and he offered crucial advice for researching the subject: "Get lots of hugs from your kids."

Three great reporters in Richmond—Frank Green, Rex Springston, and Mark Holmberg—helped me out of corners, and I'm indebted to the following authors: Nelson Lankford for *Richmond Burning*, Greg Campbell for *Blood Diamonds: Tracing the Deadly Path of the World's Most Precious Stones*, and Charles Spurgeon Johnson for *Bitter Canaan: The Story of the Negro Republic*. The latter was published thirty years after Johnson's death and depicts the painful and paradoxical beginnings of Liberia; unfortunately, it's often not mentioned in biographical sketches of this remarkable historian and university president.

For music, huge thanks go to songbird Sara Groves for her CD *O Holy Night*. For blazing trails for my heart to follow, Pastor Mark Driscoll of Mars Hill Church, and Pastor Chris Swan and my fellow Bellevue MHCers for being authentic.

My very own special agent, Brian Peterson, always stands like a rock, encouraging at every turn. And on this round, editors Amanda Bostic, Jennifer Stair, Jocelyn Bailey, and Becky Monds specialized in accountability. I can never thank them enough for their keen insights and gracious offerings.

Thanks to Dania Lee, for telling true stories that revealed forgiveness, and to Robin Sofola, for exhibiting grace rather than jumping to conclusions about race, and to all the moms at Heritage Homeschool Co-op for their good cheer and hard work. To Sara Loudon, whose Covenant Christian Middle School returns young minds to classical roots, and the CCMS families supporting this amazing enterprise, thank you.

Thanks to my always supportive, lively, and loud familia: Joe and Rita Labello and their beautiful girls, Pat Labello, Nickie and John Quinn, Roger Connor, the Simpsons of Seattle, and Maria and Tony Rainey living behind the Redwood Curtain of California. I love you all. My kinda cousin Charlie Robbs answered firearms questions but, much more importantly, served this great country. Thanks to his wife, Kris, and her fun groups of readers and doers. For cello details, thanks go to my cousin

John Simpson (okay, complete honesty: thank you for looking like Dennis Quaid). And thanks to Jim and L. A. Flynn, for their good humor.

My sons, Daniel and Nico, give an endless supply of love and generosity and challenges. Thank you for telling me to jump on the trampoline whenever the story got stuck.

But to my husband, Joe, I want to say thanks for being everything I love bundled into one man. The funniest, the toughest; the smartest, the strongest. Thanks for making it all look easy, especially since it isn't.

Author to Author

The Thomas Nelson Fiction team recently invited our authors to interview any other Thomas Nelson Fiction author in an unplugged Q&A session. They could ask any questions about any topic they wanted to know more about. What we love most about these conversations is that it reveals just as much about the one asking the questions as it does the author who is responding. So sit back and enjoy the discussion. Perhaps you'll even be intrigued to pick up one of Tim's novels and discover a new favorite in the process.

SIBELLA GIORELLO   TIM DOWNS

Sibella Giorello: Tim, I recently met a book store owner who could not stop raving about *Shoofly Pie*. She's not the first, either. That book isn't new, but people talk about it like it was just released. Aside from the obvious—great story, great voice, couldn't-put-it-down—why do you think readers still go wild for *Shoofly Pie*?

Tim Downs: It surprises me too, because I like to think my stories improve with each novel I write.

SG: And they do.

TD: Thanks. I think it has to do with the first appearance of an intriguing character—in this case Dr. Nick Polchak, forensic entomologist. I think there's a certain freshness and originality in the first incarnation of a character that readers recognize and respond to. Nick Polchak is a very strange man, and in *Shoofly Pie* you meet him for the first time in all his glorious weirdness.

SG: No offense, but I'm glad my protagonist likes rocks. Your entire forensic series features Dr. Nick Polchak, aka the Bug Man. What's with the bugs, Tim—what attracts you as an author?

TD: It wasn't bugs that attracted me, but the concept of a "bug-man". It seemed to me that in crime fiction it had all been done before: hard-nosed cops, cynical private investigators, brilliant detectives . . . Then I read an article about the emerging science of forensic entomology and something occurred to me: The people who do this aren't in law enforcement—they're just scientists who love insects and have learned a forensic application for their science. I asked myself, "What kind of person gets a PhD in bugs? What would that person be like around other people? And what would he be like at a crime scene?" I knew I had the makings of a great character, and that's when the Bug Man was born.

SG: I also heard you're a cartoonist—syndicated no less. Do you still draw? Do you sketch out the quirky characters in your books?

TD: I don't have a lot of time for drawing these days, but I think the three thousand comic strips I wrote and drew had a lot to do with preparing me to write fiction. Cartooning taught me to be creative on a deadline and to be concise with words—you have to be concise when you only have four frames to work with! It also gave me a love for humor that pervades all my writing. I can't help it; even when I try to be serious I end up being funny. Cartooning also gave me a lot of practice developing characters and writing dialogue. Most of all, it gave me the desire to break out of those four frames and try something longer—like a four hundred page novel.

SG: Stretching is good for artists and writers. Speaking of which, your new book *Wonders Never Cease* is a departure from the Bug Man series. Tell us about it.

TD: *Wonders Never Cease* is a story I waited five years to write, and finally I got the chance. It's a very imaginative story—part comedy, part romance, and part mystery. The story takes place at UCLA Medical Center in Los Angeles. The central characters are a single mother and her troubled six-year-old daughter who begins to see angels one day. Has she lost her mind, or is she seeing something that no one else can see? *Wonders Never Cease* is a story about faith and the difficulty of believing in things unseen. It's a very tender story, and it's funny too. I think I needed a break from blow flies and flesh flies and decomposing bodies!

SG: I'm intrigued! Can readers expect more books like this from you? Or did the Bug Man get jealous of your time away?

TD: I hope to write a wide variety of stories in the future. As long as it's a creative concept with oddball characters and an intriguing plot, I'm interested. And don't worry about Nick Polchak. He never gets jealous—he only cares about bugs.

Coming May 2010

Featured above are Tim's novels with Thomas Nelson.

To discover more about Tim and his writing,
visit TimDowns.net

Before The Clouds Roll Away,
the Rivers Run Dry

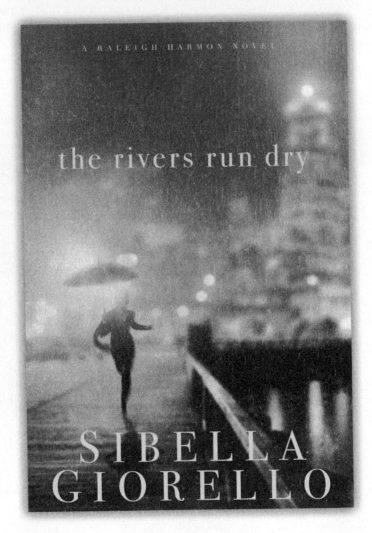

And Coming Fall 2010
The Mountains Bow Down

THOMAS NELSON
Since 1798